CW00543705

# What's so Flinking Bunny?

# What's so Flinking Bunny?

The Spoonerisms and
Misadventures of
Tristram Throstlethwaite

## Benedict Nightingale

BOOKS

First published in Great Britain in 2010 by
JR Books, 10 Greenland Street, London NW1 0ND
www.jrbooks.com

A catalogue record for this book is available from the British
Library.

ISBN 978-1-906779-93-1

1 3 5 7 9 10 8 6 4 2

Printed by Clays Ltd, St Ives plc

For Anne: much loved wife and invaluable memory stick

# ONE

When did the Great and Continuing Clope Disaster, as he came to call it, begin to threaten Tristram Throstlethwaite's peace of mind and academic career? Well, there were certainly ominous rumblings when the young lecturer got chatting with George Macdonald on the day after that genial old man officially retired from his post as head of the university's English faculty. As a promising member of the same department, Tristram had always got on well with George and was sorry to see him leave, which is why he asked him to drop by his house for a farewell whisky. And the two men drank happily and talked cheerfully, at least until the conversation turned to the professor who was to replace George at the beginning of the coming term.

'What's he like?' asked Tristram, nervously stroking his moustache, which hadn't been trimmed for, well, at least a few weeks.

'Hamish Clope?' replied George. 'He's Scottish like me

but he's not at all like me. He's not big like me. He's not fat like me. He doesn't eat and drink too much, like me. In fact, he's so thin and small I'm not sure he eats and drinks at all.'

'He doesn't sound much fun,' said Tristram.

'Fun?' bellowed George. 'Fun? No, he struck me as an earnest sort of person. Very earnest and intense. Not much sense of humour, I'm afraid. A very *good* person,' went on George in a voice which suggested that he thought very good people ought to stay safely shut up in their very good houses with their very good morals and their very good wives.

'Ah,' said Tristram just a little apprehensively.

'Mark you,' added George. 'It can't be easy being called Clope. Did you know that it's French slang for cigarette or cigar?'

'No,' replied Tristram, 'no, I didn't.'

'You'd expect a man called Cigar to be tolerant, wouldn't you?' continued George, smiling as he shook his head. 'And I've got a feeling this Clope won't be so tolerant if the Flinking Bunny makes too many appearances.'

'Ah,' repeated Tristram in a still more worried way. He began to chew his moustache, knocking off some whisky-soaked remnants of crisps that had got stuck in its nether regions. Sucking vaguely away and stepping over some papers he'd left scattered on the floor, he started to pace round the tacky old sofa on which George was sprawled as comfortably as its bulging springs would permit.

'Ah,' Tristram said again, knocking over the bowl that contained the potato crisps and absently treading them into his none-too-clean carpet.

Tristram disliked being called Flinking Bunny, but from George, who was as good-natured as anybody in the university, he tolerated the nickname he'd been given a few terms ago. It had come about this way. He was delivering a lecture on his primary subject, the Romantic poets and particularly Shelley and Keats, when he came to a climax. 'And which poets have more to say to us today than even Byron, even Wordsworth, even the great Coleridge?' he cried in a voice he intended to be impressively dramatic. 'Why, Kelly and Sheets!'

Despite his mild looks and abstracted manner, Tristram had and has quite a sharp temper; and the muffled giggles that greeted this little error annoyed him so much that he barked, 'And what's so blinking funny?' at his students. But this came out as 'And what's so flinking bunny?' which left them laughing still more and Tristram even more irked than before. It was, he realised, one of those days when he'd been invaded by the spirit of the Rev William Spooner, who became so renowned for misplaced consonants – he's said once, though perhaps spuriously, to have proposed a loyal toast to 'the queer old dean' – that he gave rise to a new word: the Spoonerism.

Anyway, news of this error quickly found its way round the university's English faculty and into the office of the large, forgiving man who right now was trying not to let the springs in Tristram's old sofa puncture his enormous rump. Fortunately for the young lecturer, George Macdonald found the formalities of his job wearisome and had an anarchic streak not usual in administrators. Indeed, he seemed almost to relish Tristram's bouts of vagueness or absentmindedness or whatever it was.

One time, a student had received back an essay on Wordsworth at the end of which Tristram had scrawled 'for God's sake, don't forget the pillowcases'. What did it mean?

# 4 What's so Flinking Bunny?

What did Dr Throstlethwaite want? The student, who was particularly conscientious, spent the rest of the day ransacking the complete works of Wordsworth in a desperate, doomed quest for an 'Ode to Pillowcases' or, at the very least, a 'Lament for Bed Linen'. And then another bewildered student brought Tristram an untidy-looking piece of paper on which he had inscribed 'quite good but you need to say more about the Lyrical Ballads'. On inspection this proved to be the laundry list that Tristram had somehow managed to get confused with the essay on Wordsworth.

The story found its way to Macdonald who, so far from showing disapproval, gave his trademark bellow of hearty laughter. 'The Flinking Bunny has been with us again,' he roared, which Tristram found embarrassing but not disturbing. He liked George and was only too aware that he was lucky to work for a man realistic enough to know that vagueness or absentmindedness or abstraction isn't exactly uncommon in universities and sufficiently tolerant not to mind when he, Tristram, called him Jim or McTavish or something else not quite accurate.

But would this new man, this austere-sounding Clope, prove equally affable? George Macdonald's twin scholarly interests were Robert Burns and the place of liquor in poetry. Why, he had recently published an article titled 'Swigging Sack, Falling Down and Throwing Up: the Tradition of Shakespeare's Falstaff in British Literature'. But Tristram had heard that Clope's specialist subject was different. It was the history of the sermon in Lowland Scotland.

'Well, this Clope is in the process of moving down from Dundee,' went on Macdonald. 'I offered to help, which was a bad mistake.'

'A mistake? Why?'

'He brought down his dog and left it with us while he went back up to Scotland to organise this and that. It's a nice wee thing but Muriel isn't at all pleased. It needs walks and it sets off her allergies. It makes her sneeze.'

Muriel was George's wife and even larger than George himself, though that didn't altogether explain why his affectionate name for her was 'dear old dromedary'. Apparently the lady, good-humoured though she was, had objected to George's original pet name, which was 'hippo', and together they had settled on the apparently less offensive 'camel' or 'dromedary', the second of which had stuck throughout their long marriage. And suddenly Tristram had a vision of enormous Muriel terrorising this tiny dog with her sneezes. They would be like typhoons or at least gusts strong enough to knock the poor little thing over.

'Maybe I could help,' he said impulsively. 'I like dogs and I like going for walks, so it could work very well.'

A second, less impulsive thought struck him as he spoke. Clope was his new boss and would be grateful. He didn't want to be ingratiating or seem obsequious or seek special favours – but why not do something that would get him off on the right foot with this tricky-sounding professor?

'I don't know,' said George slowly. But then a strange look came into his eyes, a glint or even a twinkle which, when he thought about it later, Tristram felt was a bit mischievous.

'Very good of you, Tristram,' he went on. 'I'll take you up on that. Don't forget the long walks, will you? The longer they are the better for you and the dog. Try exploring some highways and byways, especially byways. Dogs like byways.'

A few minutes later the two men were ruefully parting

company outside Tristram's small, terraced house, only to be hit by a most disagreeable stench, as of old, rotting flesh. It came from one of the dustbins just outside the front door. Tristram lifted the lid and instantly banged it back down. Flies had settled on what he recognised as the remains of a stew he had forgotten to eat, then forgotten to put in the fridge, then forgotten to throw away until it had turned a sickly yellow and began to ferment. It looked bad and smelt worse.

'You should put some mothballs in there,' said George.

'Mothballs?' asked Tristram, remembering that George had a liking for practical jokes.

'Honestly, mothballs,' said George. 'Look them up in Lizzie Evans's *100 Handy Household Hints*. The dear old dromedary swears by that book. Put mothballs in any dustbin and they'll neutralise the smell. It sounds ridiculous but it's true.'

Since the twinkle in George's eyes had been replaced by a serious look, or as serious a look as George was capable of giving, Tristram believed him. Yes, he would buy some mothballs the next time he went into the centre of town.

To Tristram's consternation, the poor little dog turned out to be a large Afghan hound that Clope had called Henryson, in honour of the medieval Scottish poet who wrote 'The Bludy Serk' and other verses that aren't much read nowadays. How on earth could he have imagined that Muriel Macdonald's sneezes could have toppled it? Come to that, how could George have called the dog 'wee'? Perhaps, being large and rumbustious himself, anything even slightly smaller and quieter was wee to him. And Henryson was certainly quiet. In fact, when George handed him over to

Tristram, he gave his new keeper a woebegone, fatalistic look, as if to say that things had always been difficult in his sad canine life and were unlikely to improve now.

But Tristram liked Henryson, perhaps partly because he could identify with all that long Afghan hair. You see, it isn't only the fuzz on Tristram's head that's apt to sprout and droop out of control. His moustache tends to grow down from his mouth to his chin, making him look a bit like Che Guevara or even John Lennon, who liked to think he resembled the South American revolutionary. But when Tristram's hair is especially long, and the two sides of his moustache disappear beneath his chin, the overall impression is harder to define. With his oval face, rather worried expression and abundance of facial fur, he begins to look like a strange amalgam of an owl and a Yeti: a creature that has made nervous people gasp in the dark, fearful of being attacked by an experiment that might have escaped from some mad boffin's lab, yet has at some stage clearly been sophisticated enough to visit an optician and get itself big, round prescription glasses.

For Tristram is certainly no fool. How could he be when he is a scholar of growing repute whose full name and title is Dr Tristram Nicholas Throstlethwaite MA PhD (Oxon)? Yes, he's absentminded, knows it, regrets it and fights against it where and when he can. However, he has a theory, which he'll tell anybody when he can't manage to cover up some gruesome blunder, like putting a pen in his mouth and trying to light it or picking a cigarette out of its packet and using it to sign what he thinks is a cheque but is actually a £5 note.

Anyway, his theory is that vagueness is an unwanted side-symptom of unusually high intelligence and, often, importance. Weren't Newton, Einstein, Beethoven and many other remarkable people famous for their absent-minded behaviour? Like Tristram, they tended to get so intensely concentrated, so focused on one thing that other things, usually of lesser significance, eluded their attention. This had even happened to the disguised King Alfred, who was thinking so hard about ways of rescuing England from the invading Danes that he didn't notice the burning smell that was coming from the cakes he had forgotten to remove from the oven of the peasant woman in whose house he was sheltering, and got an earful and a bit of a beating as a reward.

So Tristram regards himself as belonging to a great tradition and, by way of reminding himself of this, he has started *The Vague Book*, bits of which he's allowed us to print here. To be honest, this wasn't his own idea. Years ago, when he still lived with his parents, and they lived in the same town and taught at the same university where he now lives and teaches, it was decreed that a few sessions with a psychiatrist might stem his eccentricities. That's to say, they might stop him doing things like putting out a hand as he lay in the bath and grabbing bleach instead of shampoo, an event that had left his head looking as if it belonged to a deranged monk rather than to an aspiring scholar with high academic ambitions. Or taking the family car and forgetting where he'd parked it. Or, as happened on one notorious occasion, blithely driving away a car that had been left outside the house by his father's boss, who was dropping off some papers, expected his visit to last for only a moment, and so had left his keys in the dashboard.

'We'll get him to see a psychiatrist,' his parents had assured the aggrieved old man after the police had been called, only for Tristram to return home with a screech of brakes, loudly complaining that the family car was sticky to handle and badly needed to be serviced.

However, Wilhelm Furtbattler, as the doctor was called, didn't manage to change much, if anything. His most positive contribution was to suggest that Tristram do some 'journaling', which is shrink talk for writing down helpful thoughts and ideas. A record of the abstracted doings of the able and famous would, he thought, boost the young man's embarrassed ego and, as he put it, 'make you feel less alone'. And in this volume, which may one day see publication in its own right, Tristram has very belatedly followed his advice. He has started to record the stranger antics of gifted woolgatherers, brilliant scatterbrains and dozy geniuses.

Still, this isn't to say that Tristram doesn't have his normal days. He does, lots of them. Certainly, nobody could have criticised his handling of Professor Clope's Afghan hound. Even Henryson allowed himself to look, if not exactly happy, at least as if he didn't think someone was about to pounce on him and give him a bath or offer him cold haggis instead of chunks of meat. During the few days before Hamish Clope arrived to collect the dog, Henryson and his new keeper went on walks together in the part of town around Tristram's house, and nothing, nothing at all, went wrong.

Well, there was a slight problem. This was that Tristram sometimes got confused by the dog's name. In his own undergraduate days he had studied Henryson alongside another Scottish poet of the early 16th century, William Dunbar, who now is mostly remembered for two poems: 'Lament for the Makaris', which grimly celebrates dead writers, and 'The Flyting of Dunbar and Kennedie', in which

Dunbar and his rival Walter Kennedy exchange insults like *'baird rehator, theif of natur, fals tratour, feyindis gett'*. Sir Walter Scott called this the most repellent set of verses he had ever read, and the dog Henryson seemed to sense it. On the odd occasions when Tristram mistakenly called him by Dunbar's name, he got in response the melancholy, reproachful look of a creature who had indirectly been called a *'feyindis gett'* and didn't know what he had done wrong.

Anyway, just a couple of hours before Professor Clope was to appear, in order to collect Henryson and meet his helpful young subordinate, Tristram took the dog for a shopping trip. He visited the local supermarket, where he picked up some dog food that he thought he would give to his new boss as a sort of welcome gift in case he and his wife hadn't had time to pick up any themselves. Then he went to the butcher's to get something for his own supper and, as seemed often to happen, was waylaid by the man behind the counter, a friendly but irritatingly chatty bloke who liked to make heavy-handed jokes.

'What can we do you for today?' he asked, clutching his cleaver. 'Nice bit of lamb or something exotic? Bit of kangaroo or ostrich or cobra? Or dinosaur?' And the butcher bloke burst out in laughter at his own humour, even though he said much the same thing every time Tristram went into his shop.

'A nice bit of lamb would be very nice,' replied Tristram primly and, having paid for a couple of chops, released Henryson from the lamp-post to which he'd tied his lead, half-noticing that the dog was staring with curiosity and perhaps even apprehension at the butcher bloke, who could be seen through the window cheerily dismembering some defunct mammal.

Tristram started for home muttering, as he often did, lines from one of the Romantic poets, in this case Coleridge. 'I fear thee, ancient mariner, I fear thy skinny hand,' he said to himself, 'And thou art long and lank and brown, as is the ribbed sea sand.' A passing shopper looked surprised, but Henryson seemed comforted by the rhymes, and loped obediently along, waving rather than wagging his long, impressive tail. Then Tristram remembered George Macdonald's advice. 'Mothballs!' he said rather loudly, again causing mild consternation among the passers-by. 'Mothballs!'

'Sorry, Dunbar, we'll have to retrace our steps,' went on Tristram, not realising that he had just used a name which wasn't merely wrong but, like the breeze that precedes a gale, was a warning of possible confusion and trouble to come. However, Henryson just gave him a meek, rueful look, as if to say that he supposed Tristram could call him anything at all as long as he wasn't given a cold bath or ticked off for the crime of being canine.

So Tristram went back into the supermarket, again leaving Henryson tied to a lamp-post, and bought a packet of mothballs. Then he started back home, only to realise that he needed to relieve himself. So, yet again tying Henryson to a lamp-post, he popped into a gents in a side-street not too far from his house. 'Water, water everywhere nor any drop to drink,' muttered Tristram, absently quoting another line from Coleridge's 'The Rime of the Ancient Mariner' as he went about his business; words which, though perfectly pronounced, brought a half-suppressed 'harrumph' from the gentleman at the urinal beside him.

This irritated Tristram, which is why he responded with a superior sniff, a disdainful frown and a sharp retort. 'Coleridge, if you want to know,' he said.

'I don't want to know,' replied the gentleman. 'I don't care who you are.'

As flabbergasted as he was irked – what kind of idiot would confuse him with a Romantic poet who had been dead for 200 years? – Tristram finished his business, gave a bristle of the moustache, and started for home. But wait a minute. He had forgotten something. What? Some sugar for Professor Clope. He, Tristram, didn't take sugar with his tea, but Clope might have a sweet tooth and appreciate being given a lump or two. So it was back for a third time to the supermarket, where he proceeded to buy the sugar. And then he looked at his watch, realised Clope would soon be arriving and again set out for home, declaiming yet more Coleridge, this time some famous lines from 'Kubla Khan': 'Weave a circle around him thrice and close your eyes with holy dread,' he said, 'for he on honey dew hath fed and drunk the milk of paradise.'

He was almost at his front door when he began dimly to sense that something was wrong. Nobody had weaved or woven a circle around him at all, let alone thrice, but he felt like closing his eyes with holy dread. Yes, something was definitely missing. What was it? The lamb chops? No, they were in his bag. The sugar? No. The mothballs? No. The dog food? No. But why was he buying dog food in the first place? Then he realised. It was for Dunbar and, no, he wasn't holding Dunbar's lead and no, Dunbar wasn't amiably ambling beside him.

Tristram likes to think he has a cool head, but for a moment he was close to panic. Where had the dog gone or, rather, where had he left the dog? He raced back through the town streets, every now and then stopping to call out, 'Dunbar, good boy, Dunbar'. If he was anywhere, he would surely be outside the supermarket, the last place he had stopped but, again, no – Dunbar had vanished.

'Oh God, he's an Afghan hound, a pedigree dog,' said Tristram aloud. 'What will I say to Clope?'

Then he remembered. The butcher! He half-strode, half-ran back to the shop where he had bought the lamb chops, only to stop dead in his tracks as it came into view. The butcher bloke could be seen in the window with his cleaver in his right hand and, hanging from his left hand – what?

It couldn't be, but it looked very much like a paw, and a rather large, hairy paw at that. And the next moment Tristram looked down beside the lamp-post to which he seemed to recall tying the dog, only to see something that added to the picture emerging in his mind. Dunbar was gone, but a large canine turd remained. Perhaps it was a sign. Perhaps the poor creature had been dognapped but had had the presence of mind to leave a sample of DNA for those trying to find him.

At any rate, Tristram blinked and gulped and felt a dread that, this time, wasn't holy at all. Then he remembered that he was a Throstlethwaite and that the Throstlethwaites were a Yorkshire family who, in the admittedly distant past, had been celebrated for their courage. They had fought in wars, occasionally even successful ones. They had wielded broadswords and maces, often without any damage to themselves. Tristram gulped again and strode into the shop.

The butcher bloke, who had slipped into his back room, promptly reappeared, still holding the cleaver but not now the hairy paw. 'Hello there,' he said happily. 'Forgotten something, have you? Want a nice piece of camel? Or elephant? Or possum?' And once again the butcher bloke laughed heartily at his own wit.

'I'm looking for a large dog,' said Tristram hoarsely.

'Dog?' said the butcher bloke in the upbeat voice of someone who believes he's found a soulmate in the humour department. 'Dog? Well, we've got spaniel and we've got labrador. Are they large enough? What do you want? Innards – or a nice piece of tail?'

'No,' said Tristram, in his anxiety only half-following the butcher bloke's curious reasoning. 'An Afghan hound. Have you got him?'

'Well,' said the butcher bloke. 'We don't normally do Afghan hound, but I could go and look and see if there's any in the back.' And he laughed cheerily again.

It occurred to Tristram that this man was a psychopath. He had seen Dunbar in the street, slipped out, brought him into his shop and taken him from there into his back room. There, this Sweeney Todd of the butchery trade had murdered the poor, obedient, uncomplaining dog, probably without bothering to chloroform him first. Then, horror of horrors, he had cut him up. Was there nothing that some people wouldn't do when there was a chance of profit?

'So shall I have a look?' laughed the butcher bloke, giving his cleaver a jovial twirl. 'Ha, ha, ha, ha!'

Tristram was so appalled all he could do was gawp at this awful, guffawing person.

'Ha, ha, ha, ha,' went on the butcher bloke. 'And which bit of Afghan hound do you want? A nice piece of ear? I hear they're very tasty as long as you take off the hair. Ha, ha, ha, ha.'

Just then another customer, a lady in a tweed coat and skirt, came into the shop, causing the butcher bloke to break off his now one-sided conversation with Tristram. 'And what can I do you for today, madam?' he asked. 'Nice bit of Afghan hound?'

'Ha, ha, ha ha,' snorted the tweedy lady, who was clearly accustomed to the butcher bloke's inimitable sense of fun.

'We've got every sort of exotic meat on sale here,' went on the butcher bloke. 'There are no flies on us. No flies on our exotic meat either. No flies on Afghan hound when we have it in stock. Ha, ha, ha, ha.'

Then it hit Tristram. This horrible man was making one of his stupid jokes. He was a chortling idiot. And then another thought hit him. Perhaps he hadn't brought Dunbar out with him today at all. In his haste to buy things for Clope, himself and his smelly dustbin, perhaps he had left him safely at home in the kitchen.

'I've got to go,' he said and hurried out of the shop, half-hearing the butcher bloke shout after him, 'Come back when you want some Great Dane . . . ' and follow it up with a big, self-satisfied cackle.

By now quite breathless, Tristram scampered towards the gate to his house, only to realise that someone was standing at his front door. It was a man, a man so thin he looked like a wizened meerkat or an elongated tadpole or an emaciated winter shrub or the cigarette he seemed to remember George Macdonald mentioning. Most of all, he reminded Tristram of a human needle, though a needle that happened to have two eyes rather than the customary one. It must be the new professor. What was his name? Carp? Clip? Yes, Clope, Professor Clope, Professor Hamish Clope. But why was he here? It was only four o'clock and Tristram had asked him for four-thirty – hadn't he?

'Dr Throstlethwaite, I presume?' said Clope in a stiff, needle-like way, holding out his hand.

Tristram grabbed it, in his sweaty desperation attempting a joke about a celebrated meeting in deepest, darkest 19th-century Africa.

'And you must be Mr Stanley,' he said, panting and heaving as he forced himself to smile.

'No,' said Clope even more stiffly. 'The name is Clope. Professor Clope. Are you expecting a Mr Stanley?'

'No,' replied Tristram. 'No, sorry, it was just a joke. Livingstone, you know.'

'No,' said Clope. 'I don't know any Livingstone either. And I don't think I quite understand your joke,' he went on, sounding as if jokes were things to be picked up in hygienic tweezers, preferably by surgeons wearing disposable plastic gloves.

'Never mind, it's very good to meet you, professor,' lied Tristram. 'I'm so glad you managed to get here early.'

'Early?' said Clope, removing a tiny Filofax from his pocket and opening it. 'I believe we agreed on four o'clock. 'Yes, it was four o'clock. I have it here in my own hand-writing. I am not usually early and very seldom late.'

'Oh dear,' said Tristram, checking his watch, which read ten past four. 'Then I have kept you waiting. My mistake. I'm so sorry. Not a good start to our relationship, eh?' And he tried to laugh, only to be cut off by Clope's attempt at magnanimity.

'No doubt you had very pressing business,' he said, wrinkling his nose slightly as he spoke.

Unsurprisingly, Tristram took this nasal quiver as a mark of disapproval, but then he realised it might have another cause. He had kept Clope waiting in the small space between his front gate and front door and that small space contained his dustbin. And that dustbin was emitting the same vomit-like smell of fermenting decay that he and George Macdonald had noticed before, only more strongly. This was, he thought, decidedly not the way to welcome your new boss to your house for a first encounter.

'Yes,' he said. 'I'm so sorry. I've had problems with my dustbin. That's why I went out. To buy some mothballs. Mothballs are a very good way to deal with tough smells. It's well known. Lizzie Evans says so,' he added lamely. And he took a packet from his shopping bag, yanking out some of its contents, and dropping them into the bin.

He did this quickly and, he thought, surreptitiously because he didn't want Clope to see the once yellow and now yellow-green stew or the flies, even more of which were buzzing about inside the dustbin. But Clope saw as well as smelt. And what he saw was a sweaty, long-haired young man with a big, bushy and doubtless unhygienic moustache throw a bunch of sugar lumps at flies who looked as if they already had more than enough to keep them busily chomping away for months. Yes, sugar lumps, for in his disarray Tristram had grabbed the packet he'd bought for Clope's tea, not the one containing mothballs.

'And now let's go in and reintroduce you to Dunbar,' said Tristram, hoping that all this embarrassment was at an end. He had, you see, managed to convince himself that of course he'd left the dog in his house. It was all the fault of that dreaded vagueness. He had imagined he had taken the dog to the shops when he had very sensibly done the opposite. Anything else was too awful to be conceivable.

'Dunbar, Dunbar,' cried Tristram as he opened the door. 'Professor Clope is here and eager to see you again.'

Clope was mystified. Dunbar was and is a small town near Edinburgh. Why was this Throstlethwaite shouting its name? And why did he think that he, who barely knew Dunbar, wanted to go there and look at it? And who was this strange and sinister-sounding woman, this Lizzie Borden or Lizzie Evans or whatever she was called, that Throstlethwaite had been talking about? Were mothballs a codeword for criminal substances? Was this Englishman on drugs? If so, he would have to deal with the problem very firmly, as his position as the new head of the English Department demanded.

Or was this some strange, malicious joke? Clope remembered that Throstlethwaite had also spoken irrelevantly about Livingstone, another lowlands town that he, Clope, knew slightly but also had no particular intention of revisiting. Yes, it must be a subtle sneer, and if there was anything he disliked more than drugs it was subtle, anti-Scottish sneers. Indeed, he saw them as a sort of heroin of the mouth and privately thought that dealing in them should be an imprisonable offence.

'I think I would like to see my dog Henryson now,' said Clope, pursing his lips and, like the needle he somewhat resembled, looking sharp and pointed and even dangerous. If some traveller had packed him in his hand-luggage, and he would just about have fitted there, he would have been confiscated at airport security.

Certainly, his words pierced Tristram like a hot needle in the head. Why had he started calling the dog by the wrong name? Henryson was Henryson, not Dunbar. Even though this mistake showed his familiarity with early Scottish poetry, and so emphasised his credentials as a scholar with unusually broad interests, it couldn't have made a wholly good impression on his new boss. And, even worse, where was Henryson himself? Apologetically muttering, 'I seem to have got my Scotsmen a bit confused . . . ' – a remark that Clope took as some cryptic and possibly racially motivated gibe – he rushed into the kitchen, then raced upstairs, then returned to the living room looking, well, distraught.

'Where's my poor wee dog?' asked Clope with a bluntness that implied that Tristram might well have sold this very valuable creature to finance his dope habit or his career as a comedian with a line in racist jokes or, of course, both evils at once. But Clope's words, coming as they did like the crack of a canon at Edinburgh Castle, shifted something in Tristram's head. Now he remembered. He'd popped into the town gents for a pee and had emerged thinking, not of the dog tied outside, but of the philistine at the urinal who had irritated him by harrumphing at Coleridge and then assuming he was actually called Coleridge. As often with absentminded people like him, the one thought had banished the other.

'Oh no, oh dear, oh Spooner,' he said inwardly, as he often did when things didn't seem to be going all that well, while he decided that outwardly he would put on as bold face as he could.

'So sorry, Professor,' he said in his humblest, most subordinate voice. 'I left Henryson in a safe place. I'll go right out and fetch him now. Do sit down. Can I get you tea and biscuits while you wait?'

Tristram had tidied up his living room in readiness for this visit. At least there were no papers on the carpet. However, this wasn't altogether a good thing, because its stains were all too evident and the odd bit of squashed potato crisp was visibly sticking out from under the sofa.

'I'll bide the tea and biscuits until you return,' said Clope, sitting abruptly down on a protruding spring, bouncing back up, then cautiously settling down on a flatter, safer-looking section of Tristram's sofa. 'But perhaps you would be kind enough to tell me where my dog Henryson is.'

There was a long, awkward pause, after which Tristram gave what he hoped was a big, reassuring smile.

'Well,' he said slowly. 'He's tied to a lamp-post.'

'A lamp-post?' said Clope, fixing him with a piercing stare.

'He seemed very much to like it,' added Tristram weakly. 'I wanted to please him. You know how dogs are. They're very keen on lamp-posts, aren't they?'

'I don't know anything of the sort,' replied Clope. 'Neither I nor Mrs Clope have ever left Henryson tied to a lamp-post and then gone home to have afternoon tea. And where is this lamp-post?'

'Well,' said Tristram. 'It's quite close. Don't worry. It's at a gentleman's loo.'

Clope's stare stopped being merely piercing. It thrust its way through to Tristram's backbone and froze it up.

'You are telling me,' said Clope, 'you are telling me that you have left my wee dog Henryson at a public convenience?'

'Please don't worry,' gasped Tristram. 'I'll be back with him in just a moment. Do make yourself comfortable while I'm away.'

The last thing he heard as he leapt for his front door was a half-growl, half-wail of 'comfortable?' It was the sound of Clope lengthening his 'o's, rolling an 'r', and then snapping out a 't' in a mixture of indignation and dismay.

So would Henryson still be safely tied to the lamp-post,

wondered Tristram as he raced through the streets, too anxious even to quote something appropriate from Coleridge or something about the woes of dog-walkers from Keats.

But Henryson was. He was seated beside the lamp-post looking calm, patient and perhaps a little sad. He hadn't been dognapped, still less dismembered by any chortling butcher bloke.'Good dog,' panted Tristram, untying him. 'Good dog,' he repeated as he began to hurry with Henryson back to his house. 'Good dog, your master's come to fetch you.'

It seemed to Tristram that Henryson put on the brakes for a moment, but he decided that this was probably imagination, because the dog continued to lope along beside him. However, he didn't exactly leap, bound and roll on the floor with delight when he and Tristram came panting through the door and encountered the needle-like figure that was Hamish Clope.

'Heel, Henryson,' said Clope in an authoritative voice. The dog's head sagged slightly forward, his long hair seemed to shrivel and, though he was almost as tall as his master, he looked a quarter of his size as he sat wanly down. If there had been a white flag around, he would have picked it up in his big brown paw and given it a long, abject wave. Everything about him signalled his surrender to the world of cold baths, chilly haggis and orderly conduct.

'Good dog, Henryson,' said Tristram, hoping this sign of warmth towards the Afghan hound would thaw this frosty-seeming professor.

'Adequate dog,' corrected Clope as Henryson stared abjectly up at his master. 'Adequate dog.'

As for Tristram, he summoned up all the brightness he

could muster. 'I'll make you some tea,' he said, 'After all this, it's the least I can do. And then perhaps you'd like a discussion about the English Department. Just a short discussion. A wee discussion as you might say.' And he gave a forlorn sort of laugh that was meant to be comradely or collegiate but, judging by the glint in Clope's eyes, wasn't taken as such.

At any rate, Clope didn't reply, which struck Tristram as a bit rude. Instead, he lifted Henryson's lips and started to inspect the dog's teeth and gums, which Tristram thought still ruder. However, the young lecturer gave another bright smile, hurried into the kitchen, put on the kettle and, while it slowly boiled, returned to his guest in the living room.

There was a long, pregnant pause, so very long that Tristram decided it had to be broken and so heavily pregnant it clearly had to be lightened. Desperately, he reached for a joke sophisticated enough to amuse Clope more than his earlier reference to Livingstone and Stanley.

'What do you call someone who speaks two languages?' Tristram asked Clope with what he hoped was a disarming grin.

'What?' said Clope. 'What?'

'Bisexual,' cried Tristram, quickly correcting himself, 'sorry, bilingual, bilingual.'

Clope simply stared at him as Tristram ploughed feverishly on: 'And what do you call someone who speaks three languages?'

'What?' said Clope.

'Trilingual,' chirruped Tristram, adding, 'it's a German joke, so you can probably see where it's going.'

Clope continued to stare.

'And what do you call someone who speaks one language?'

'What?' said Clope.

'English!' cried Tristram as jubilantly as he could. 'Or, rather, British!'

The long silence that followed somehow contrived to be even more pregnant than before. In fact, it sounded as if it was at the nine-month stage and was about to give birth to something not altogether nice. And so, indeed, it proved.

'I am British,' said Clope. 'But like many men from the Dundee area I am extremely well educated. I speak three languages and, as the son of Scottish missionaries, I can also make myself understood in Swahili. I hope that is good enough for you, Dr Throstlethwaite.'

'Quite enough, tremendously enough,' replied Tristram in what, to be frank, was a rather flatter voice than before. Nobody likes their jokes to go down like lead balloons, and this one now felt so full of dense metal it could have anchored a large liner.

By now Tristram's kettle was feverishly whistling, so he dashed back to the kitchen. There, he nervously but briskly assembled a plate of his favourite garibaldis, or 'squashed-fly biscuits' as their covering with currants means they're often called. Then he swiftly opened the packet of moth-balls he had bought at the supermarket and, carefully dropping them into a sugar-bowl with one hand, made a pot of tea with the other.

'Tea's up,' cried Tristram gamely, proffering the biscuits. 'Hope you like squashed flies. I've heard they're very popular north of the border.'

'No,' said Clope slowly, peering with the deepest suspicion at biscuits which did indeed look rather as if a few of those dustbin flies had been caught, fried and stuck to their surfaces. 'No, I don't think so.'

'Then a nice cup of tea should do the trick,' said Tristram even more brightly.

'Thank you,' said Clope curtly. 'And I'll have one sugar with it if you please.'

'I do please,' said Tristram with a sort of desperate cheeriness. 'I certainly please. After all the trouble I've caused, I absolutely and utterly please.' And he dropped a mothball into Clope's cup, put in a little milk, and began to pour tea from the teapot, only to sense from the professor's expression that something new might be amiss.

'Oh dear,' said Tristram. 'I should have asked you if you wanted milk before I put it in.'

But Clope let go of Henryson's collar, which he had been gripping, leaned forward towards the sugar-bowl and gave it a long sniff. Tristram thought this another example of rudeness, but of course didn't say so. As far as he was concerned, Clope could wander around the living room sniffing his books and his computer if it would help to ensure that their joint future in the English Department was a success. So Tristram smiled what he hoped was the very friendliest smile he had ever smiled.

'Let me pour you another cup,' said Tristram. 'This time without milk, but of course with all the sugar you want.'

'I wanted milk,' said Clope. 'I certainly wanted milk in my tea. I also wanted sugar in my tea.'

'Good, good, good,' said Tristram with a smile that now seemed glued-on. 'I can certainly arrange that.'

'What I didn't want in my tea,' went on Clope, ignoring the interruption. 'What I didn't want was a mothball.'

Tristram did a sort of treble-take. He blinked, jumped, sniffed the sugar-bowl and then, for good measure, sniffed the squashed-fly biscuits, lifted the lid of the teapot and sniffed the tea inside.

'Oh dear,' he said. 'I think there must have been a small mistake.'

'Dr Throstlethwaite,' said Clope. 'I must now ask you a serious question. Think carefully before you answer. Have you been feeding mothballs to my wee dog Henryson?'

'No,' replied Tristram feebly. 'Certainly not.'

'Or squashed flies?' went on Clope.

'No,' gulped Tristram. 'They're a bit too much of a delicacy for a dog, don't you think?'

'Let me ask you one other question,' said Clope, pointedly ignoring that remark. 'I have an extremely good memory and I recall what you said when you were keeping me waiting outside your front door.'

'Ah,' said Tristram, trying not to sound as hopeless as he was beginning to feel.

'You quoted a woman to the effect that mothballs were effective in dealing with tough smells. Are you now implying that there is a tough smell emanating from myself?'

'Oh dear, oh Spooner, oh no, not at all,' was all Tristram managed to say or, rather, croak.

'I think it's time I and my wee dog Henryson made our way home,' went on Clope. 'And I think we will defer any discussion about the department of which I am now head.'

'Fine,' gulped Tristram. 'Jolly good. I am at your disposal.' And he followed Clope out into the porch, hoping the professor would ignore the buzzing that was coming from a dustbin that, if anything, smelt even more gruesomely rotten than before.

'Just a moment,' went on Tristram, remembering perhaps the one thing that would add a little hope to a first encounter which, he had to admit, hadn't gone all that brilliantly well. He rushed back to the kitchen, grabbed the tin of dog food and thrust it into the one hand of Clope that wasn't tightly gripping Henryson's lead.

'I'm sorry about the mothballs,' he said. 'I'm also sorry the squashed flies weren't to your taste. But maybe this will atone. It's, well, one of the better brands. And it's meant to be a sort of welcome gift. I thought Mrs Clope might appreciate it since she can't have had time to get to the grocer,' he added lamely. 'I'm much looking forward to meeting her.'

Clope said nothing, but stared at the tin disbelievingly, his two eyes bulging so widely that they might almost have been one, making him look like a very small, very thin Cyclops. Tristram took this as the beginnings of gratitude and therefore a good sign.

'This is for Mrs Clope?' Clope finally stammered, his voice taking on a note that Tristram dared to hope reflected astonishment at his consideration and generosity.

'Assuming it's a brand she likes,' said Tristram in what he hoped was a solicitous voice. 'I wouldn't want to give her anything cheap.'

'I'm lost for words,' said Clope.

'So all's well that ends well,' said Tristram.

'We'll see,' said Clope, inexplicably failing to take the tin of dog food. 'We'll see.'

Funnily enough, George Macdonald said much the same thing when Tristram phoned him up at his house on the edge of town and recounted to him the events of that day. 'There's a long way to go before we see how this story ends,' he said with a self-satisfied relish that struck Tristram as not wholly appropriate in a senior academic of very mature years.

It was that very evening that a humbled Tristram got to work on the tome we mentioned earlier and he provisionally titled *The Vague Book*. A remark by a character in one of Joseph Conrad's novels, he couldn't remember which, had come to his mind: 'in the destructive element immerse yourself'. Well, absentmindedness was sometimes pretty destructive for him, as the incident with the dog, the moth-balls and the emaciated professor had managed to demonstrate. So why not immerse himself in real-life stories of the vague, abstracted, dozy, distracted and absentminded, just as the psychiatrist Furtbattler had once suggested?

Yes, it would be cathartic. Yes, it would surely boost his troubled ego. Yes, he would collect stories of the remarkable men – for some weird reason they were almost always men – who had succumbed to forgetfulness, confusion, addled idiocies and so on. Maybe he could even establish that there was such a thing as a Vague Community, much as gay people talked of a Gay Community with members like Michelangelo, Oscar Wilde and Ian McKellen. Tristram's fantasies began to escalate, until he was thinking of Vague Pride Days and Vague Pride Marches with himself in the front, carrying a banner reading 'VAGUES UNITE' and leading choruses of 'memory out, out, out'.

But it was time to get writing in earnest. He opened his laptop, turned it on and in his creative excitement forgot the password. What was it? Once it had been 'Thross', in tribute to an old girlfriend. She was called Meryl and liked calling Tristram Thross while playfully and sometimes not so playfully thumping him on the shoulder. After falling out with her, he had changed it to 'funerals', because of something, he couldn't recall exactly what, which had happened at roughly the same time. But what was the password now?

Perhaps one of the Romantic poets he loved. Shelley? Keats? No. Then he remembered. It was 'moustache', after the item he wore proudly if shaggily above his upper lip. Anyway, he typed in the word and off he went.

*THE VAGUE BOOK 1*

*OK, let's open the Throstlethwaite files with a question that has dogged me for years. No, let's start again because I don't much feel like talking about dogs at the moment. Let's begin with a question that has exercised me for years because I'm a self-confessed vague person and it involves the faltering memory of another vague person.*

*But what vague person? Can anybody tell me the identity of the man who just couldn't put a name to the familiar-looking face of the small, chic woman with whom he found himself chatting at a smart London party? He did what any self-respecting vague person would do. He tried slyly and subtly to winkle her identity out of her. He mentioned friends he thought that this woman and he might have in common, but that didn't get him anywhere. Nor did she say anything when he asked after her children. She just said thank you, they were well, and kept smiling. He seemed also to recall that this pleasant person had a connection with some company or other and he asked her about the health of 'the firm', as he put it, and again got back the answer that it was doing fine, thank you very much.*

*Then he remembered. She had a sister. If he could get some information about this woman from her, maybe he would at last learn who this small, smiling person was. 'Your sister,' he said. 'Still doing the same thing, is she?'*

*'Yes, still Queen,' replied Elizabeth II's younger sister, Princess Margaret.*

*History has consigned this particular vague gentleman to undeserved oblivion, but history has remembered and recorded plenty of others, some of whom managed to cause embarrassments that were literally right royal. Back in the 19th century a certain Lord Portarlington approached another small, well-dressed woman at a grand reception, saying, 'Damn it, Madam, I know your face but I can't remember your name.' It was Queen Victoria. Much more recently the novelist Beryl Bainbridge went to a royal reception and, annoyed that she wasn't allowed to smoke, reportedly complained to a woman she assumed was the singer Vera Lynn about how horrifically boring the occasion was. Unluckily, this Vera Lynn wasn't Vera Lynn. She was the same Elizabeth II.*

*It's a problem that has of course involved many a commoner too, and many a commoner has found the answer equally elusive. A famous 18th-century actor called Thomas King ran into an old friend whose name he just couldn't remember and took him home for dinner, where they were joined by another of King's old friends. Together, the actor and this second friend devised a ruse for prising out the first friend's identity. 'My dear sir,' said King, 'my friend and myself have had a dispute about how to spell your name. Indeed, we have laid a bottle of wine upon it.'*

*'Oh, with two "p"s,' came the not-so-helpful reply.*

*But few people have attracted as many anecdotes about absentmindedness as my special hero: the Rev William Archibald Spooner, who was the Master or Warden of New College, Oxford, in the early 20th century and a brilliant scholar. He often confused the faces and names of the young men in his care, persistently reproaching a virtuous undergraduate called Malloran for the misdeeds of an unruly undergraduate called Mallet and going so far as to summon another, unnamed, student to his rooms and grimly inform him that he was to be sent down or expelled from the university.*

*'But what is my crime?' asked the distraught young man.*

*'Oh, ah,' said Spooner, 'I am very pleased to inform you that you have been awarded a scholarship and would like to offer you my congratulations.'*

*Once the Warden happened to see a young college lecturer called Casson and said to him, 'Do come to dinner tonight and meet our new Fellow: Casson.'*

*'But I am Casson,' replied Casson.*

*'Never mind,' said Spooner. 'Come all the same.'*

*And another time he went up to a young man in the street and earnestly asked him, 'Was it you or your brother who was killed in the Great War?'*

*Spooner was a brilliant scholar, but there was something topsy-turvy about that mind of his. He kept getting things the wrong way round. Indeed, once he's supposed to have said to an acquaintance, 'I remember your name perfectly but I just can't think of your face.' Another time, he was walking through Oxford with a friend and lifted his hat to a passing lady dressed in black, remarking afterwards of her husband, who had apparently discovered the hard way that people preaching the gospel in distant places could still fall foul of cannibals, 'Poor soul, very sad, you know, a very sad death, eaten by missionaries.'*

And then there was the time Spooner spilt some salt during a college dinner. Now, it's pretty well known that, if you spill red wine on a tablecloth, it's a good idea to pour salt on it, because it will absorb and soak up much of the wine, making a permanent stain less likely. The Warden clearly knew this, but put his knowledge to a very Spoonerish use. He reached out for a decanter of claret and slowly and carefully poured it on to the pile of salt, creating a wet, red and completely unnecessary splodge in the middle of the tablecloth.

But more often he got words, or at least consonants, the wrong way round. For instance, during one of the sermons he preached in New College's chapel, the sentence 'which of us has not felt in his heart a half-formed wish?' is said to have come out as 'which of us has not felt in his heart a half-warmed fish?' Again, he's supposed to have reproached idle undergraduates with 'you have tasted a whole worm', 'you have hissed my mystery lectures' and 'you will leave on the town drain', meaning the down train from Oxford to London. I suspect that some of these are apocryphal. Did Spooner really spend an evening vainly trying to find a pub called the Dull Man in Greenwich when the friend he was supposed to meet was actually at the Green Man in Dulwich? Well, maybe.

However, Spoonerisms like these are to be found in all places and walks of life. A once-famous actress, Maude Adams, turned a line in A Midsummer Night's Dream from 'You spotted snake with double tongue' into 'You potted snake with ham and tongue'. Over in America, the cast of a Broadway thriller regularly had to stifle its giggles when a particular actor bungled the line, 'This is the chair Schmidt sat in when he was shot'. Try saying *the sentence yourself, and you'll quickly get the idea. And then there was the radio broadcaster who years ago reduced the American nation to hilarity by mispronouncing Herbert Hoover as Hoobert Heaver.*

*Had a later president of the United States, George W. Bush, a similar problem? Quite often he opened his mouth and strange things came out. For instance, when he meant to say 'the family is where our nation finds hope, where dreams take wing', he ended up saying 'families is where our nation finds hope, where wings take dream'. Again, he came out with a Spoonerism when he was talking publicly about weighty matters of economics and trade: 'If the terriers and barriffs are torn down, the economy will grow.' Mr Bush even managed to get the Antipodes muddled up with central Europe, commending the Australians for being Austrians. Nor did he impress a conference on the scourge of malaria in 2008 by referring to sufferers from the disease as 'malarians'.*

*Actually, he wasn't the only American president who had strange lapses. According to Tom Friedman's 1,000 Senior Moments, an indispensable guide to our subject, Dwight D. Eisenhower couldn't remember the name of the Department of Health, Education and Welfare, which he himself had created, and kept calling it Health, Welfare and Whatnot. Truly, there were times when President Eisenhower was indeed President Eisenhowever, as a vague sub-editor on the* Guardian *immortally renamed him. Again, Lyndon Johnson was apt to discover he couldn't recall names that should have been familiar, once grabbing aside a* New York Times *journalist called Russell Baker, telling him how important he had been to the administration, and then slipping his secretary a note which, Baker later discovered, read, 'Who is this I'm talking to?' And Jimmy Carter sent a suit to the cleaners, forgetting that one of its pockets contained the codes needed to launch a nuclear strike.*

*But luckily for the survival of the species these men weren't habitually absentminded and abstracted, as Spooner certainly was. George W. Bush was probably just a very confused and confusing president who didn't always get his grammar right. And some people have been rude enough to suggest that he lacked the one thing so many of us vague people paradoxically possess in abundance: a very good mind.*

# TWO

The new university term arrived and, with it, the inevitable encounters with Clope, who, Tristram felt, was unaccountably hostile to him. Hadn't he looked after the professor's dog for several days, and all without thanks or reward? Yes, there had been a minor problem or two at the very end. But so what? Henryson hadn't been dognapped, nor had Clope drunk or otherwise consumed any mothballs. There hadn't been an offence bad enough to leave a normal person refusing to talk to him about the English curriculum or other university matters, but then Clope didn't strike Tristram as particularly human or normal. Rather, he thought of the spindly little professor as oddly metallic; a sort of semi-human needle that stood upright and stared in a severe, disapproving way at other people through its own eye or, rather, the two eyes it had somehow acquired.

The trouble was that Clope's chilly manner had an unsettling effect on Tristram's mind, which was anyway none too reliable when a name had to be remembered but especially shaky when someone made him feel nervous. Why, oh why couldn't Clope follow George Macdonald's example and call himself something that matched his Scottish accent, like McTavish or Macbeth or, he supposed, McClope? Tristram knew it was important he didn't alienate him further by calling him Clip or Clump, but how, oh how was that to be achieved? What was wanted, he decided, was a special word or series of words in order to call up the Clope surname. In other words, he must devise a mnemonic – but what? Rope, slope, dope, grope, mope, Pope or soap?

One or two of these words seemed appropriate, but especially the last, for Clope's face had a pink, flayed look, rather as if it had been scrubbed by a phalanx of large, determined washerwomen armed with pumice stones. But Tristram's choice of the word 'soap' was also unfortunate, for during his boyhood and even afterwards Clope had been teased about his looks. No small, sensitive boy likes hearing shouts of 'Hey, Titch, mother been washing off your face then?' Nor does any small, important professor like it when an underling walks down the departmental corridor muttering for all and sundry to hear, 'Clope, soap . . . soap, Clope . . . Clope, soap.'

For that's what Tristram did, unaware that he was talking aloud, still less that Clope had come out of a door and overheard his words. And for the professor this was pretty much the last straw. Here was this Englishman, this mad Englishman who had tried to feed him mothballs and squashed flies and his wife dog food, this animal-hating Englishman who had imprisoned his pedigree dog in an urinal, this offensive Englishman who had gratuitously insulted his linguistic skills, this snobbish Englishman whose abstracted, head-in-the-air manner persistently suggested he was looking down his nose at anyone who hadn't been born and brought up in Belgravia or Tunbridge Wells or Cheltenham or some other pretentious English place – here was this vainglorious viper of a Sassenach comparing him, Professor Hamish Clope, with cleaning materials. It was outrageous, intolerable.

'Dr Throstlethwaite,' said Clope in a voice that did in fact sound rather as if it had been washed in the sort of carbolic soap that cruel stepmothers used on innocent children in Victorian novels. And the Clope voice combined with several other things: the Clope frown; a narrowing of the eyes that Tristram was to get to know as the Clope squint; and a rustling of the nose that was the Clope sniff. All this made the young lecturer so nervous he promptly forgot the Clope name.

'Professor,' said Tristram feebly. 'Professor . . . ah, um, Professor.'

'You have a problem with my name?'

'Er, not really,' said Tristram.

'Not really?' asked Clope sounding like what he doubtless was: a man who had never forgotten anything in his life and, on the occasions when he wore his kilt, took care to ensure that his wife ironed it twice and polished his sporran as well. 'Not really?'

'No,' said Tristram even more feebly. 'No, Professor . . . um, Professor.'

Not for the first time, Clope decided Tristram was the sort of Englishman who had made the lives of the Scottish people a misery for centuries, sometimes by defeating them in unjust wars, sometimes by cutting down their forests, sometimes just by being snide and sneering.

'Clope,' said Clope. 'Clope. And I come from a long and, if I may say so, distinguished line of Clopes. We are the Dundee Clopes because we come from the fine old Scottish town of Dundee. I hope that is good enough for you, Dr Throstlethwaite.'

'Oh, more than enough,' said Tristram. 'Terrifically enough.'

'I should hope so,' said Clope, giving the Clope squint and the Clope sniff, and disappeared through another door, leaving behind a faint aroma of, well, carbolic.

But Clope was no fool. True, he had concluded that Tristram was the worst kind of English snob, very likely a dope fiend and possibly also certifiably insane. True, he did his best to ignore and avoid him where he could. Nevertheless, he knew he was important to the university's English Department. For Tristram was gaining a reputation for his essays on the Romantic poets, especially Shelley and Keats. It was even rumoured that a great American university was keen to employ him. However much Clope detested Tristram – and how could he do anything but loathe a man who had tried to poison his tea with mothballs, drown his Afghan hound in a public convenience and force dog food down his wife's throat, and imply that he, Professor Hamish Clope, was an ignorant person with a questionable smell? – he couldn't yet afford to lose him.

So when the top people at the university suggested that Tristram was the person to give the annual lecture that was named after one of its most generous benefactors, Clope was forced to agree. The prospect of sitting in the front row while this cursed Englishman babbled self-indulgently away about poetry, and maybe made subtly insulting remarks about Scottish people in general and Clopes in particular, was not at all pleasing to him. Aside from anything else, he was a world expert on the Lowland sermon between AD1300–1500 and thought most poems and poets trivial by comparison.

'Dr Throstlethwaite,' said Clope, giving a thin smile that Tristram found even more disconcerting than the usual Clope squint, frown and sniff.

'Yes, Professor?' replied Tristram meekly, wondering if he'd done something absentminded, like putting one of Clope's endless memos about departmental discipline into the departmental shredder while fixing a pizza ad to the space on the wall reserved for important edicts. But, no, the latest memo was where Clope expected his subordinates to place it, pinned among three or four others just above his desk.

Anyway, Clope drew himself up to his full height and breadth, which was roughly 5 feet by 15 inches, again forced his lips into that tight rictus he was passing off as a smile, and said in his prim, proper way, 'I have to ask you if you would be good enough to give the Annual Fanny Carter Lecture at the end of term.'

Tristram was flattered, very flattered, but also so surprised that all he could do was stare at Clope in a way the professor thought strange and probably malicious. But just as the Clope squint and sniff began to appear, Tristram replied in his most polite voice, 'Yes, thank you Professor Clope, I would be delighted to do so.'

Clope thought that Tristram's careful politeness was probably a supercilious sneer, but decided to say nothing. Again he gave a forced, thin smile and, this time looking like a needle whose eye had suddenly twisted into a mouth, he left the room.

Tristram decided to take the Annual Fanny Carter Lecture very seriously indeed. For one thing, he had known the late Mrs Carter before she died at the age of 90 and had much admired her dignity and her kindness. She was, he thought, a grand old lady. Also, it was an honour to be asked to give the lecture. The university's great hall would be packed. Everyone who was anyone would come. If the lecture was a success, it would be published and Tristram would be read by English professors all over the world. And that would help his career no end.

But which poet or poets should he choose as his subjects? Why, Shelley and Keats of course. He had plenty to say about them, and some of it, he thought, was fresh and new. So he set about preparing and writing and doing all the things bright young academics do when an important occasion looms. And well before the official date he had finished a lecture he felt he knew so well that he could recite it without notes.

But the very fact that Tristram could behave erratically, and knew it, made him in many ways a pretty careful person. He was only too aware there were dangers for someone as absentminded as him. Therefore he must not dare deliver his lecture unless he had a written copy of it ready as a back-up. Without that, he might get nervous and forget or omit passages. And he must not mislay the written lecture itself. In fact, he must make several copies of the original and keep them safely in his desk. And, of course, he must speak meticulously, avoiding Spoonerisms and other such errors. No Kelly and certainly no Sheets!

Anyway, life at the university went on pretty much as usual. There were embarrassing incidents, though not very many of them. For instance, he realised at the end of one lecture that he had misnamed the poet he was discussing. Funnily enough, that had also happened to the great Spooner himself. Once he preached an entire sermon in which he kept calling one of the founders of Christianity by the name of the greatest of Greek philosophers and just before he left the pulpit was impelled to tell the congregation, 'Where I said Aristotle, I meant St Paul.' Well, Tristram did much the same when several times he called that swashbuckling poet Byron by the name of a Hollywood actor whose adventure films he admired and had recently been watching in a special season on television.

'By the way,' he said stiffly at the end of his lecture, 'I meant Byron on every occasion where I said Clint Eastwood.'

One or two undergraduates sniggered, which was something, as a dignified and self-respecting person, Tristram did not like at all. When such things happened to Spooner, he could rely on his wife to ensure there was no laughter as a result. Once he chatted at dinner to Julian Huxley, who was to become well known himself, and managed to confuse a notable figure from English medieval history with the tip of Scotland, saying how far it was from Land's End to 'John of Gaunt'. 'Mrs Spooner, who was a large and majestic woman, fixed me with a stony look,' wrote Huxley later. 'I didn't even smile.'

Since Tristram is unmarried, and so doesn't have a large and majestic Mrs Throstlethwaite to defend him, he has developed a stony look of his own. In tribute to his native Yorkshire landscape, he goes into a sort of tufty boulder mode. So on that occasion, as on others when it was necessary to be intimidating, he glared at the giggling undergraduates through his glasses, made his moustache bristle like tough old grass, and muttered in a dark, forbidding way – and they shut up.

He even managed to avoid tricky scenes with Clope, who every now and then squeezed out one of his citrus smiles and asked him how the lecture was going. Mostly Tristram simply replied, 'Fine, thank you,' but sometimes he managed to remember the mnemonics he had devised to help him when he was in danger of forgetting Clope's name. One was now a rhyming word: 'grope'. The other was 'cake'. That was because it would remind him of Dundee, which Clope had told him was his birthplace. And Dundee was even more renowned for Dundee cakes than it was for Dundee Clopes.

So on these occasions the words 'grope . . . cake . . . Dundee . . . Clope' went slowly through his head and he managed successfully to reply, 'Fine, thank you, Professor Clope.' And each time Clope gave his sour little smile and went on his way, thinking that Tristram's long, ruminative pause before he answered a perfectly simple question showed that somewhere inside his head this Englishman was mocking him or, almost as bad, plotting to filch his wee dog Henryson and do him to death in a lavatory.

Anyway, the big day approached. The lecture on Shelley and Keats was not only finished but, Tristram thought, really quite good, since it proved beyond doubt that both poets were as topical today as they had been 200 years ago. Also, Tristram made every effort to ensure that nothing could go wrong. He duly made many copies of the finished lecture, placed them in his desk, and even put a note on top of the desk saying 'all copies of my new lecture are inside this desk'. And on the great day itself, he put these carefully in his briefcase, trimmed his moustache so as to ensure it looked neat, made sure he wasn't wearing odd socks or odd shoes, checked that his watch was on his wrist and working OK and, just in case the battery ran out, placed his bedside clock in the pocket of a jacket that had recently returned from the cleaners, along with the most sober tie that he could find among the bright ones he favoured.

Was he nervous? Of course he was nervous, very nervous. But he knew that the worst thing he could do was soothe his nerves with whisky, gin or anything of that kind. He had read Kingsley Amis's novel *Lucky Jim*, in which a frightened university lecturer swallows alcohol and tranquillisers before giving a major lecture and ends up making rather a fool of himself. If Tristram swallowed anything, it would be coffee or caffeine pills or both. Together, they would keep him alert and sharp throughout the lecture.

So before setting out from home, he swallowed four caffeine pills with his usual breakfast cups of strong coffee and jammed the caffeine pill packet alongside the little clock in his jacket pocket. When he got to the lecture hall, his audience was still arriving, which meant there was plenty of time for a couple more cups of coffee in the anteroom. And since his mouth was dry, he took a long, deep swig of water and realised he had forgotten whatever it was went with water. Yes, caffeine pills! So he swallowed two more, took his lecture and its copies out of his briefcase and sat down to wait for someone to ask him to go on to the platform at the front of the hall.

It was time. In came a porter to summon him into the hall. Just to be on the safe side, Tristram swallowed three more caffeine pills, swigging the rest of the jug of water as he did so and, carrying all ten copies of his lecture and his empty briefcase, strode out into the lecture hall and on to the platform. And, yes, he felt nervous, but nervous in all the right ways: smart, brisk, hyped-up, as full of energy as a nuclear reactor.

What Tristram didn't realise was that, thanks to all that caffeine, he looked rather as a nuclear reactor might look if it grew a body and a head. His face was a glorious crimson. His eyes didn't merely glitter with determination. They sort of fizzed. He looked as if he might explode with the sheer excitement of what he was about to say, dazzling the audience with brilliant ideas, like a human H-bomb at the point of explosion.

The university's Vice-Chancellor, who was a large, sleepy man weary at the prospect of listening to yet another academic deliver yet another lecture, didn't notice. But Tristram's former boss George Macdonald, who had come from the edge of town to show his support, certainly did. 'Dear old dromedary,' he said to his wife Muriel, who had also made the trip, 'look at the Flinking Bunny. He looks like the Mad March Hare.' And his new boss, who was sitting in the front row beside the Vice-Chancellor, also noticed, but couldn't understand why Tristram looked so different from his usual, abstracted and, as he thought, supercilious self. 'It must be some sort of plot,' thought Clope, but what sort of plot he couldn't yet tell.

Anyway, Tristram strode on to the platform and gave the audience a truculent look, as if daring it to dislike what he was about to say. Then he put all ten copies of his lecture on to the lectern, creating a pile of paper many inches high. At that the Vice-Chancellor, who didn't know that Tristram was only going to deliver the contents of the few pages at the top, gave a tiny gasp. And Tristram, who mistook that gasp of horror for a gasp of appreciation and support, gave the Vice-Chancellor a fierce, bold grin, mouthing the words 'thank you' as he did so.

Up on to the platform walked Clope, and called for silence. 'It is my happy duty,' he said, trying not to look as if he was lying, 'my very happy duty to introduce Dr Throstlethwaite, who will be giving the Annual Fanny Carter Lecture, which this year is on the subject of Shelley and Keats. I know he will have plenty...' At that moment he saw the height of the pile of lecture copies and, like the Vice-Chancellor, assumed that Tristram was going to read them all. That was Throstlethwaite's evil plot, thought Clope, as he stopped halfway through his sentence. He was going to humiliate the English Department and its leading light, Professor Hamish Clope, by talking for hours and hours. Not content with trying to murder him, humiliate his wife with dog food and submit Henryson to water torture in a lavatory bowl, he was going to bore the university's top people to death. And those who survived the ordeal would certainly blame him, Hamish Clope, for failing to give him a clear time limit in advance. But what could he do now?

'  .  .  .  Plenty to say,' finished Clope with a croak, staring at the pile of paper in barely disguised misery and consternation, as if it was a pile of bills he had unexpectedly been asked to pay.

'Plenty indeed, plenty indeed,' cried Tristram in a loud cheerful voice, giving a smile so huge his teeth looked as if they would shoot out and impale Clope to the wall of the lecture hall. He felt good, very good. He knew that one's nerves could work for one as well as against one, and this time, thanks to that extra bit of caffeine he remembered that he had been wise enough to swallow, he felt they were working for him.

'Thank you very much, Professor . . . ' cried Tristram, but then stopped dead. His mind had suddenly gone blank. Professor what? Grope – but why Grope? Cake – but why cake? Birthday cake? Christmas cake? No, Dundee came into it somewhere – but where? Dundee cake, that was it – but why?

Then and there Tristram's mood went into reverse. He felt as bad as he had previously felt good. His nerves were suddenly, horribly working against him. His moustache began to droop, twitch and shudder, which was always a bad sign. What he didn't realise was that he was saying aloud to himself, 'Why should anyone grope a Dundee cake?' though so softly that nobody but Clope, whose ears were as acute as his knowledge of Lowland sermons, could hear his words. All that the audience could see was their lecturer muttering inaudibly and turning from crimson to white while his professor just stood there, his own face turning from its usual scrubbed pink to dark red. The Biblical needle through which the camel tried unsuccessfully to pass must have looked as uncomfortable and indignant as Clope did at that moment. Indeed, his face bulged and boggled, as if a whole caravan of humped mammals were pushing their way through that human needle, Hamish Clope.

Tristram gave up. 'Thank you, Professor . . . um, Professor,' he said aloud in what was now a high, gibbering, alarmed voice and, trying desperately to smile again, bowed at Clope and ushered him off the platform in what was meant to be a polite, apologetic way but actually gave the impression he was shooing him off, like a stray goose. And the audience uncomfortably shifted in their seats, feeling that they were witnessing some strange, deep academic argument beyond their power to comprehend.

Anyway, Clope bulged, boggled, sniffed, frowned and furiously squinted his way back to his seat in the front row and Tristram turned back towards the lectern, only to stop in surprise. What the hell was that enormous pile of papers doing there? He didn't remember having prepared as lengthy a lecture as this one appeared to be. But he knew he must not panic. He was alone up there now and only he could help himself. All he could do was return to the lectern and do what he had to do, which was first to give a graceful tribute to Fanny Carter, the benefactor who had made the lecture possible.

'Before I begin,' stuttered Tristram, 'I must pay tribute to the great lady who instituted this lecture and did so much for this university. So very much that everywhere you go you can sense her presence. I refer, of course, to Canny Far...'

Fortunately, Tristram stopped before the spirit of Spooner led him over the edge into verbal disaster, but not before a group of undergraduates at the back began to giggle. Oddly enough, that made Tristram feel more in control. He had experience of that kind of behaviour and, as a proud scion of the battling Throstlethwaite dynasty, he knew how to deal with it. Suddenly he felt a lot better. Suddenly he felt that, thanks to the caffeine, his nerves were once again working for and not against him.

'I refer,' he said very carefully and slowly, 'to the great, the unforgettable Fanny Carter.' And he glared across the hall at those troublesome undergraduates, some of whom were still snorting and snuffling. They shut up and the whole audience stiffened, as if called to attention by an army sergeant.

There would be no further problems, Tristram decided.

He was in charge now and intended to remain so. There would certainly be no Kelly and Sheets.

'I shall now begin my lecture on Shelley and Keats,' said Tristram in a way that was so emphatic and sounded so aggressive that the audience didn't just stiffen. It slightly cowered. But he didn't realise the effect he was having. He just wanted to be clear and reassuring, especially to Clope, whom he knew he must have embarrassed by his earlier hesitancy. By way of making up things with the professor, Tristram decided he would direct the lecture largely at him, smiling whenever he could. That would be a compliment that even the grudging Clope could not fail to appreciate. Besides, he wanted to impress the Vice-Chancellor, who was sitting in the front row beside Clope and whose eyelids were already beginning to droop.

So Tristram, his nerves once again in tip-top, razzle-dazzle condition, also decided that whenever he came to the word 'Keats', he would say it particularly loudly. That way, he would ensure that the Vice-Chancellor, who was famous for falling asleep during lectures, would stay alert and attentive.

Anyway, he gave Clope one of his biggest, toothiest smiles, returned to his place behind the lectern and, to his relief, saw that almost all the papers on it were copies he had made of the lecture. The solution was simple. He would get rid of them. So he picked them up, gave a carefree chortle, opened his briefcase and more or less hurled them into it. Again, the audience stiffened. Why was this strange, laughing man throwing away the lecture he was supposed to be giving? Faces puckered with astonishment, though there were also some sighs of relief.

But Tristram quickly realised his error. He flashed

another smile at Clope, grabbed one of the ten copies of his lecture back from the briefcase, and began.

'What do Shelley and Keats have in common?' he asked. 'What do they have to say to us today? My view is far more than some people – dare I say some misguided and foolish people? – choose to believe.'

Again, Tristram gave a big smile at Clope, though this didn't have quite the effect he hoped. The rest of the audience, still puzzled by what had looked like a private argument between the professor and the lecturer, thought that Clope must be one of the misguided and foolish people who went out of their way to think that neither Shelley nor Keats had much to say to the world today. Even worse, Clope thought that this was exactly what Tristram was saying. How could this snide Throstlethwaite make such an accusation when he, Clope, knew next to nothing about Shelley and Keats and had never even uttered an opinion on them? And why did he keep opening his mouth and baring his teeth at him while he propagated this vile slander? Clope curled up in his chair, sniffing and squinting and frowning and looking like a twisted needle, while the Vice-Chancellor did indeed fall asleep beside him.

The lecture continued. 'Some people think of Shelley and KEATS, and especially KEATS, as being pretty, decorative poets. No thought could be more wrong.' And Tristram, who felt he was really buzzing now, glared round the hall as if looking for wrongdoers or wrongthinkers to behead on the spot. There was a complete silence from his audience, except from Clope, who was emitting the Clope sniff, and the Vice-Chancellor, who had started gently to snore.

Exhilarated though he was, Tristram noticed both these

things. He couldn't understand why Clope kept squinting and sniffing in such a hostile way and he decided that the only answer was that, whenever he came to a pause, to give him a still bigger, friendlier smile. Nor could he think of any way of awakening the Vice-Chancellor except to shout louder.

'Who is the greater? Shelley or KEATS . . . KEATS . . . KEATS?' yelled Tristram, his moustache bristling in warlord style and his voice sounding like Tamburlaine the Great rallying his troops before going into battle. So intimidated was a lady in the third row that, without thinking, she audibly replied, 'Keats, if you say so.' And for her pains she received the kind of look that once preceded the burning of a major city.

'At the present time, Shelley,' went on Tristram. 'Keats may use language more richly but Shelley has so much to say to us that he might be alive today.' And he paused for effect and directed a huge smile at Clope, who frowned, squinted and emitted a whirring, gurgling noise that was now as much a snarl as a sniff, all the time twisting in his seat like a corkscrew trying and failing to get a bottle open.

The lecture was halfway through and, boy, it was going well; or so Tristram felt. He had never been more excited. If a Formula One racing car could have talked, it would have sounded like him. There was a vroom-vroom about the way he was speaking. But those caffeine tablets, which had given him this energy, started to have an additional effect. Tristram had remembered much – his briefcase, all ten copies of his lecture, and two timepieces – but he had forgotten one thing. He had forgotten to relieve himself before he started to speak. And the coffee and caffeine tablets, combined with the swigs and sips of water he was still taking from the glass on the lectern, were making him feel more and more uncomfortable. To be blunt, he began desperately to want to pee.

But obviously he couldn't just stop the lecture, walk off the platform and go to the gents. That would be embarrassing for everybody. All he could do was invisibly to clench the relevant parts of himself. But the strain was tremendous and, without wanting to, Tristram started slightly to hop.

'Let us reconsider the case of KEATS here.'

Hop.

'In our admiration for KEATS let us not forget Byron and Wordsworth.'

Hop, hop.

'If Shelley and KEATS were with us today, what would they be saying?'

Hop, hop, hop.

'They don't call him the Flinking Bunny for nothing,' whispered George Macdonald to his wife Muriel. 'But until now I'd never realised what flinking meant. It means jumping up and down like a rabbit and flashing your teeth like Bugs Bunny.' And George's dear old dromedary couldn't quite stifle one of her hearty chuckles.

The Vice-Chancellor didn't care, because he was deeply asleep and having a dream in which he was drinking port with old friends, but Clope was getting angrier and angrier. Perhaps Throstlethwaite was saying sensible things about Romantic poetry – he had no opinion on something essentially so trivial – but why was he behaving like this? Why did he keep shouting 'KEATS', feverishly jumping up and down, and exposing his teeth in a way that suggested he was threatening to bite or swallow him, Clope? And why had he earlier muttered insulting things about Dundee and Dundee cakes? This wasn't just madness. It wasn't even the result of heroin addiction. It was some sort of attack on his Scottishness. For a moment, Clope squinted so hard that his eyes shut and he had a brief vision in which his hero, Robert the Bruce, conquered an English force and hanged its leader, Tristram the Troublesome, Evil Earl of Throstlethwaite.

On went the lecture in its vivid, vital way, always making perfect sense but, thanks to Tristram's need to visit the gents, even faster than before. Then, quite suddenly, it came to a halt. Tristram had scrupulously put together all those copies, ensuring they were in the right order, but he had still managed to place one page the wrong way round.

Now, this shouldn't have mattered. Once he had realised his error, all Tristram had to do was turn the page the right way round. But the spirit of Spooner, who was so adept at getting things diametrically the wrong way round, momentarily seized him. His knees tight together, Tristram half-walked, half-jumped to the other side of the lectern and, still hopping like a man in a sack race, continued to deliver his lecture, reading the offending page with his back to the audience.

Since little could be heard but an occasional shout of 'KEATS', the audience shifted in its seats even more. George Macdonald couldn't help chortling in his Falstaffian way, and several undergraduates at the back began to laugh too. Clope sniffed and snarled. The Vice-Chancellor snored. And then an even odder sound was heard. It was a distinct ringing. What was it?

Tristram swivelled round in the middle of a sentence, more outraged by the intrusive noise than he was embarrassed by the sudden realisation that he had been addressing a wall at the back of the stage. He could not believe it. Somebody had failed to turn off his or her mobile phone. He stopped speaking and let his gaze sweep piercingly through the audience, pausing only to give a quick grin at Clope. The impression he gave was that the wages of this particular sin might indeed be death.

And yet wasn't it an unusual sound for a mobile phone? Had someone brought a conventional telephone into the lecture hall? And, if so, how had they managed to connect it to a socket in the wall? Yet the noise wasn't right for a land line either. It was a loud, long, ceaseless ring and, Tristram realised, it wasn't coming from the audience at all. No, it was coming from him.

Oh no, oh dear, oh Spooner, it was his bedside clock, the alarm clock, the clock he had conscientiously put in his jacket pocket in case his wristwatch went wrong. Tristram realised that the only way of saving the situation was to act quickly. So instantly he reached into his pocket. The trouble was that he was so keen to turn off the alarm that he reached into his pocket with both hands and, since his pocket was not very big, they got stuck. And the more he tried to pull them out, and the clock with them, the more stuck they managed to get.

What was to be done? All the astonished audience could see was a red-faced Dr Tristram Throstlethwaite having a desperate wrestling-match with his own jacket, hopping and emitting a ringing sound as he did so. What had this to do with Shelley and Keats or, come to that, Wordsworth, Byron and Coleridge?

But then the fight was over, because the jacket ripped and the torn pocket opened, showering the remaining caffeine pills on to the floor. Tristram yanked out his bedside clock and hammered its top so hard against the lectern that the alarm stopped ringing, gave a sort of metallic gulp and burst open. An undergraduate at the back gave a cheer. His friends clapped. And one or two audience members even managed to convince themselves that the whole event was deliberate. Words like 'post-modern' and 'deconstructionism' wafted knowingly across an aisle, reaching George Macdonald, who suppressed a guffaw and whispered, 'Post-flinking or flinkism, I think,' to Muriel, who this time burst out laughing herself.

But nothing so sympathetic came from Clope. He knew when he was being got at. He knew when the English Department was being deliberately brought into disrepute. He even felt a sense of relief. Surely this meant he could now sack the mothball assassin, dog-killer and all-round troublemaker without any reasonable person opposing him. Surely this meant he could look forward to life without a Throstlethwaite in his hair, still less a Throstlethwaite baiting him or yelling 'KEATS' while flashing his teeth and threatening to bite him.

But Clope was wrong. In an instant, Tristram had hopped, skipped and jumped behind the lectern again, given Clope another enormous smile, glared at the rest of the audience as if daring it to argue with him, and started to speed through the remainder of his lecture. And he was in luck too, for the sound of the alarm had worked where the shouts of 'KEATS' hadn't. The Vice-Chancellor had woken up from his dream just as he had finished drinking a particularly rich and satisfying glass of port to discover to his delight that he would have to listen to very little more lecture. Indeed, young Throstlethwaite wasn't only setting a fine example to all academics by talking at a rate of knots; he was bouncing up and down with the sort of enthusiasm for his subject that it was incumbent on universities to encourage, applaud and reward.

As Tristram came to his close, triumphantly shouting out the names of both 'KEATS' and 'SHELLEY' and then following it with a tiny, hopping sort of bow, the Vice-Chancellor clambered to his feet and started to clap. Seeing this, the rest of the university staff rose from their chairs and joined in what was now a standing ovation. 'Good old bunny,' cried George Macdonald, and a group of under-graduates chorused 'flinking, flinking, flinking bunny!'

The Vice-Chancellor hadn't a clue what this meant, but concluded it must be a good-natured rallying cry, a sort of literary football chant, that had just been introduced into the English Department, presumably by Clope himself. He was pleased to find that one of his most recent appointees had taken so original a step towards improving staff morale. Yet when he turned to congratulate Clope, he was shocked to discover that the professor was sitting, not standing, and, so far from clapping, was staring at Throstlethwaite in an odd, hostile way.

'Clope,' said the Vice-Chancellor reproachfully, assuming that this was a display of professional jealousy. 'Clope, don't you think the young fellow deserves our thanks?'

Clope gave a start, blinked, forced a thin, sour smile on to his face and slowly, very slowly stood up and began to do something with his hands you couldn't call applaud or clap. He sort of brushed them together, as if getting rid of a coating of powdery dirt. Even more shocked, the Vice-Chancellor gave Clope a frown, marched on to the platform, grabbed Tristram by the hand, held his arm aloft, and delivered the public thanks that had been Clope's prerogative.

'A distinguished effort,' the Vice-Chancellor told the audience. 'A brilliant chap and a credit to the university. A real – what's your department's term of appreciation? – a real *flinking bunny*! We must see to it that this lecture is published and distributed as widely as possible. Professor Clope will, of course, see that this happens, won't you Clope?' And he looked down at Clope in a manner that was at once commanding and accusing.

Clope couldn't speak, so he just gave a ghastly nod. As for Tristram, he couldn't hold himself in any more. He gave Clope a quick grin, muttered, 'Thank you, Vice-Chancellor,' and bounded off the platform, forgetting to take his lecture or his briefcase as he left the auditorium and ran like a hare towards the gents' loo.

The Vice-Chancellor wasn't the least offended by this. It meant that, like him, Tristram liked to get through public occasions as quickly as possible, and it meant that he was the sort of person who didn't think time should be wasted on congratulations.

'A modest chap too,' said the Vice-Chancellor, beaming at the audience. 'A man without envy. An example to some of us. We need more young men like him.'

And, just for a moment, he frowned again at Clope, who simply stood there, still looking like a needle or a corkscrew, but one that was blunt, rusty and old.

## THE VAGUE BOOK 2

*Who was the vaguest man who ever lived? That would be a hotly contested position, attracting competitors who would range from Thomas Edison to Adam Smith, from*

*W.A. Spooner to the actors Ralph Richardson and John Gielgud, to the gentleman who absentmindedly poured an evil-tasting, medicinal ointment instead of oil on the asparagus he gave Caesar at a Roman feast. (Caesar ate the dish, explaining afterwards that he didn't want to be rude to his host.)*

*King George III once shook hands with a tree in Windsor Great Park in the belief that he was greeting Frederick the Great; but then George was probably a bit mad at the time, so he would be excluded from competing. Indeed, Ronald Reagan should be similarly excluded, although it was when he was still the American president and long before he succumbed to a serious ailment of the mind that he indulged in such 'Bushisms' as going to Brazil and calling it Bolivia and greeting Princess Diana as Princess David.*

*We are concerned here with the hale and the sane, the intelligent and the gifted. People whose otherwise good and sometimes superb minds are apt to drift in unwanted directions, waft about in unexpected areas, and settle in unusual places. People – well, people a bit like me, Tristram Throstlethwaite, if that's not too boastful.*

*Actually, a finalist and maybe a surprise winner would be Ronald Duncan. He was well known as a poet and playwright in the 1950s, though, like so many of the items that belonged to him in his lifetime, his reputation got mislaid in the years afterwards. He once went to one of the larger London termini to catch a train to Cambridge, where he was due to give a lecture. He was afraid of being late and, as he wrote afterwards, was in an agitated, anxious state of mind. 'Is this the train for Cambridge?' he asked the inspector at the barrier.*

'Straight on,' came the reply – and Duncan thanked him, hurried through the barrier and went straight on.

Straight on and on. Duncan walked the length of the platform. He walked off the end of the platform on to the tracks. He walked beside the tracks over crossings and through tunnels, all the time earnestly rehearsing the lecture he was to give that evening. A quarter-of-an-hour and almost a mile later he met a platelayer, who asked him where he was going.

'To Cambridge,' snapped Duncan, irritated to have his thoughts so rudely interrupted.

'Wouldn't a train be quicker?' asked the platelayer.

'Oh yes, I suppose so,' said Duncan as he suddenly realised where he was and how he had got there.

Travel had a funny effect on Duncan. On one occasion he sat in the waiting room at Salisbury station for five hours, wondering why he was changing trains and where he was going before it occurred to him to look at his ticket, which told him what his destination actually was. Another time he was driving his car from London to Bristol when he switched on the radio. On it was a game show he disliked so much that, when he had heard it before, he had rushed out of the room to avoid listening to it. 'I now found myself doing the same thing,' he wrote later, 'but travelling at 60 miles an hour, the door half open, myself hanging out and nobody steering the car.'

On yet another occasion, a small, mild-looking man sat down beside him in the first-class compartment in which he was travelling by rail to London and, to the testy Duncan's intense irritation, took out a large pack of smoked salmon sandwiches, put them on his lap and prepared to devour them. Hoping to ignore the sound of *munching, which he hated, Duncan opened his newspaper with a 'harrumph' and began to read.*

*Later, the restaurant car attendant came round to ask if anybody wanted a ticket for lunch and the small man said yes, he did, at the first sitting. Duncan was revolted. How could anybody be so greedy? 'These spring mornings give one quite an appetite, don't they?' he said sarcastically to the small, mild man, who gave him a wan smile in return.*

*'And will you be taking lunch, sir?' the attendant asked Duncan.*

*'Yes, at the second sitting,' replied the poet emphatically, since he was determined to avoid the sight of the small man gorging himself in the restaurant car.*

*But there was a surprising response to Duncan's decision. 'That's some relief to hear,' the small man muttered.*

*Duncan was outraged. How dare this dreadful little glutton say something so appallingly hypocritical and rude? 'Do you mind explaining yourself?' he yapped indignantly.*

*'Not at all,' replied the small, mild man. 'I'm relieved to hear that we're not having lunch together.'*

*'Do you mind telling me why?' gasped Duncan, barely able to get out the words in his anger.*

*'Because I was afraid that if we'd gone to the restaurant car together you might have eaten my lunch too.'*

*Never had Duncan been so insulted. 'British Railways are probably able to provide a meal for two people,' he shouted.*

*'Even so,' replied the small man. 'That might not have prevented you eating mine.'*

'Sir,' bellowed Duncan. 'You're obsessed with food.
You're the greediest little man I've ever travelled with.
First, you wolf a great pile of sandwiches...'

'But I haven't eaten anything,' moaned the small,
mild man. 'You ate them all. That's why I want the first
lunch.'

At that point a man on the seat opposite intervened.
The small man was right. It seemed that every time
Duncan's neighbour made to eat a sandwich, Duncan's
hand shot out from beneath his newspaper and seized it.
Indeed, before the poet had finished one sandwich, he
reached out to grab another.

'You didn't even leave him one,' said the man opposite.

'It's true,' wailed the small man, 'and I'm very partial
to smoked salmon.'

Duncan began to expostulate that it couldn't be true
but, as he spoke, he realised that there was a telltale taste
of smoked salmon on his tongue. And, to do him justice,
he took the small, mild man to the dining car and paid for
his lunch there.

This story is recorded in more detail in Duncan's
memoirs, How to Make Enemies, along with several
others. Why, for instance, did he get on a London bus and
ask for a ticket to Calcutta, getting the reply from the
conductor, 'You'll have to change, we only go as far as
Oxford Circus.' He couldn't explain the error until he
remembered there had been a story in the evening paper
about that city. Why did he then ask the waitress in the
café where he went on to have tea, first for 'hot buttered
monsoons', next for 'mangoes'? For the same reason,
presumably. Duncan's own theory was that his
subconscious thoughts, which this time happened to

*concern India, had come bubbling up into his conscious mind and from there into his mouth. And, yes, that's very much the sort of thing that happens to us vague and abstracted people.*

# THREE

One of the things Tristram most likes to do is go to the theatre that's situated near the university campus and, even though it stages professional productions and brings in professional companies, calls itself the University Theatre. There are other regular members of the audience, too, some of whom he has got to know. One of these is a beefy, cheerful man called Valentine, who has a round face, a big smile and not only a moustache but also a neat, black beard. In fact, Valentine and Tristram have become friendly enough to share a glass of wine – or 'bright red snifter', as Valentine jovially calls it – in the interval of whatever play they're seeing. They will discuss the acting and sometimes talk about their interests, which in Valentine's case is hill-climbing and mountaineering. Then they'll return to their seats, feeling better for the chat and the drink. Tristram even feels he knows Valentine well enough to call him Val.

But it doesn't always happen like this. There are, of course, times when Tristram and Valentine don't happen to go to the theatre the same night. There are other times when Valentine's shape and personality mysteriously change. As it seems to Tristram, he gets fatter; his face gets redder; his beard gets messier; he no longer looks cheerful. In fact, he looks grumpy and becomes a bit smelly.

At all events, he clearly doesn't want to share a glass of wine or even a conversation. When Tristram greets him with a cry of 'Hi, Val', and jokily calls out 'Bright red snifter ahoy!' he doesn't react with the enthusiasm he normally displays. Instead, he blinks and looks the other way, muttering to himself in a low, not-very-friendly tone. And yet, when Tristram sees him at another performance a few weeks later, he's back to his old self: smiling, chatting, drinking that bright red snifter as cheerfully as ever and looking physically a lot trimmer.

At first Tristram shrugged off these weird inconsistencies. Everybody has mood changes. Everybody has up moments and down moments. Many people have periods when they eat and drink more than they normally would and so get fatter. Sometimes people wash a lot and sometimes they don't. But with Val the changes were unusually marked. And one night at the theatre it seemed to Tristram that his friend's body was not just fat but obese, his face not just red but florid, and his body-odour sort of fungoid, like an old damp cellar that's been invaded by mice, some of whom have perished and haven't yet completed the process of rotting. And when Tristram hailed him and began to suggest they share a bright red snifter, he thought he heard the sadly changed Val growl 'maniac' in a way that wasn't pleasant at all.

'My God, Val has let himself go this time,' Tristram said to himself and began to worry about him. These changes just weren't normal. They suggested that poor Valentine had problems. Nice as he was, he clearly had trouble with his nerves and maybe with his head. Really, he needed advice from a well-qualified doctor or psychiatrist, since he was presumably suffering from manic depression or bipolar disorder and, as nobody seemed to have told him this, Tristram felt that he had to do so. He didn't know Val all that well, but he liked him and felt some sense of responsibility towards him. And Tristram knew just the medical man to help his friend. As we've mentioned before, he had once lain on his couch, discussing the vagueness that had been worrying his parents, and knew him to be a well-qualified, sensitive psychiatrist who, like many of the best of his profession, had a German name: Furtbattler.

But clearly he had to choose his moment. It would be no use approaching Val when he was in one of his big, fat, smelly, mice-infested, muttering moods and asking him if he would like to see Furtbattler. Tristram knew he had to raise the subject carefully and tactfully when his friend was looking relaxed and feeling happy, preferably over a glass of red wine. And the time for that came sooner than he expected, only a few weeks after he had seen Val looking horribly bloated at a production of Arthur Miller's *Death of a Salesman*.

It was the interval of a performance of *Hamlet* and Valentine gave every appearance of having returned to his usual cheery, robust self. He was again beefy-looking but certainly not obese, and he was again offering Tristram a glass of wine or 'bright red snifter'. How could a man puff up and puff down like a balloon, wondered Tristram. How could his mood go up and down so quickly? Human beings were strange.

In fact, Valentine was in an unusually cheery, very 'up' mood during the interval. 'God, that Hamlet!' he cried. 'Why is he in such a state? Why does he keep moping about the stage mumbling, "To be or not to be"? I'll tell you what he needs. He needs a good day on the tallest mountain he can find in Denmark. That'll put some lead in his pencil!'

He was half-joking, but Tristram was so concerned about his mental state he didn't fully realise it. He thought his friend was talking the sort of pernicious nonsense that sometimes cropped up in undergraduate essays. He was saying eccentric and possibly mad things about a tragic hero who was understandably feeling a bit flustered, having just been ordered by his father's ghost to murder an uncle who happened to be the king of Denmark. And Val's manner confirmed this diagnosis. This was exactly the way manic depressive or bipolar people behaved: up and down, up and down, up and down.

So Tristram, who seldom forgets he comes from the great Throstlethwaite warrior clan and likes to think of himself as a pretty proactive sort of chap, took his courage in both hands. 'You seem very up today, Val,' he said.

'Well, so I am,' replied Valentine. 'Or so I have been. I've just been doing a bit of mountaineering. I've been up Snowdon. Up, up and up!' And he gave a big, hearty laugh, as if he'd never had a moment's trouble in his life.

But Tristram wasn't fooled. 'Yes, but sometimes you're down,' he said in the careful, soothing way he'd planned.

Valentine looked slightly surprised. 'Well, yes, if you go up you have to come down,' he said.

'Precisely,' said Tristram in a meaningful way. 'I'm sure that's what Furtbattler would say.'

'Furtbattler?' asked Valentine, looking still more puzzled.

'Never heard of him. Swiss, is he? Alpine expert or something?'

Well, it's true that many psychiatrists study in Switzerland, often in Zurich or Geneva, both of which offer fine views of the Alps. Even the great Carl Gustav Jung, who actually was Swiss, could at a stretch be described as an Alpine expert, as could many of his followers; or so Tristram thought.

'Actually, Furtbattler is Austrian in origin,' he said, 'and, yes, very expert in his field.'

'I don't know about fields,' said Valentine, 'but when it comes to mountains, and especially the Alps, the Swiss and the Austrians are the best.'

Why was Val babbling about the Alps, Tristram asked himself. He must be sicker than anybody knew. Like many mentally ill people, Val was refusing to confront the real problem. He wanted to talk about his hobby, which was mountaineering, and not his illness, which was bipolar disorder or manic depression. But then Tristram remembered; to be fair to Val, he hadn't made it clear who Furtbattler was or what he did.

'Actually, Furtbattler is a doctor,' he said.

'Oh,' said Valentine, sipping at his wine, 'and he's a bit of a climber too?'

'In a way,' whispered Tristram, for he didn't want to be overheard. 'He climbs minds.'

Unsurprisingly, Valentine misheard that. He thought that Tristram was telling him, for some unexplained reason, that this Austrian doctor climbed in and out of mines. This Furtbiggler or Furtfighter was presumably a potholer, meaning that he spent his leisure time climbing into deep underground caves, often with the help of ropes.

'Well, that's nice,' said Val uncertainly. 'But I expect he

prefers the real thing. There's nothing to beat a good mountain, is there?'

'Would you like to meet him?' asked Tristram. 'I'm sure you'd find him helpful, especially when you're really down.'

'Really down?' repeated Valentine, now sounding truly baffled. 'But I'm down most of the time. Down is where I live. And I don't need anybody's help when I'm down, do I?'

Oh dear, thought Tristram, he's worse than I imagined. And he said, this time talking very slowly, solemnly and tactfully, 'I know it's not my business, but I do want to help. And I could give you an introduction to Furtbattler any time you want. I think you'd find him very sensitive to all your anxieties.'

Valentine didn't know what to say. He couldn't imagine why Tristram thought he needed a very sensitive, mid-European doctor to help him come down mountains or even clamber down mines or potholes. A fit, sensible, courageous person was what he wanted on his team in such places, and it didn't matter whether that person was a doctor, dentist, plumber or astronaut. Moreover, he was offended by Tristram's suggestion that he got anxious when he went climbing. He never, ever felt that way. Hadn't he climbed dangerous crags and reached far-off peaks without any problem? Hadn't he stood on an Alp chortling with happiness as he looked at the sun? Wasn't he, well, a pretty bold sort of bloke?

But the bell sounded for the second half of the play, so all Valentine did was say stiffly, 'Well, see you,' and go back into the theatre to see Hamlet stop hesitating, avenge that pushy spook by killing his murderous uncle, and then die himself, along with a distressingly large portion of Denmark. And after the performance he didn't speak to Tristram at all.

He just gave him a curt nod and left the University Theatre.

Tristram was worried. He had to admit that the conversation hadn't gone all that brilliantly well. Indeed, he had failed Val. He hadn't been tactful enough. All he seemed to have done was upset the poor, afflicted man. By bringing his troubles into the open, he might even have made him sicker. And his worst fears were realised when he next saw Val, which was a month or so later, at a performance of Chekhov's *The Seagull*. His friend wasn't just fat, wasn't just bloated, wasn't even just obese. He looked like the coupling of a mammoth and a gorilla. You could almost smell the stench of the zoo emanating from him. And he sighed and grunted as he lumbered across the theatre foyer.

Also, he ignored Tristram. Or maybe he just didn't notice him. So what was Tristram to do? He couldn't pretend he hadn't seen an old friend who was clearly even more in need of help than before. In fact, it would be rude, cowardly and perhaps even criminal not to offer Valentine a drink and a chat, because *The Seagull* was surely not the play for a manic depressive to see when he was in a down phase. As Chekhov *aficionados* will recall, it's a sad play and at the end sadder than sad, since the heroine runs out of the french windows to be even more unhappy than she already is and the hero, who is a writer, tears up all his manuscripts and then shoots himself dead. So Tristram walked nervously towards poor, overblown Valentine and hailed him in his jolliest manner.

'Hi, Val,' cried Tristram, putting on as big a smile as he could muster. 'Bright red snifter ahoy!'

Poor, overblown, hairy Valentine didn't just give a start. He stopped, lurched and looked as if he was about to explode. Then he gave Tristram a look of pure hatred.

'Who the hell are you?' he growled.

'Er . . . ah,' replied Tristram, horrified to find his old chum so utterly and inexplicably upset he couldn't even name his name. 'Er . . . um . . . Tristram, of course.'

'Well, Tristram,' said overblown Valentine, 'I don't know what you want. I don't know why you keep calling me by a woman's name and I don't know why you think I'm a red-coloured snifter. And if you say anything to me again I will call the police and demand that they arrest you as a stalker. That's a promise.'

And he lurched and lumbered murderously away, puffing and wheezing and muttering that he might have a red face, but that was because he suffered from high blood pressure, not because he was a snifter.

Tristram stood where he was, feeling aghast. He had clearly offended Valentine so much that he had gone completely to seed and become seriously ill. What was he to do to rectify a situation that had become so distressing? But then a strange thing happened. Tristram looked up and saw a familiar face and a familiar body come through the door at the other end of the theatre foyer. It wasn't! It couldn't be! Yes, it was. It was Valentine.

Moreover, it was a Valentine who had been restored to normal. His beard was pretty neat and tidy. His stomach stuck out only a little bit. His face was pinkish white, not red, not florid. He wasn't at all like a mammoth or hairy gorilla, still less a blend of the two. He didn't look like a man who stank of cellars or mushrooms or rotting mice or zoos or, indeed, was exuding any sort of stench. It was highly likely that he had washed. The only different thing was that, instead of greeting Tristram with a cry of 'Time for a bright red snifter', he pretended not to see him.

At long last Tristram asked himself the obvious question: how could Valentine change his appearance so quickly? And at long last he came to the obvious conclusion.

Beefy Valentine and Obese Valentine were two different men. Beefy Valentine was Beefy Valentine and Obese Valentine was someone else altogether: a George or a Harold or, perhaps, a Godzilla. Beefy Valentine was his friend and maybe now his ex-friend, and Obese Valentine was his enemy and maybe now his mortal enemy.

Tristram gave a low moan of 'Oh no, oh dear', followed by a stuttery wail of 'Oh Spooner!' and felt his moustache begin to shudder and sag. How could he have been such a fool? Both men had black beards, wore dark suits and were roughly the same height, but they weren't identical twins. They looked somewhat similar but, no, they weren't the same.

Again Tristram looked across the theatre foyer, hoping that at least one of these Valentines was a beardy mirage. But, oh no, oh Spooner, it was all too true. There was his old friend, Beefy Val, dusting himself down and still refusing to look at Tristram, and there was Obese Val, or whatever he was called, glaring at Tristram as if daring him to come and call him a girly name or shout 'bright red snifter' at him. And Tristram just stood there, wishing that he, like the hero of Chekhov's *Seagull*, could shoot himself with a pistol or, like the heroine at the end of the same play, run into the night crazily shouting 'I'm a seagull'. What *was* he to do?

Yes, what *was* he to do? That was a question Tristram had sometimes had to ask himself before, because, if the truth were to be told, this wasn't the first time he had mistaken someone for someone else. In fact, the problem took two forms. There were days when he didn't recognise people he knew quite well. Like the unnamed party guest who didn't know he was talking to Princess Margaret, he had more than once tried to coax people's identities out of them by asking them questions he thought might well help to reveal who they were. And Tristram will admit that, as with Princess Margaret, this has sometimes led to serious embarrassment.

Well, he denies the tale of the time a middle-aged woman had stopped him in the street with a cheery, 'Lovely to see you, Tristram.' According to his friends and relatives, it wasn't until he asked, 'And how are the children?' thinking that this might lead to a reply that would unmask this familiar-seeming stranger, that the truth came out. 'Well, you should know,' said his mother, 'I've only one child, and it's you.'

'I can't remember that incident at all,' Tristram usually says stiffly, waiting for the inevitable riposte, which is: 'That doesn't prove anything, does it?' But then a memory hits him, which is of this unknown woman's features slowly morphing into his mother's face – and he hastily changes the subject.

The other problem is the very opposite. Unfamiliar faces somehow turn into familiar ones. Passers-by seem to look like people he knows or once knew, causing Tristram to greet genuine strangers with cries of 'Hello, Jack' or 'Good to see you, Jill'. This can also lead to awkwardness. When he was a very young man he was a huge fan of the actor Alec Guinness, whom he had seen playing the part of the spymaster George Smiley in *Tinker, Tailor, Soldier, Spy* and several other television adaptations of novels by John le Carré. And who should he see when he entered the lift in a

big, local department store but, as he thought, the great
man himself?

Tristram just couldn't contain himself. 'You are a great
Smiley,' he blurted.'A great what?' said the man.

'A terrific Smiley,' said Tristram. 'In your wonderfully
quiet, understated way.'

'What?'

'You couldn't be more Smiley if you tried, which of
course you do,' gushed Tristram. 'Try, I mean.'

'I think you've got the wrong bloke,' said the man in
what seemed to be a slight cockney accent.

'And you can do funny voices,' burbled Tristram, adding,
'don't worry, your secret is safe with me.' And he tapped his
nose in what he hoped was a conspiratorial sort of way.

At that the man got out of the lift, which had reached the
top floor, and as soon as Tristram followed him, got back in
and pressed the down button. That left Tristram, first with
a feeling that he had been intrusive, then with a dim but
growing sense that he had made an embarrassing mistake.

And sometimes such encounters have been worse than
merely embarrassing. Tristram may have a bad memory,
but he'll never forget the day when he was convinced that a
skinhead wearing a Millwall Football Club shirt was his
cousin Sebastian from Wales. Skinheads don't like being
solicitously asked why they have suddenly gone bald. They
don't like being asked how things are in Wales, a place they
think is populated by gay foreigners with long hair. Even
less do they like being called Sebastian, which is a name
seldom heard on the terraces or the pitch at Millwall.
Fortunately, a police car was passing, so Tristram didn't
end up strangled with a football scarf, only told he was
something he doesn't care to recall.

Anyway, the Valentine Problem, as he called it, began to obsess Tristram and keep him awake at night. He had to apologise to Beefy Valentine and, if possible, he had to try to explain himself and apologise to Obese Valentine or whatever his name was. He couldn't have people sitting near him in the theatre either being angry at him or hating him so much they would call the police if he said the wrong thing. That way, he would never enjoy a play again. But how was he to put right the wrong he'd committed? With Beefy Valentine that should be relatively easy because, until recently, he and Tristram had been friendly enough to talk about plays and drink wine together. But Obese Valentine, the semi-human mammoth? That was quite another matter.

First things first. Tristram next saw Valentine at a performance of Lorca's *The House of Bernarda Alba* – in which a lot of Spanish women spend two hours complaining about having to be Spanish women – and went boldly up to him in the interval.

'I owe you an apology, Val,' he said. 'I was very confused when I saw you last and I think I may have said some things which confused you too.'

'Well, yes, you did,' replied Valentine cautiously, adding, 'I could certainly do with a bright red snifter.'

Tristram took this as a good sign. Val wanted a reconciliation. So he bought him a glass of red wine and began to try to explain himself.

'Yes, I may have given the impression I thought you were mad,' said Tristram. 'And I don't. I want to assure you it was all a mistake on my part.'

'Thank you very much,' said Valentine in a voice that didn't sound exactly grateful. 'But do you mind telling me why you thought I was mad?'

'Not because you are mad,' repeated Tristram earnestly. 'Please don't think that.'

'Actually, I don't think I'm mad,' said Valentine, again sounding not altogether thrilled with what Tristram was saying.

'No,' went on Tristram. 'Absolutely not. You see, I was confusing you with someone else.'

'Someone mad?'

'No, no, probably not,' said Tristram quickly. 'Not as far as I know. Though he is a bit odd. He's much fatter than you and has a much redder face and a much hairier beard. And, well, he stinks. He's not really like you at all.'

'Well, thank you very much,' said Valentine again, still not sounding as if he meant it.

'And I'm sure he's not a mountaineer,' went on Tristram. 'He looks as if he would find it difficult to climb a staircase. He puffs and wheezes a lot.'

'Thank you very much indeed,' repeated Valentine not very nicely at all.

This conversation was not going exactly as Tristram had planned it, but it was too late to go back and too difficult to explain much more.

'So I hope you understand,' finished Tristram weakly.

'Well,' said Valentine evenly. 'Well. What I understand is that for some reason you have been confusing me – *me* – with a large, red, hairy man who is very smelly, may be mad, and gets so tired climbing the stairs he should probably stay in bed waiting for a doctor, a psychiatrist, or both. Doesn't quite sound like someone who has conquered Mont Blanc, does it?'

'I did say I got very confused,' said Tristram feebly.

'Maybe you should see Fartbelcher or whatever his name

is.' And Valentine put down his glass of wine, even though it was unfinished, and walked away, his chin pointing defiantly forward, as if he was ready to scale every peak in the world, starting with Everest itself.

Tristram had to be honest. Once again, a conversation with Val hadn't gone all that well. But (he reminded himself) it wasn't for nothing that he belonged to a clan whose ancient motto, stolen without acknowledgement by a certain American president, was '*nihil timeo praeter timorem ipsum*' or 'I fear nothing but fear itself'. No, it wasn't for nothing that he was descended from the great Yorkshire warriors who fought behind and sometimes beside those other great Yorkshire warriors, the men who started the Wars of the Roses 500 years ago. How could a scion of the Throstlethwaite dynasty be afraid of confronting anyone, even someone large and murderous-looking? Somehow (Tristram told himself) he had to talk to Obese Valentine, or the Anonymous Hulk as he had begun mentally to call him, and try to befriend him. Or if not actually befriend him, at least ensure he didn't keep glaring horribly at him, at least make some sort of peace.

But how to do it? Telling Val he had confused him with a great, grunting man-mountain hadn't really worked. He had to admit that. But if he told the Anonymous Hulk he had confused him with someone neat and trim, the Hulk would surely be flattered. It would be like telling an ogre he was a bit like a prince, or a gorilla that he was Tarzan, or a Quasimodo that he was really Cary Grant. If he said to the Hulk, 'I'm sorry I mistook you for a handsome, athletic mountaineer,' well, the Hulk might even end up thanking him.

Tristram's chance came several weeks later and in a very unexpected way. He was once again in the University

Theatre's foyer, this time during the interval of a play by David Hare called *Plenty*, which is about a British woman who performs a series of brave deeds in Nazi-occupied France, comes home, gets disillusioned and bored, and goes violently insane. Tristram was in one of his daydreams, vaguely wondering if there was an essay to be written about Shelley's influence on David Hare, when he felt a jolt in the back. He turned to see who had bumped him and got the shock of his life. It was large man in a dark suit with a florid face and a black beard. It was Obese Valentine or the Anonymous Hulk – wasn't it?

'Oh my God,' gasped Tristram and reeled back, in his panic thinking that the jolt in the back might be the prelude of something worse, like a kick on the shin or a bite on the chin.

'Sorry,' said the Anonymous Hulk, giving Tristram a look that was neither friendly nor unfriendly, neither nice nor nasty. It was the sort of calm, unsurprised look you might give to something you had every day for breakfast, like a boiled egg or a piece of toast.

That thought worried Tristram, since he didn't particularly want to be the Hulk's breakfast. So he answered nervously but politely, 'That's all right.' Then he recovered his courage, adding, 'That's quite all right, especially when it's me who owes you an apology.'

'Is that right, Tristram?' said the Anonymous Hulk. 'And what makes you think that?'

Tristram was beginning to find all this calmness sinister, especially as he thought he detected the hint of a German accent in the Hulk's voice. It might just be the calm before some awful Prussian storm or neo-Nazi onslaught. And how did the Hulk know his name? Then he remembered that he had told him he was called Tristram just after he had invited him to have a bright red snifter and just before Obese Valentine, or whatever he was called, had taken this as a slur on the colour of his face and had threatened to call the police. But what was he to say in answer to the Anonymous Hulk's question?

'Well, I didn't mean to be rude when I last saw you,' said Tristram. 'But I was rude and I'm sorry.'

'Ah,' said the Hulk in his strangely quiet way. 'And what makes you feel that?'

Tristram again found this menacing. Why did this Hulk keep asking him what he was thinking and feeling in a voice that put him in mind of Markus Wolf, the famous East German spymaster and Stasi supersleuth? The thing now was clearly to do what he had planned and try to appease him.

'Well, I mistook you for a mountaineer I know,' said Tristram. 'A very fine, strong mountaineer, actually.'

'Interesting,' said the Hulk. 'You are in need of the company of very fine, strong mountaineers?'

'Also I got your name wrong,' said Tristram, deciding it would be wiser not to reply to this curious question. 'Badly wrong, stupidly wrong.'

'Many people get my name wrong,' said the Hulk, giving a laugh that wasn't exactly a laugh, more the sort of long, satisfied purr a cat gives when it brings a dead mouse or bird to its master or mistress. 'Tell me, do you feel guilty about this?'

This was so unlike Obese Valentine's reaction to being called Val or a red snifter that Tristram found himself thinking two things more or less at the same time. Either this man was softening him up for the kill, lulling him into a mental state when he would be unprepared for the explosion of Hulk rage when it finally burst out. Or he was another person, a third Valentine or, rather, a sort of in-between Val and Hulk.

'I am rather absentminded after all,' thought Tristram and, without realising he was speaking aloud, added to himself, 'I have to be very careful.'

'And what makes you think that?' asked the In-Between Hulk again, smiling a smile that wasn't quite a smile. 'Why do you have to be so very careful? What is the reason for that?'

But Tristram didn't answer. Instead, he gave the questioner as complete a look as he could while pretending not to look too hard at him. Beard, face, suit? Well, they weren't exactly neat but perhaps they were a bit more tidy than Tristram seemed to remember they were. Body? That was stout, even fat, but perhaps not as enormous as he recalled it being. Smell? Tristram just couldn't prevent himself leaning forward and, while trying to pretend he was recovering from a slight cold, gave the Hulk a long, lingering sniff. No, there was no mushroomy stench. This hulk didn't smell like an old dungeon or a cellar packed with defunct mice, as the Anonymous Hulk did, and so perhaps this hulk wasn't a hulk at all. Perhaps he was just an overweight but perfectly pacific person – a bulk rather than a hulk – who happened to exist somewhere between Valentine and the man-monster.

'Atishoo!' cried Tristram, thinking he was being sly. 'I wish this wretched cold would go away.'

But it isn't easy to disguise it when you are sniffing at someone in an inquisitive sort of way. And it isn't particularly pleasant to be sniffed at by someone else, even someone who sounds apologetic. But this hulk didn't seem to be offended at all. He remained very, very calm. It was as if something soothing, like camomile tea, had acquired a voice.

'It is your cold that you believe is the problem?' asked the In-Between Hulk. 'And what makes you think that?'

Tristram had had enough. He felt confused and alarmed and generally in a sadly familiar sort of muddle. He felt the way he feels when he settles down for a cup of tea and realises he has assiduously put coffee into the pot; only worse, much worse. It was time to come to the point. 'Please, what is your name?' he asked politely but desperately.

'Why, Tristram, what makes you ask that?' replied the In-Between Hulk in his solicitously downbeat way. 'Why do you not see that I am your friend? Why do you not know that I am Furtbattler?'

And of course he was. Tristram knew him. Why, he had briefly if unsuccessfully consulted him. Like so many psychiatrists, Furtbattler had a beard and a dark suit as well as a German name and a slight German accent. Like many, he also had a serene, detached manner and couldn't speak two sentences without asking a question, usually about the way the patient was thinking and feeling. In fact, he had asked precisely that question when, some years ago, Tristram had asked him if his persistent vagueness might have come from some forgotten psychological trauma. Perhaps something awful had happened to him in his infancy. Perhaps he had suffered something similar to being put into a large handbag and checked into left luggage at a railway station. After all, that icon of absentmindedness, Miss Prism, was revealed in Oscar Wilde's *Importance of*

*Being Earnest* to have done exactly that to the baby John Worthing. Couldn't Tristram too be a victim of Creeping Prismosis or whatever the disease was called?

But after quizzing Tristram further and further, Furtbattler had intimated that this probably wasn't the case. He thought Tristram used absentmindedness to evade deeply repressed aspects of his psyche. He had said things like, 'And when you forgot to see the dentist to have that tooth pulled do you think or do you feel that the dentist reminded you of your father? Do you think you may be suffering from castration anxiety?' Furtbattler had even coined a name for Tristram's affliction: Generalised Aphasia Syndrome or GAS.

Anyway, it was clear that GAS had struck again. GAS had overcome Tristram's already addled head. He had been well and truly GAS'ed. Talking to those supposed Valentines had put Furtbattler into his mind. The three men had merged together in that very original brain of his. And, yes, they were alike but not totally alike. Val was beefy; the Anonymous Hulk was obese; and Furtbattler was, yes, somewhere in between.

'Three different men, all with the same black beard,' said Tristram, again failing to realise he was talking aloud.

'Very interesting,' said Furtbattler. 'And how do these three different men manage to share this black beard?'

But Tristram didn't answer, because just then the theatre's bell went. It was time for the second half of *Plenty*. And Tristram spent it in much the same mood as the heroine, who at one point runs amok, rips all the wallpaper off a wall and throws valuable furniture out of the window while her husband wails that she doesn't really love him. In fact, if you had asked him how he was thinking and feeling he would have gone further and said he was thinking and feeling in the identical way as that heroine, that furniture and that wall.

And that's that. Valentine still looks the other way when his and Tristram's paths cross in the foyer of the University Theatre. Hulk still sends Tristram scuttling the other way when he sees him or thinks he sees him. Only Furtbattler is pleasant – and, judging from the gentle, earnest way in which he asks him what he's thinking and how he's feeling, it seems likely that he thinks Tristram's psyche is pretty drastically churned.

'Oh well,' says Tristram either to himself or vaguely out loud after these encounters or near-encounters have occurred. 'Oh well, I suppose those reactions are only to be expected.' After all, he had sent Furtbattler's professional brain-cells whirling and he had offended beefy but trim Valentine. But the anger of Obese Valentine or the Anonymous Hulk still puzzled him. Why was the man-mammoth quite so hostile? Wasn't his rage pretty disproportionate? After all, there were many worse things than 'bright red snifter' to shout at a man, even a man whose face veered from scarlet to purple. But for now, Tristram shelved his surprise and alarm to the back of his mind, ready for inspection at some later date.

## THE VAGUE BOOK 3

*Unsurprisingly, there's plenty of absentmindedness in the theatre. Why else is a prompter often ensconced at the side of the stage, feeding the author's lines to actors who can't recall them? 'Jolly useful chap, that,' the late Sir Ralph Richardson remarked to the audience after just such a moment of forgetfulness. 'What's the line?' John*

*Barrymore once hissed at the prompter. But the man was in a churlish mood, having been insulted too often by the great American actor. 'What's the play?' he tauntingly replied.*

*Barrymore was noted for drunkenness, which addles the mind but is not to be confused with absentmindedness, but Richardson was genuinely and famously dreamy and sometimes had difficulty learning and recalling his lines. In Garry O'Connor's biography of the actor there's an account of how he maddened David Storey, the author of a play called* Early Days, *by phoning him and letting him know how he was progressing in learning the part he was about to play at the National Theatre. One weekend he'd call up saying he knew his lines up to page 33, the next up to page 27, the next up to page 12. And when rehearsals were over and Richardson was finally performing onstage, he simply couldn't remember the bizarre insult his character was supposed to direct at an actor playing his son-in-law. It was supposed to be 'fetish', but it became 'mollusc' and even 'croissant'.*

*Richardson could be pretty vague off the stage too. Invited to address an Anglo-French society, he managed to praise and finally toast 'Anglo-British relations'. Laurence Olivier, then in his third marriage, once asked him to call his wife and tell her he'd be late for dinner, so Sir Ralph obediently got on the phone and passed on the message. Unfortunately, the woman on the other end was Jill Esmond, the first of Olivier's wives. 'Well, I haven't seen Larry for 30 years,' she dryly replied, 'so I suppose I can wait another 30 minutes.'*

*Actually, Richardson's relationship with Olivier's wives wasn't always easy. He maddened the second one, Vivien*

*Leigh, by setting off a rocket in celebration of her birthday, only to see it zoom from her garden into her drawing room, where it set the curtains on fire and destroyed some valuable porcelain. 'I mustn't put my foot in it again,' he reportedly said to his own wife as they drove to the Oliviers' next house, a converted abbey, but this time he literally did. He stepped back to admire a fresco that Olivier was showing him in the attic and, to Vivien Leigh's consternation and fury, crashed from a rafter into the plaster, leaving his leg dangling through the ceiling of the guest bedroom.*

*Another time, the now-famous theatrical knight was waylaid by a man in the street as he, Olivier and others hurried off to an important meeting after having shared lunch in a pub. 'I'll join you in a minute,' he said, but turned up an hour later. 'Who the hell was that?' asked Olivier. 'I don't know,' replied Richardson. 'He thought he'd seen me somewhere before and I was trying to help him remember where.'*

*Actually, Olivier himself wasn't always as mentally on-the-ball as all that. The critic Sheridan Morley once asked him if Merle Oberon, who had appeared with him in the film of* Wuthering Heights, *had been David Niven's lover. Olivier replied that, yes, that was the case, but 'though Niven and I were both deeply in love with Merle Oberon, I was the one who married her'.*

*'No you didn't,' said Morley, 'it wasn't Merle Oberon you married, it was Vivien Leigh.'*

*'My dearest boy,' exclaimed Olivier, 'you are so right.'*

*Olivier and Richardson's great friend and fellow actor John Gielgud had his moments, too, many of them combining absentmindedness with a propensity for* dropping bricks. *At the first rehearsal of a new theatrical company he was forming he reminisced about the success of his Hamlet in New York, saying, 'Of course, I had a really terrible Horatio,' only to realise that one of the actors he'd assembled, Harry Andrews, had been playing the part. 'Oh, it was you, Harry,' he said. 'Isn't it wonderful how much better you've become since?'*

*Again, Gielgud was having lunch with a once-celebrated dramatist with the unusual name of Edward Knoblock and, in the course of their conversation, managed to describe a friend as being 'nearly as boring as Eddie Knoblock'. 'No, no, not you, of course,' he improbably corrected himself, 'I mean the other Eddie Knoblock.' Much the same thing happened to Athene Seyler, who was present when Gielgud absently remarked that a certain foreign actress was 'as dreadful as poor dear Athene on a very bad night...Oh not you, Athene,' he quickly added, 'no, of course not. Another Athene entirely.'*

*In a short book about Sir John, Gyles Brandreth records that and several other 'Gielgoofs', as the actor himself called them. After the opening night of his own Broadway production of* Hamlet *in 1964, he struggled through the crowds into the dressing room of Richard Burton, whose prince he privately didn't altogether admire. And when Gielgud discovered that the star would inevitably be delayed before joining him for dinner he said, 'I'll go ahead. Come when you're better — I mean, when you're ready.' He also Gielgoofed badly when, rather later, he ran into Elizabeth Taylor, whose husbands had of course included Burton. 'I don't know what happened to Richard Burton,' he said to her in his mild and gentle way. 'I think he married some terrible film actress and had to live abroad.'*

*Actually, Brandreth suspects that this last anecdote may be apocryphal. One Gielgoof that certainly wasn't, though, happened to Brandreth himself when he was an MP and, together with Glenda Jackson, asked Sir John for a 90th birthday celebration lunch at the House of Commons. 'A great honour that you should join us, Sir John,' he said.*

*'Oh, I'm delighted to have been asked,' he replied. 'You see, all my real friends are dead.'*

*As with many abstracted people, Gielgud's unguarded thoughts and Freudian slips were apt to bypass the barriers that warier men and women manage to put up against tactless blunders and unintentional self-revelation. But theatrical vagueness more often takes the form of failing to remember lines, which Richardson did but Gielgud seldom did even in extreme old age. For instance A.E. Matthews, famous as a character actor in the mid-20th century, picked up the phone during a play and, forgetting what he was supposed to say into it, handed it over to an aghast young member of the cast helpfully declaring 'It's for you'. Another time, he swore to an untrusting director that he'd be word perfect 'even if we were to open next Monday'.*

*'But, Matty, we do open next Monday,' came the reply.*

*And Sir Frank Benson, one of the 20th century's great Shakespearian actor-managers, once had a junior member in his company who, forgetting his lines in his panic but remembering that he had to display contempt for the hero, stared blankly at the man – then simply spat in his face and walked offstage.*

*But Benson, too, was notoriously absentminded.
Among other things, he's remembered for walking about
on stage trailing a lead on to which he'd omitted to attach
his dog – but I'll come back to him and one or two other
theatrical people another time.*

# FOUR

In defiance of caffeine tablets, the alarm clock and the problems that had occurred that day, Tristram's lecture on Shelley and Keats had been pronounced a success, and not merely a success at the time he delivered it. Its subsequent publication in a learned journal and its enthusiastic promotion by the Vice-Chancellor led to other things, prime among them an invitation to take part in a conference on the Romantic poets in New York.

It was Tristram's first visit to America, and naturally he wanted to ensure that there were no problems when he arrived there. So he decided it would be wise to get a visa for visiting academics stamped into his passport, which meant he had to go in person to the American Embassy in London for an interview with a consular official.

Now, the most on-the-ball person in the world would have found this difficult and time-consuming. For Tristram, it was trying to undo a very complicated knot with his toes or maybe his knees. First, he had to call the embassy to find out what was wanted, which meant he ended up lost in one of those telephone mazes in which soothing voices tell you to press buttons and play you baroque music while you wonder whether the right choice is button 1, button 2, button 8 or something weirdly called 'hash'.

'Hash,' said Tristram unhappily to himself after being told he could press it if he wanted to start all over again. 'That's what I'm making of this. One hell of a hash.'

Eventually, he realised that he shouldn't be on the phone at all, but on the Internet, which to Tristram is pretty much what a jungle is to an ant. Yet finally, after mistakes galore and the waste of loads of paper and oodles of ink, he somehow managed to print out and fill in what was called an 'Application for a Visa', the very form that he needed to take to the American Embassy.

The only problem was that Tristram had to get a letter from his boss at the university proving that he was who he claimed he was and that he did what he claimed he did; and that boss was, of course, Hamish Clope, who was making it pretty clear how little he liked him. Mostly he did this by squinting, sniffing and scowling, but he had also taken to muttering, 'Come back, Culloden,' when he saw Tristram, referring to the famous battle in which the English had inflicted a bloody defeat on that great Scot, Bonnie Prince Charlie. Though Tristram didn't realise it, Clope had fantasies of staging a rematch in which revenge would occur and the whole clan of Throstlethwaites would be utterly routed and then annihilated.

Anyway, Clope squinted, scowled, gave his squeezed-lemon smile and then shied away when Tristram politely tried to hand him the Application for a Visa form. For Clope had instantly got the wrong idea and silently started to ask angry questions. Why was Throstlethwaite tormenting him? Why did he want him, Clope, to acquire an American visa? Was it part of the great Throstlethwaite plot to humiliate and, eventually, get rid of him?

'I have no plans to go to America,' hissed Clope.

'Oh, I'm sorry to hear that,' replied Tristram, trying to make himself agreeable. 'There's so much to see, or so I'm told. Tall buildings, a real buzz in the streets, theatres, museums . . . so much you'd never want to leave.'

Clope squinted so thinly that for a moment his eyelids looked as if they had been stuck together with superglue. Though he was talking in a sly, indirect, English way, this Throstlethwaite couldn't have made himself clearer. He believed that he, Clope, belonged in a museum so that he, Throstlethwaite, could one day take over the English Department and teach nothing but effeminate English poets.

'Come back, Culloden,' he muttered to himself.

Tristram was puzzled. He knew that Clope was peculiar and maybe a bit mad. But why did he keep mentioning Culloden? Tristram was well aware that it was a great 18th-century battle between the English and the Scottish, but he couldn't remember anything more about it. Indeed, he vaguely believed that the reason it provoked such strong emotions in the Scots was because they had won it. Anyway, Clope clearly had to be humoured. So Tristram gave him his friendliest smile and replied in what he hoped was his most soothing voice, 'Terrific . . . great victory. Jolly good. You Scots deserved it.'

Clope was so enraged by Tristram's apparent cheek, especially as he seemed to him to be speaking in that maddeningly superior way and giving the same insulting smirk he had flashed at him during the lecture on Shelley and Keats, that he grabbed the visa application form out of his hand, only to squint and blink in amazement at the name he saw on it. That was, of course, Throstlethwaite.

'Why have you put your name on my visa application form when I didn't even ask you for a visa application form?' gasped Clope.

Not for the first time in his dealings with Clope, Tristram was completely nonplussed. Had he done a Spooner? Had he muddled hash with star or pressed button 8 instead of button 1? No, that couldn't be it. Had he somehow managed to spirit up Clope's form on the Internet and put his own name in it instead? Oh no, surely not.

'Sorry, Professor . . . um . . . Professor,' he said nervously. 'I didn't know you planned to go to America too.'

'Go to America too?' wailed Clope. 'What do you mean, "too"?'

'As well as me, I meant.'

'You think I'm going to America with you?' shrieked Clope, his squint suddenly giving way to a bulging of the eyes so pronounced that Tristram thought they might shoot across the room, like miniature cannonballs. 'In your dreams, laddie, in your dreams.'

Tristram knew it was not good to be called 'laddie' by a distraught Lowland Scotsman. Next thing, Clope would start calling him 'Jimmy', which would be really dangerous. But why was the professor so angry? All Tristram was asking him to do was write a letter supporting his application for an American visa. Suddenly, he saw the problem with rare clarity.

'No,' said Tristram, once again smiling as warmly as he could. 'It's me that's going to America.'

'Then why did you tell me I was going to America?' asked Clope hoarsely. 'Why were you linking me with American museums?'

Clearly it was necessary to humour Clope again, so Tristram simply said, 'Must have been one of those little misunderstandings. Like Culloden, eh?' And he gave a laugh, hoping to relax Clope, who continued to stare at him, this time looking like a needle whose eye had suddenly multiplied many times in size.

But when Tristram asked Clope for a letter of support for his visa, he was surprised by the alacrity with which the Professor agreed and the ferocity with which, muttering, 'There's for you, laddie,' he thrust a very brief letter into his hand the next day. This read: 'Dr Tristram Throstlethwaite, a junior member of the university English Department of which I am chief, requires a visa in order to take part in an academic conference in the United States of America. I hope you will agree not only to let him into the country for this purpose but to let him in many times in the future for visits of long and even indeterminate length. Signed, Hamish Clope, MA (Dundee) PhD, Professor of English.'

There was something slightly odd about this letter, thought Tristram, but then Clope was odd. He had a dog called Henryson, a wife who was rumoured to oil as well as polish his sporran, and an obsession with the Battle of Culloden. Anyway, Tristram put the letter carefully in his desk, alongside the other items the embassy required – the completed visa application form, his passport, two photos that made him look like the result of an owl's coupling with a walrus, and the receipt for the money that he had already paid into the embassy's bank account for the privilege of being allowed to go to America.

A few days later, he was in the embassy itself, having queued outside for two hours, been frisked by security men, seen his briefcase X-rayed, been ushered into a large hall that was already crammed with people, given a ticket stamped with a number that would be called out when it was time for his interview and – oh no, oh dear, oh Spooner! He had brought along everything the Americans wanted except Clope's letter. Either he had dropped it or had somehow managed to leave it in, on or near his desk. Tristram felt panicky. Oh, wait, perhaps it was in one of his pockets. So he pulled out everything that was in them, including used bus tickets, old theatre tickets, bits of Kleenex, a crumpled £5 note, a couple of unposted letters, several nuts, a sock, a left-hand glove, some keys to God knows what, a tiny, model cuckoo clock from one of last year's Christmas crackers, an ad for pizza, a cufflink, a bit of burst balloon, an unwrapped toffee with bits of fur sticking to it, three or four receipts, and a dozen pieces of paper on which he had scribbled people's phone numbers or inscrutable messages to himself, and a handkerchief which inexplicably had a knot in it; but, no, there was no letter from Clope.

'No littering,' said an American voice just above him. Tristram looked up to see a severe face jutting out from a severe-looking uniform.

'I'm not littering . . . I'm looking,' he replied feebly.

'For a needle in a haystack?' asked the face.

'No, for a document I need if I'm to go to America.'

'You some kind of Pilgrim Father?' asked the face sarcastically, picking up an ancient-looking envelope from the embassy floor and giving it to Tristram.

'No,' replied Tristram in a hurt voice. 'This stuff isn't as old as that. I'm a professor going to a very important conference in New York.' Even junior university lecturers are called 'professor' in America; but, if Tristram thought the word or the conference would impress the face, he was wrong.

'Expect to be fined if you litter in New York,' said the face in its severe way and disappeared, leaving Tristram still rummaging round the debris of his pockets and, to his consternation, not finding Clope's letter.

So when his number was finally called, he loped out of the hall to a room nearby, shedding bits of paper and mumbling some of the lines that Shelley directed to the West Wind: 'Wild spirit, which art moving everywhere; Destroyer and Preserver; hear, oh hear!' But these changed to a private prayer to St Jude, the saint charged with dealing with hopeless causes and desperate people, as he approached the window to which he had been summoned.

But the face behind the glass was elderly and, for an official at this scary embassy, surprisingly sympathetic. 'Are you a holy man?' asked the official, who had heard the last of Tristram's fervently muttered amens. 'A reverend? A minister?'

'No,' said Tristram in a flustered voice. 'I'm a professor.'

'Ah, you minister to minds,' said the official with a pleasant smile. 'And can you confirm your name please?'

Tristram was so taken aback by this that his own mind went completely blank. 'Yes,' he managed to say. 'I do have a name.'

'So do I,' said the official encouragingly. 'And what is yours?'

'Oh . . . em . . . erm . . . er,' haplessly burbled Tristram.

'Mr O'Murmur,' repeated the official rather doubtfully.

'No,' said Tristram, feeling more and more flustered. 'I'm sure it's longer than that.'

'Well, it seems to begin with an O,' said the official helpfully. 'You are of Irish origin, I assume.'

'No,' said Tristram, fumbling for his passport, opening it at the page with his photo and name on it and handing it to the official, who took a long look at it.

'You're right,' said the official triumphantly. 'It is longer than O'Murmur. It's Throstlethwaite,' he went on, pronouncing the name 'Throst-le-thwaity'.

'Is it?' replied Tristram, by now feeling that a cloud had descended on his brain cells and shrouded them in a thick Dickensian fog. An attack of Generalised Aphasia Syndrome, or GAS as Furtbattler called it for short, had clearly struck him.

'That's what it says here,' said the official. 'You must be of French origin.'

'I don't think so,' said Tristram.

'You should try one of those websites that tells you about your ancestors and your origins,' said the official solicitously. 'You never know, you might be Italian. Or Greek. Or anything.'

Tristram decided to come clean. 'I'm afraid I seem to have left behind the letter from my boss explaining that I work for the university,' he said, hoping against hope that this nice official would take pity on him and grant him the visa he needed.

'Sorry, Mr Throst-le-thwaity,' said the official. 'I'm afraid we will need that.'

Tristram's shoulders slumped in despair, which was a good thing because, amazingly, he suddenly felt a papery rustle between his jacket and his overcoat. It couldn't be!

But it was. He hadn't a clue how Clope's letter had found its way there, quite separately from his passport, his application for a visa and the photos of himself. But it had. It was either the Curse of Clope or that damned GAS. Feeling foolish and looking embarrassed, Tristram pulled the letter from its nestling-place beside his neck and pushed it through the window to the official, who smiled sympathetically. 'You're going to tell me you put it in a safe place, aren't you?' said the official as he read Clope's letter. 'But I know that there's no safe place less safe than a safe place. And I know that you're the original absentminded professor.'

Tristram agreed. 'Oh . . . um,' he said glumly, thinking that this helpful official had put it in a nutshell. Truly, there was no safe place less safe than a safe place.

'Think of dogs,' sighed the official. 'They're quite sure they've put their bones in safe places when they bury them in the garden. But have they? Have they, hell. I've watched dogs scrabble around in all the wrong places and find nothing at all. I've seen pedigree spaniels in suicidal despair.'

Tristram thought of pedigree spaniels, bones, gardens and suicide, and agreed. 'Oh . . . ah,' he said.

'I'm not a dog but I suffer from absentmindedness myself,' went on the official in his gloomy but friendly way. 'Why do you think I'm down here, looking at visa applications, when I could be an ambassador, sitting in comfort somewhere upstairs? Years ago, I made a big mistake. I ushered the United States Ambassador to France into a closet, thinking it was an elevator. Then I locked the door after him and pressed the keyhole, thinking I was dispatching him to the fourth floor. He was stuck there for hours until someone heard him desperately singing "The Star-Spangled Banner". My career never recovered.

'So please, please look after yourself when you get to America. Be sure you know who you are and which way you're going. Have you,' went on the official, 'have you heard of Wrong-Way Corrigan?'

No, Tristram hadn't, which was a pity, because Douglas Corrigan really existed and possessed a mind that was often literally as well as figuratively in the clouds. He was an American pilot in the early days of flying. One night in 1938, he took off from New York, planning to take his little plane across the United States to California. Unfortunately, he went in the opposite direction and 3,000 miles later landed in Ireland, where he and Irish immigration greeted each other with mutual surprise. Nobody knows how he failed to notice that there were no lights blinking below him. Perhaps he thought there was a lot of low cloud around that night or that there had been a power cut across the whole of America. Perhaps he thought that the bigger waves were really the Rocky Mountains. Or perhaps he was just a sort of airborne Spooner. Anyway, poor Corrigan was always known afterwards as Wrong-Way Corrigan.

'He's a hero to me,' said the official sadly. 'But also a warning to us all.'

'I quite understand,' said Tristram gratefully. And he picked up the receipt for his visa application and his passport, which was due to be returned a week later with a stamp in it that would allow him to enter America – and most carefully and conscientiously he deposited it in the wastepaper basket just below the official's window.

But this didn't matter because the official let out a great chuckle of comradely understanding when he saw it happen, and called out to Tristram to pick up the receipt and put it safely in his briefcase, which he rather sheepishly did. All was well; or so he thought as he tried to exit through a door marked 'Entrance' and, politely apologising to the grimly suspicious Marines guarding the embassy, at long last found himself safely in the street.

In fact, everything proceeded to go surprisingly well with the big trip to America. Tristram remembered to collect his newly stamped passport, remembered to take it to the airport, remembered his briefcase and the lecture inside it, remembered the rest of his luggage, remembered his name when he checked in, and remembered to go to the right gate at the right time, get on the right plane and sit in the right seat.

   In fact, the whole journey would have been an unalloyed success if he hadn't been sitting next to a passenger who was both talkative and nervous. Charlie, as he was called, wasn't just afraid of the plane crashing or being hijacked by terrorists. He was afraid of New York, where he lived. Apparently, the people were surly and rude; the taxi drivers were incompetent crooks; the policemen were corrupt and violent; the streets were dangerous; and the city was full of robbers and muggers and crazed drug-addicts, some of whom at first seemed perfectly respectable. Why, Charlie knew of someone who had been brushed by a man in a tracksuit and discovered afterwards that his pocket had been picked.

   'Watch out for dark streets and watch out for thieving joggers,' were his last words to Tristram as they left the plane.

   'I certainly will,' said Tristram, hastily scrawling the letters 'TNT' on the back of his right hand, just in case the mental blankness that had proved so embarrassing at the

American embassy again overcame him. If the immigration officers or Customs people rattled him by demanding his full name, he would be able to look down and remember that he was, of course, Tristram Nicholas Throstlethwaite.

But things continued to go well, in spite of an awkward moment as he passed through immigration control. These days, visitors to America have to provide fingerprints on their visa applications and these are checked against their actual fingerprints when they arrive in the country. Tristram's fingerprints matched perfectly, but when he put his hands forward to have them checked on the electronic reader, the TNT was visible, puzzling the immigration officer.

'Excuse me, sir,' he said. 'Could you tell me why you have "TNT" written on your hand?'

'Oh,' replied Tristram, feeling embarrassed. 'It's a sort of *aide memoire*. Just in case.'

'Just in case you need some explosives?' asked the immigration officer in what Tristram thought wasn't an especially friendly way.

'Oh no,' said Tristram, aghast. 'Not that sort of TNT. Not explosives. No, TNT are my initials. They tell me my name.'

'I see,' said the officer in a voice that suggested he didn't see at all. 'You need to be told your name. Could that be because you are travelling under an alias?'

'Oh God no,' replied Tristram, feeling aghaster and aghaster. 'I've always been who I am.'

'But you don't know who you are?'

'Oh yes, I know who I am today,' said Tristram.

'And who were you yesterday and who will you be tomorrow?'

'Tristram Nicholas Throstlethwaite every time,' said Tristram, trying not to glance down at his hand to check that this was correct. 'It's in my passport and on my visa. But I'm afraid I'm a rather forgetful person.'

The immigration officer fell silent and stared at Tristram for what seemed a full minute, taking in his long, untrimmed moustache, cloudy glasses and hair that had clearly been on a plane for seven uncomfortable hours, as well as his facial expression, which made him look as lost as a sheep in a shopping mall. The officer seemed to be thinking this way: if this man is a murderous fanatic, he is so deeply disguised that America is powerless against him and might as well admit defeat in its war on terror.

So, finally, the officer gave a hopeless sigh, handed Tristram back his passport and said, 'Well, Dr Throst-le-thwaity, welcome to New York. It's a big city straight ahead. You can't miss it – or maybe you can.'

But an hour later Tristram had been deposited, together with all his luggage, in a hotel called the Sherwood Forest in mid-town Manhattan. It was a modest place, despite boasting amenities that included the Maid Marian Honeymoon Suite, the Friar Tuck Eaterie and the Little John Big John, which appeared to be an ample loo. And behind a desk in the foyer stood a large, dark-suited man with a countenance so grim that Tristram was instantly reminded of the Sheriff of Nottingham.

'Yes?' he said curtly.

'Throstlethwaite,' replied Tristram stiffly.

'What kind of name is that?' asked the Sheriff.

'Yorkshire, if you want to know,' replied Tristram even more stiffly, spelling his name out letter by letter in what he hoped was a sarcastic sort of way but not having any apparent effect on the Sheriff, who continued to scowl as he worked his computer.

'Major credit card,' demanded the big, burly Sheriff still more brusquely.

What was a major credit card? Was his a minor card? Frowning in what he hoped was a superior sort of way, Tristram handed over a card that seemed somewhat to irritate the Sheriff, though he gave it back after making some notes on his computer.

'Room 405,' said the Sheriff, handing over a plastic key with what Tristram thought was a sneer. 'Have a nice day and welcome to Sherwood Forest, Mr . . . ' – and he checked his computer again – ' . . . Mr Throst-le-thwaity.'

'Thank you,' said Tristram in his most superior voice. 'It's "Dr Throstlethwaite" actually. Or "Professor Throstlethwaite" as you would presumably say over here.'

'Huh,' said the Sheriff, sounding about as impressed as an ogre who had been served too small a portion of person for his supper.

Charlie on the plane was clearly right about these surly New Yorkers – or at least about some of them. But in spite of the Sheriff's abruptness, everything else started and continued to go pretty well. Tristram had a nice evening meal, slept well in his dull, anonymous hotel room, and had quite a hit with his lecture on Shelley and Keats at the conference the next morning and with his more informal contributions during the two days that followed.

Almost everyone seemed to want to discuss the Romantic poets with him, from an eminent professor from Michigan called Hiram Boon to a New York policeman called Al Gotti, who, as Tristram was impressed to discover, had a serious amateur interest in Coleridge. There were none of the problems that had occurred back in England. Indeed, the only things that disconcerted his American hosts were the ferocity of his refusal to drink the coffee on offer, muttering 'it's a diuretic' as he did so, and his insistence on visiting the loo very frequently. But it was generally assumed that he was gallantly battling a bladder illness, so neither did his reputation any harm.

Anyway, after the drinks and farewells that closed the conference, Tristram felt good enough to take a late-evening stroll through the city. It was February and pretty cold, but the weather was fine and the walk would be invigorating. But then he remembered the warnings of Charlie, his neighbour on the plane. Beware of muggers! He had, he thought, better put his more valuable possessions somewhere safe before he went out on to the streets at night. But where? Then he noticed that there was a small key sticking out of the drawer next to his bed, so, after removing a few dollars, he carefully locked away his wallet along with his passport, went out into the street and started to walk towards what he thought was Fifth Avenue to the east but – as if in tribute to Spooner and Wrong-Way Corrigan – was, in fact, the Hudson River to the west.

Tristram doesn't notice much when his mind is on other things as it was now on Gotti, Boon, the other people at the conference and, of course, the Romantic poets they had so enthusiastically been discussing. 'In Xanadu did Kubla Khan a stately pleasure dome decree . . . ' he happily muttered to himself as he continued, ' . . . Where Alph the sacred river ran through caverns measureless to man down to a sunless sea.' But even he couldn't help noticing that there were no pleasure domes in sight, though the cavernous streets were getting sort of measureless and something not unlike a sunless sea appeared to be ahead. In other words, the entire area was becoming emptier, less interesting and darker.

But just as he had decided to turn round and start his return journey he saw trotting towards him a spindly man, who was wearing a tracksuit and listening to music through earphones. Tristram stepped to the left in order to avoid him, but the spindly man turned right at exactly the same moment, so there was a slight collision between them.

'Sorry,' said Tristram instinctively, only for an awful thought to hit him. What was a jogger doing out at night? Was this spindly jogger actually a fake sort of jogger? Could he be one of the muggers Charlie had been talking about on the plane? Tristram's hand flew to his wallet pocket and, oh no, his wallet wasn't there. He had clearly been robbed by a jogger who, Tristram saw as he swivelled round, was continuing to trot up the street at a pace so slow it struck him as deliberately insulting.

Now, Tristram isn't feeble. It's not merely when he's alarmed, as in the case of confrontations with Anonymous Hulks or Hamish Clopes, that he remembers his family motto, which is, of course, the Latin version of 'I fear nothing but fear itself'. It's the same when he's been wronged. That reminds him that he comes from a Yorkshire clan which shed blood, often other people's, in the Wars of the Roses. So almost without thinking, he raced after the splindly jogger, grabbed him by the shoulders, whirled him round, and thrust him against the railings that he was passing at that moment.

'Give me that wallet,' shouted Tristram, his eyes bulging, his nostrils flaring and his long, rough moustache bristling with such fury it seemed as if it was a hairy creature with a venomous life of its own; a giant killer-caterpillar from a rainforest yet to be discovered by any explorer.

The spindly jogger seemed to get spindlier. 'What?' he

stuttered, turning white and beginning to shake.

Tristram ripped the earphones from the man's head. 'Listen to me and listen good,' he said in what he hoped was the proper, tough-guy manner, repeating very slowly and significantly, 'Hand over that wallet.'

'Wa-wallet?' stammered the spindly jogger, quaking even more.

'And be quick about it,' hissed Tristram, 'or it will be the worse for you.'

Hands juddering, the jogger reached into his tracksuit, took out a black leather square and gave it to Tristram, who jammed it into his breast pocket.

'You can have my Walkman too, if you leave me alone,' gasped the spindly, quaking jogger.

This enraged Tristram. This weedy runt hadn't only robbed him; he was trying to bribe him not to report the robbery. It was doubly intolerable.

'You can't get away with it as easily as that,' snapped Tristram, jabbing the gasping jogger in the ribs. 'I'd think of something better, if I were you, or you can kiss your freedom goodbye.'

'I haven't got anything else,' jabbered the jogger, looking as if he would faint or throw up or both.

Suddenly, Tristram's rage evaporated. This was a pathetic opportunist, not worth the trouble of reporting and seeing prosecuted and imprisoned. Besides, he was returning to England on a flight early the next morning and didn't need the hassle. But he owed it to society to give the man a lecture and a warning.

'All right,' he hissed. 'Just think yourself lucky I'm a tolerant man. And make very, very sure our paths never cross again, because next time I might not be so tolerant.

And remember this: *nihil timeo praeter timorem ipsum. Nihil... timeo...praeter...timorem...ipsum.*'

The spindly jogger nodded, as it seemed to Tristram, with a mix of stricken gratitude and beaten bafflement.

'I have a good friend in the New York police – Al Gotti. Remember that name. Gotti. So you'd better behave yourself in future,' went on Tristram, thinking of the friendly conference cop with the interest in Coleridge. 'And no more jogging.'

And Tristram repeated the warning very slowly and solemnly – 'No . . . More . . . Jogging' – and strode off eastwards, not even bothering to look back at the defeated mugger.

Seldom had Tristram felt so fully in control. Although New York didn't know it, he had played a proud part in the great and unending war between the forces of good and evil. He even felt powerful enough to go up to the large Sheriff, who now seemed to be on a night shift at the Sherwood Forest Hotel's reception desk, and fix him with the steely, defiant glare of Robin Hood himself.

'Goodnight,' he snapped, his voice as piercing as an arrow as he crossed the drab acreage of the Sherwood Forest Hotel's foyer. 'A very good night to you.'

'Goodnight, sir,' said the Sheriff, looking perplexed as Tristram strode over to the lift, gave the up-button a ferocious bang and, trying now to look like an avenging cowboy making a grand entrance into a Wild West saloon, swaggered through the opening doors, hoping that the fact that he bumped into one of them hadn't spoiled the John Wayne effect.

It wasn't until he had sat down in the fake-leather

armchair in his room and prepared to switch on the television that Tristram began to feel that something might
possibly be a little bit amiss. Very, very slowly he did a kind
of double-take, which meant that his eyebrows rose, his
moustache quivered, and his eyes bulged, somewhat in the
manner of Macbeth when he learns that Birnam Wood has
very unreasonably decided to relocate in Dunsinane. No, it
couldn't be true – could it?

His hand went to his breast pocket, extracted the wallet
he'd just placed there, and opened it. The first thing he saw
was a driving licence belonging to a Mr Elwood G.
Mackintosh of 440 West 56th Street, New York City.

No, that wasn't his name. His name was surely Tristram
N. Throstlethwaite, not Elwood G. Mackintosh. No, the
photo on the licence wasn't him either. Unmistakably, it
was the jogger, though looking pinker and happier than
when they had parted. The awful truth had to be faced – the
mugger hadn't mugged him. Tristram had mugged the
mugger. He had taken the jogger's wallet while delivering a
lecture on social morality that the jogger must have thought,
well, a trifle hypocritical. He had even harangued him in
Latin. And, oh no, oh dear, oh Spooner, he had ordered the
jogger to give up jogging.

But now Tristram was beginning to think of himself
rather than of poor, spindly, misunderstood Mr Mackintosh.
Probably the New York Police were out looking for him at
this very moment, and probably they wouldn't find him
hard to trace. After all, how many youngish men of his
height had been roaming the streets of far-western
Manhattan, equipped not only with a shaggy moustache
and a fierce stare but with an English accent?

He would be found. He would be arrested. He would

very likely be imprisoned or at least deported, because what all-American judge would listen to a plea of not guilty to street robbery because of extreme absence of mind? He would lose his job at the university and his reputation. Clope would triumph. The Vice-Chancellor would disown him. Even friendly old George Macdonald, his former boss, would stop speaking to him. Though he seldom now saw his one-time girlfriend Meryl, she, too, would pretend she'd never met him. He would become a pariah on both sides of the Atlantic and probably of the Pacific too. His career, his prospects, his very life would be over. Oh dear, oh Spooner! What, oh what, should he do?

Make himself less identifiable for a start. Tristram grabbed his razor and, not pausing for a moment's regret at the loss of so proud a possession, got to work on his moustache. But halfway through shaving, a thought struck him. If, as he planned, he was going to check out of the hotel very soon and take a taxi to the airport, he would need his money, his credit cards and, above all, his passport. And, yes, they were in the drawer in the little table beside his bed.

Throwing down the razor, Tristram rushed from the bathroom back into the bedroom and tried to pull the drawer open. But then he remembered; he had locked it. So where was the key? Tristram started rummaging through his pockets, then his luggage. He looked under the bed, then under the sheets, then just about everywhere: below the television set, behind the smiling portrait of Robin Hood on the wall, in the water tank above the loo. But even though he thought he had probably put it somewhere where it would be secure, the key had vanished. He had forgotten the sage advice of the helpful official at the London embassy – 'There's no safe place less safe than a safe place

. . . ' – and now he was paying the price. He had brought upon himself a possibly terminal attack of the dreaded GAS or Generalised Aphasia Syndrome.

So Tristram tugged and tugged again at the drawer, imploring St Jude, patron saint of the totally defeated and utterly hopeless, to make a personal intervention. He jabbed at it with his toothbrush and, in his desperation, he even tried to bite it open with his teeth, but, no, it remained firmly closed. What was he to do? He had no crowbar, not even a pair of scissors. He needed a knife. Badly.

There was no alternative but to ask the hotel for a knife under the pretext of using it to eat. So he picked up the phone, dialled zero and, when the Sheriff replied, made his request in a voice that he hoped was firm yet casual.

' . . . And the bigger and heavier the knife is, the better,' he added with what he intended to be a breezy chuckle but, if truth were told, sounded a little strange.

The Sheriff was taken aback. Why was this weird-looking Englishman who had just yelled 'Goodnight' at him, and then walked into the elevator door, asking for a big, heavy knife and laughing crazily as he did so? It was odd and it was disturbing. But the Sheriff was a New Yorker born and bred and knew the great rule of the city from his forehead to his heels – don't get involved with anyone and, especially, don't get involved with nuts. However, he also knew that his boss might not be entirely happy if the Englishman ran amok and stabbed a large number of other guests to death, so he cautiously asked a question.

'Aha. And what would you like with your knife, sir?'

This struck Tristram as a pretty obtuse enquiry. 'I don't want anything *with* the knife,' he said. 'I just want a knife. Now if you please.'

'Aha,' said the Sheriff warily. 'It's just that here in New York folk usually have something with their knives, like a sandwich or a piece of fruit or something. We don't usually get asked for knives on their own.'

Tristram was momentarily at a loss. 'An apple,' he improvised. 'I have an apple here and I want to eat it, so I need to cut it.'

'Aha,' said the Sheriff. 'And you need a big, heavy knife to do that?'

'It's a big, heavy apple,' said Tristram defensively. 'I don't want to hurt my teeth. I don't want to hurt my dentist either. He's a very strict person and he gets upset when his patients don't look after their teeth.' Tristram didn't add, because it seemed irrelevant, that his dentist had threatened to remove him from his list after he had forgotten one appointment too many.

'Aha,' said the Sheriff. 'And would you like a plate with your apple and your knife?'

'No,' said Tristram, adding as an afterthought, 'thank you very much.'

'We'll see what we can do,' said the Sheriff. 'Aha.'

A few minutes later there was a knock on the door. Tristram opened it to see the Sheriff, but a much changed Sheriff from the curt, rude giant who had barely given him a glance downstairs. He seemed slightly to have shrunk. He looked wary and nervous and, when he saw Tristram, his face froze and he took a big step backwards, holding out a not-very-big, not-very-heavy knife in an almost pleading way.

'Thank you very much,' said Tristram with what he hoped was a reassuring smile and took the knife from the Sheriff, who stepped even further backwards as he did so.

If only we could see ourselves as others see us! What had met the Sheriff's eyes was not, as Tristram supposed, the benignly beaming face of a youthful professor with a love of people and poetry, but that of a feverish-looking foreigner with half a moustache. And this red-faced, bulging-eyed, sporadically hairy creature was giving a mad grin and, now, taking hold of a knife.

The Sheriff said nothing but 'Aha' and disappeared down the corridor at a canter, leaving Tristram to close the door and start prising away at the drawer with what seemed to him far too light a knife. It was no good. Tristram applied more force, then even more force until the knife handle broke off from the blade and the drawer snapped open with what sounded to him like a minor nuclear explosion, leaving bits of half-broken wood sticking upwards.

Tristram was horrified, then relieved, then horrified again. He pulled open the drawer and tried ineffectively to force the jagged wood back into its original position, ending up with a splinter in his finger and blood running down on to his palm, but his own wallet at long last in his hand. He sat on the bed, too exhausted even to mumble a piece of life-enhancing Shelley to himself. What next?

Next, he had to send the jogger's wallet back to its owner. Next he had to try to fix the drawer and the knife, so as to ensure he wasn't arrested for vandalism as well as for street robbery. Next he had to get out of town and to the airport. But the first of these nexts was to sit down and get a grip on his nerves. It was time to draw on the spirit of his legendary ancestors. And by sheer force of the Throstlethwaite will, Tristram began to breathe very deeply, in and out, in and out, picking up the phone as he did so.

'Yes?' said the Sheriff, this time rather shrilly.

'I want two things,' said Tristram, still breathing slowly and loudly in and out. 'One is some brown paper and some string and some postage stamps . . . ' – pant, wheeze, pant – ' . . . and the other thing I want is to check out of the hotel as quickly as possible.'

The Sheriff's voice took on an upbeat tone Tristram had not heard before. 'Check out?' he said. 'Yes sir! Any time, sir! As soon as you like, sir!'

And a few minutes later an even more shrunken Sheriff was at his door, gasping slightly when he saw Tristram, still inanely beaming, still with only half a moustache, but now with a bleeding finger and a blood-stained hand in which he was holding the handle of the knife he'd broken and had forgotten to put down.

What was going on in Room 405, the Sheriff wondered. He had seen streaks of fresh blood and pieces of knife that gave every sign of having been thrust deep into something or someone. He had heard breaths that sounded as if they belonged in a film about vampires or werewolves. And now he had given this British nut brown paper and string! Was the man indulging in some kind of Druidical ritual? The Sheriff had never been to England, but he had seen that cult film, *The Wicker Man*, and he knew that they put men in cages and burned them and did other primitive things in the ancient stone circles just outside London. So could there be a dead body somewhere in Room 405? Or did this particular Druidic ritual consist of self-harm? Was this lunatic about to cut off his own or someone else's finger and mail it somewhere? It was wiser not to ask, decided the Sheriff, as he reached out from a safe distance and handed Tristram some brown paper, some string and stamps and, with them, a hotel bill.

'Thank you very much,' said Tristram, adding as he realised that the knife handle was still in his hand, 'I'm sorry to say I had a little accident. The fruit's flesh wasn't as soft as I thought.'

The fruit's flesh wasn't soft enough? As the Sheriff well knew, 'fruit' was an offensive name for gay men that had sometimes been used in America in the bad old days. So for an awful moment he thought a homophobic murder had occurred in Room 405. Then he recalled the apple. And then he remembered that he hadn't believed in the existence of the apple. Thoroughly confused, the Sheriff said, 'Never mind about the knife,' and galloped away jabbering, 'It's not my business . . . it's not my business . . . ' to himself.

Hastily, Tristram packed his clothes. Hastily, he took the fateful wallet, wiping it with a towel so as to ensure there were no fingerprints on it, wrapped it in the brown paper, tied up the parcel with the string, stuck several stamps on it and, cannily using his left hand instead of his usual right in order to disguise his identity, carefully wrote: 'Mr Elwood G. Mackintosh, 440 West 56th Street, New York City, New York. From a Wellwisher.'

He had little luck making the drawer look normal but, once he had pulled the lamp to the front of the bedside table, the splinters didn't seem to him too obvious. Certainly, they wouldn't be noticed until he had left for England on his early flight. That is, if he succeeded in getting on that flight and flying away before the New York Police caught up with him.

There was little time to waste, and Tristram didn't waste what little time there was. He hurried to his suitcase and packed, hurried to the lift and hurried up to the reception desk with the bill that the Sheriff had given him. Then a new worry hit him. Suppose the spindly jogger had recovered his courage enough not only to give the police a description but to help them construct an Identikit picture of his face.

It was too late to hide that face altogether, for the Sheriff had already seen it several times, but there was no point flaunting it. In fact, the less the Sheriff saw it, the less able he would be accurately to reconstruct it for a police Identikit artist. So as he went up to the desk, Tristram bent his head so low that he was looking at his own chest, not at the Sheriff, and pulled out his wallet from the breast pocket where he had carefully placed it, meaning to give the Sheriff his credit card so he could finally settle his bill.

Except it wasn't his wallet and it wasn't his credit card. Both, he suddenly realised, belonged to Mr Elwood G. Mackintosh. In his fluster, he had wrapped his own wallet in brown paper and put the jogger's wallet in his breast pocket. What was he to do, especially since he knew the Sheriff would be staring suspiciously at him? Giving what he hoped was a casual, carefree laugh, Tristram turned away and started undoing the brown paper parcel, hoping the Sheriff wouldn't notice.

But, of course, the Sheriff, who by now was looking less like a giant than a somewhat overgrown dwarf, did notice. After all, it's hard not to pay attention to a weirdly cackling man checking out at the dead of night when he has half a moustache, while trying so hard to hide his face that he's pointing the crown of his head rather than his mouth at you, and cramming one wallet hurriedly into his breast pocket, pulling a credit card from the second wallet he had inexplicably tied up in bloodstained brown paper and...

But here we'll leave Tristram, hoping to return to him and his predicament in a moment or two.

## THE VAGUE BOOK 4

*With one big exception, there aren't many anecdotes about the vagueness of the major Romantic poets, though there are several about their friends and lesser contemporaries. For instance, Coleridge and Wordsworth knew a minor poet who was also a clergyman, the Rev William Bowles, and celebrated for presenting a parishioner with a Bible as a birthday gift and, when asked to inscribe it, writing on the flyleaf 'From the author'. Once, he kept his guests waiting for dinner while upstairs he searched desperately for a sock to put on a bare foot, unaware he'd put both socks on the other foot while thinking of a new poem. On another occasion he paid a gatekeeper two pence for entering a toll road. 'But why?' asked the man.*

*'For my horse, of course,' replied Bowles.*

*'But, sir, you have no horse.'*

*'Oh, am I walking?' said Bowles, looking behind him in surprise.*

*But the big exception I just mentioned was Coleridge, who often drifted into a contented daze, not necessarily induced by drugs. Once, the organisers of a lecture on the fall of the Roman Empire he was supposed to be giving in Bristol felt impelled to tell the prospective audience that had been impatiently fidgeting for over half-an-hour that 'a circumstance exceedingly to be regretted' had prevented him from making his scheduled appearance. The disappointed audience trickled away, assuming that Coleridge had broken his leg or suffered some terrible family loss. In fact, he was sitting in his rooms, having forgotten that he had anything to do except composedly smoke his pipe.*

*But even more often he was so busy talking – and usually talking brilliantly, like many absentminded people, with an extraordinarily acute memory for the subjects that interested him – that he went into another kind of daze. 'His large, grey eyes assumed a dead, dull look,' wrote a friend of Charles Lamb called John Payne Collier, 'almost as if he were not looking out of them; and I doubt if external objects made much impression upon his sight, when he was animated in discourse.'*

*And Lamb himself claimed to have met Coleridge on the public highway and, even though Lamb told him he was in a hurry, Coleridge took him by the button of his coat, closed his eyes and got talking and talking. So Lamb gently severed the button from his coat with his penknife and decamped, returning five hours later to the same spot, where he found Coleridge 'with closed eyes, the button in his fingers, and his right hand gracefully waving, just as when I left him: he had never missed me!'*

*As we'll see later, Lamb was mightily amused by absentmindedness and surely elaborated that particular memory. However, another friend, Bryan Waller Proctor, wasn't exaggerating when he recalled Coleridge coming from Highgate, then a village on the edge of London proper, to the city itself to consult yet another friend about his worrying son, Hartley. He arrived at about one o'clock, got talking, talked through the afternoon and then through dinner about history, law, medicine, divinity and other subjects until at five minutes before eight a servant came in and told him the stagecoach back to Highgate was waiting for him. Coleridge had completely forgotten the purpose of his visit.*

*But on that particular occasion, Coleridge at least left*

*in the orthodox way and caught the stagecoach. Anne
Matthews, the sister of a once-famous comic actor called
Charles Matthews, became the poet's neighbour and, like
her husband, delighted in his brilliant conversation.
However, he'd usually try to leave, 'his benevolent
features beaming with good-humour and kindness',
through the large, floor-to-ceiling mirror that Mr and
Miss Matthews had placed in their drawing room. So
when he prepared to leave they made a habit of grabbing
him and leading him to the door, 'to which he would
submit, talking and laughing upon the point which
prevented his knowledge of outward things, until the
entrance-gate was closed upon him'.*

*Actually, Coleridge was absentminded from an early
age. Indeed, he himself wrote that his appetite for
day-dreaming was reinforced by a boyhood incident in
which he was walking down the Strand in London,
thrusting out his hands as he imagined himself to be a
mythic hero swimming the Hellespont. But one hand
came into contact with the pocket of a gentleman who
accused him of trying to pick it, whereupon Coleridge
began to sob and explain he was pretending to be
Leander. This so impressed his supposed victim that he
made him a member of a circulating library, a gift that
enabled him to indulge his love of reading and become a
man who perfectly illustrates the thesis that a superb
intellect and a fine memory are sometimes inseparable
from abstraction and forgetfulness.*

*Maybe the same was true of Coleridge's contemporary,
de Quincey, who is still remembered as the author of*
Confessions of an English Opium Eater. *Is it really
true that at night he sometimes got so absorbed in his*

books that he didn't notice that the candle he was using had set fire to his hair? Or he fell asleep, knocking over the candle and setting light to his papers? Well, perhaps; but perhaps he was rather more the drug-addict than Coleridge, despite his own liking for narcotics, ever allowed himself to become. However, there's no doubt that Walter Savage Landor, who began publishing his verse in 1795 and was extremely well known as a poet and essayist by his death in 1864, was genuinely absentminded.

On one trip to see his sister in Warwick, he forgot to bring the key to his portmanteau, or suitcase, meaning that it had to be broken open. So on his next visit, he greeted the lady by triumphantly waving the key at her, only to discover that he had left the luggage itself at the railway station in Cheltenham. The suitcases, which included not only his clothes but all the prose and poetry he'd written in the last three months, were never recovered.

Though Landor once said that his memory for faces was so bad that 'I may converse a whole evening with a person and forget both his features and name before the next,' he was mostly renowned for mislaying things. 'He used to stick a letter in a book,' wrote his friend and biographer Eliza Lynn Linton, 'then, when he wanted to answer it, it was gone, someone had taken it, the only letter he wanted to answer, he would rather have forfeited a thousand pounds than have lost it, and so on. Or he would push his spectacles up over his forehead, and then declare they were lost, lost for ever. He would ramp and rave about the room at such times, upsetting everything that came in his way, declaring he was the *most unfortunate man in the world, or the greatest fool, or the most inhumanly persecuted.'*

*Mrs Linton would persuade him to sit him down and let her look for the lost property, at which he'd sigh in deep despair and say it was no use, the object was gone for ever. 'When I found it, as, of course, I always did,' she added, 'he would say "thank you" as quietly and naturally as if he had not been raving like a maniac half a minute before.'*

*Landor was a lively, forceful man, the model for Boythorn in Dickens's* Bleak House, *a genial, outgoing character described by the author as 'impetuous and hearty'. But that impetuosity could take not-so-lovely forms. Once he threw an Italian cook who had displeased him out of the window, only to realise that his absentmindedness had brought about an error that seemed to trouble him more than the poor man's distress. 'If I'd remembered that our best tulip bed was under that window,' he said, 'I'd have thrown the dog out of the other one.'*

# FIVE

When we left Tristram, he was trying to conceal his face and outwit the sleuths at the New York police department by hanging his head down towards his chest while paying his bill at the Sherwood Forest Hotel. He was also in a state of terrible anxiety because he expected at any moment to be arrested for mistakenly mugging a jogger called Elwood G. Mackintosh and seizing the wallet that was now tucked next to his own wallet in his breast pocket. All he wanted to do was catch a taxi, get away from Manhattan, and hurry to the airport, where he was due to take a flight back to England early the next morning.

But Tristram, glancing up for a moment, saw that the man at the hotel desk – the Sheriff of Nottingham, as he privately called him – was looking at him in an anxious, watchful way. It was clearly vital that he threw him off the scent in case he phoned the police or the police turned up at the hotel asking hard questions. But how? Then he had an idea. New York has three airports: John F. Kennedy, La

Guardia and, over the Hudson River in New Jersey, Newark.
He, Tristram, was flying from JFK and now planned to take
a taxi there. But he would tell the Sheriff he was going to
Newark. That way, it would take the police longer to catch
up with him.

'Well, yes, that should throw the cops off the scent,' he
said to himself, or rather to his chest, not aware that he was
speaking aloud.

'Aha,' said the Sheriff, unsettled still more by what
seemed to him a new display of dangerous criminal lunacy.

'I'm going to Newark,' Tristram told him, again directing
his words somewhere near his stomach.

'You're going to Newark,' said the Sheriff. 'Good plan.'

'I'm going to Newark in a bus, not a taxi,' added Tristram,
thinking that this lie would throw the Sheriff even more off
the scent.

'You're going to Newark in a bus,' repeated the Sheriff,
this time rather breathlessly. 'Very good plan.'

Still without raising his head, Tristram nodded, reached
out a bloodstained hand and signed the credit card paying
for his stay at the Sherwood Forest Hotel.

'I like the bus,' said Tristram with sudden, startling
emphasis, hoping to make sure the Sheriff remembered the
lie.

'I like the bus too,' half-panted the Sheriff, who by now
seemed to have shrunk so far from his original gigantic self
that he might have been mistaken for the smallish chap
who nervously climbed up the beanstalk. 'I love the bus.'

'Then we understand each other,' said Tristram, nodded
again and, his head still looped downwards, carried his
suitcase and briefcase past the picture that adorned the
hotel foyer, which was an enormous fresco of Robin Hood,

who, as in the room upstairs, was happily smiling, this time at a pack of men who looked not just merry but in states of terminal hilarity. He hurried out into the cold February street where, as luck had it, a taxi was passing.

With a grunt that seemed to express both relief and foreboding, Tristram threw himself and his cases into the back. 'Newark Airport,' he said.

But of course he was a fugitive and couldn't relax. He spent the journey wondering what to do with the poor jogger's wallet. Apart from belonging to someone who presumably needed it back, it was incriminating evidence. He resisted the temptation to wipe it clean of fingerprints and throw it out of the taxi window, partly because that would be immoral, partly because the driver might think it strange and suspicious if his passenger started hurling wallets out of the window.

As it happened, the driver was one of the curious, chatty sort. 'You goin' a long way?' he asked.

A new idea for throwing any potential pursuer off the scent suddenly struck Tristram. He would disguise his English accent. Instead, he would adopt a French one. That would confuse the driver and, if the driver was ever quizzed about him, the New York police.

'A long way, *bien sûr*,' replied Tristram. 'La France. France, as you call her.'

'They wear their moustaches that way in France?' asked the driver.

Tristram's hand darted to his upper lip and he realised for the first time that half his moustache was missing. In his earlier panic he had shaved off the right side while leaving on the left side. Could he restore it all? Hardly, or at least not in time for a morning flight. There would be a little fur on one side of his upper lip and a long hairy bush on the other. Having half a moustache must have made him more recognisable in the hotel and, if the police came in search of him, would certainly make him easier to identify. Besides, people didn't walk around with half-moustaches in New York or England or, he thought, France.

He must cut all the hair off as soon as he could. Meanwhile, it was important to talk as little as possible to the taxi driver.

'I do not like to speak about it,' said Tristram. '*Bien sûr.*'

'Please yourself,' said the driver and kept silent for the rest of the 30-minute trip.

They arrived at Newark Airport, at which point a horrible realisation hit Tristram. He wasn't supposed to be there at all. He had mentioned Newark to the Sheriff only to throw him and the police off the scent. But the name must have stuck in his mind when he was telling the taxi driver where to go. He had sent the cab to the wrong airport. He was supposed to be at JFK. His flight for England left from there at nine o'clock the next morning, And here he was at Newark, several miles away. What was he to do?

'Sorry,' said Tristram, forgetting in his fluster to use his French accent. 'I've, um, gone to Newark when I should have gone to JFK. Could we please drive there at once?'

The cab driver turned round and gave Tristram a long, hard, searching look, as if wondering whether this Frenchman with the interchangeable English accent and half a moustache was mad and dangerous or mad and harmless. He evidently decided that the second option was true, for he sighed, started up the taxi again and drove silently to JFK.

By the time they arrived the meter was showing that Tristram owed the driver $80, whereupon another awful realisation dawned on him. He hadn't enough money to pay for the trip. In his anxiety, forgetfulness and desperate attempts to evade detection he had failed to change a travellers' cheque in the Sherwood Forest Hotel, and so had only about $40 in cash.

'Ah, um, you'll take zee cheque for zee traveller?' asked Tristram hopefully, this time remembering his adopted accent.

'No,' said the driver in what struck Tristram as a very blunt, New York kind of way. 'Cash only. Dollars only.'

What was the poor fugitive to do? Get arrested and face the music for two crimes, mugging a jogger and failing to pay for a cab ride? Try to find a booth where he could change his travellers' cheques inside an airport terminal which, since it was now about midnight, looked pretty closed up? Give the driver the watch that he'd bought at a market stall a few months after somehow mislaying all its predecessors? Or simply get out of the taxi and scream?

'Can't give you your luggage until you pay,' said the driver. 'They's the rules.'

For a moment Tristram was tempted to tell the driver to keep his luggage. But then a thought struck him. There was money in the jogger's wallet, wasn't there? So with a sickly grin Tristram extracted the remaining $40 from his own wallet and put it down on the taxi seat, took poor Mackintosh's wallet out of the breast pocket where he'd placed it, extracted another $50 from it and, with an even sicklier grin, gave it to the driver, who received the money with the weary expression of a man who has now seen everything and can never be surprised any more.

'Got any more wallets?' asked the driver in what Tristram thought was a sneery sort of tone.

'No, only two,' replied Tristram. 'Or *seulement les deux*, as we say in la France.'

'They sure talk English well in la France,' said the taxi driver as he handed over his suitcase and briefcase.

By now Tristram was too exhausted to reply, or even come up with a sentence in a French accent, so he just flashed his sickly grin once more and walked into a JFK Airport that was mostly dark and looked all but abandoned.

It was then that another realisation, even more horrible than the others, struck him. He had the jogger's wallet. But he had left his own wallet on the back seat of the taxi. Deserting his luggage for a moment, he dashed outside – but the taxi, the driver, his wallet and all his credit cards and other bits and pieces had gone.

Desperately, Tristram rushed back into the terminal, only to find that his luggage wasn't to be seen. Briefcase, suitcase and all had apparently evaporated. Oh no, oh dear, oh Spooner! He had only been gone a few minutes, but one of New York's authentic, full-time thieves had struck.

'Fool, fool that I am,' wailed Tristram, swivelling around in his agony, dementedly dancing about, and then tripping over a black something-or-other and falling flat on his face. What? What now? Who had left such an article in such a stupid, dangerous place? But wait. Half-crouching on the floor, he stared hard at the black leather something-or-other. It was his own briefcase next to his own suitcase. He had misidentified the seat next to which he'd left his luggage before dashing out of the terminal building. Thank God, everything was still safely in place.

Feverishly, he got up, checked the briefcase and again thanked providence. He still had his passport and his ticket.

He could get home to England, at least if the New York police didn't catch up with him first. He was already a mugger and a thief and he was all too likely soon to become a convict inside one of those American jails from which people are always trying to escape in old films. How would he survive the steel bars and the striped uniforms and the evil warders with thin, tiny eyes and thin, tiny moustaches? Why, he had heard of a sheriff who dressed inmates in bright pink pyjamas and then humiliated them by parading them about in chain gangs. He imagined Clope rubbing his hands vindictively at the sight while the world's Keats and Coleridge scholars gravely shook their heads and turned away.

Then Tristram remembered. He wasn't only a crook but a crook in disguise or, rather, a crook with an upper lip that was in half-disguise by virtue of having no hair at all on the right-hand side. How was he to get rid of the remainder of his moustache? A quick look round the terminal showed that all the shops were now closed, meaning he couldn't buy a razor. They probably wouldn't open again until well after the time had come for him to check into his flight to London. And that would be at about six-thirty in the morning, over six hours from now. How was he to spend the time until then?

An airport terminal in the small hours of the night is a desolate, spooky place. The ceiling looks higher and more shadowy, the walls dingier and greyer. For Tristram it was a great, gaunt version of the sort of prison where convicted men wait before being taken out and shot at dawn. There were a few would-be passengers slouched or sleeping here and there. The occasional official also drifted by, among them one or two security men and, as Tristram was horrified to see, a New York policeman. So Tristram curled up in the most remote, unobtrusive seat he could find – and waited and waited and, without meaning to do so, fell asleep and began to dream.

First, Clope appeared in a kilt, squinting, thinly smiling and waving a caber three times the size of his body. With a great sniff of glee he threw this awesome object at Tristram, who dodged it, only to find it had turned into a Sheriff of Nottingham who had been restored to even more than his original size. And the Sheriff started to bark in an American accent: 'Who are you? Where do you come from? Why would anybody give someone like you a major credit card? Why are you wearing green?'

Tristram couldn't answer any of these questions, but looked down to discover he was dressed as Robin Hood. But where, oh where were his bow and arrows? Why, in his wallet. But, oh no, oh dear, oh Spooner, he must have left that in the Friar Tuck Eaterie or in the Maid Marian Honeymoon Suite or even among the urinals in the Little John Big John. So he backed away from the accusing Sheriff and sank down into what he realised was an electric chair. 'Goodbye for ever, laddie,' cried Clope, who had mysteriously rematerialised, this time with one huge eye in his forehead, like a Cyclops. 'Remember Culloden!' And the chair began to shake and judder like a cake-mixer – and, suddenly but gratefully, Tristram woke up.

An airport terminal at 6.00am, which is what the time now was, is an even grimmer, greyer place than an airport terminal at midnight. That's what Tristram thought as he saw people beginning to bustle and check-in counters to open. Suddenly alert, he made a prompt if not very ethical decision. He would simply drop the jogger's wallet and walk away from it. Some honest person might find it and hand it in or even mail it back to poor Mr Mackintosh. And when he was back in England he would mail him the money he had taken from the wallet.

Tristram stood up, checked that his briefcase and suitcase were still beneath his feet, took the fateful object from his breast pocket. Then he carefully wiped his fingerprints from the wallet and, using his knuckles, let it fall beside the bank of seats where he had been sitting. And, in the most casual manner he could muster, he began to stroll with his luggage towards the check-in area.

'Hey, sir, you dropped this.' Tristram stopped and turned. A huge policeman had appeared from nowhere and was holding the jogger's wallet out towards him. Tristram didn't merely freeze. He felt as if he'd just been parachuted into Antarctica with not even a penguin costume to protect him. Inside, he turned to ice.

'Good thing I was passing,' said the policeman. 'You want to be careful. There are thieves about in New York. We don't want a law-abiding person like you going away with a bad impression of us, do we?'

'Um, ah, um,' gulped Tristram, reaching out and taking the proffered wallet as if it was a poisonous snake.

The policeman gave him or, rather, his half-moustache an odd look. 'Does one side grow more slowly than the other?' he asked.

'It's a fashion statement,' replied Tristram in a moment of inspiration, adding after a moment, 'I come from England.'

The policeman paused and gave Tristram a long look. 'Well, I guess that explains it,' he said. 'Have a good flight.' And he walked away, leaving a palpitating Tristram to put the jogger's wallet back in his breast pocket.

By now Tristram was almost beyond caring. After all this time, the police must have a description of him. If it was circulated there was a hotel receptionist, a taxi driver and now a cop to confirm his identity. It wouldn't be hard to recognise a man who had made himself recognisable by sporting half a moustache and speaking in more than one accent. He even thought of going back to the policeman, admitting his crimes and revealing his name, which was, yes, Tristram Throstlethwaite. But the blood of the Throstlethwaites, or at least those Throstlethwaites who, 500 years ago, had fought their fellow-countrymen with ferocity and sometimes even with success, kept him going. Was this the spirit of the Wars of the Roses? Let cowards shave. He would keep his half-moustache to the bitter end.

'It's a fashion statement, I come from England,' he said to the puzzled check-in clerk. 'It's a fashion statement, I come from England,' he said to the security people as they frisked him, ignoring their cheery suggestion that he get himself some fertiliser to help grow the right side back. 'It's a fashion statement, I come from England,' he said to an air stewardess as, hardly believing his good fortune, he settled into his seat on the plane. 'It's a fashion statement, I'm going back to England,' he said to himself as, more exhausted than he had ever been in his life, he felt the plane take off and fell deeply and dreamlessly asleep.

Tristram's troubles weren't quite over, of course, but they didn't continue for long. The immigration officer at London's Heathrow Airport gave both him and his passport a strange look when he repeated the mantra that had been effective in America – 'It's a fashion statement, I come from England' – but eventually nodded him through, saying dryly, 'Well, if you decide to make a fashion statement with your eyebrows, it might be better to shave off both.'

In the main concourse Tristram bought some disposable razors with the British coins that were still in his pocket, went to the gents and, resisting the temptation to tackle his eyebrows, regretfully shaved off the remaining half of his moustache. Then he found a branch of his bank, explained that he had left his credit and debit cards in a New York taxi, cancelled them, ordered new ones and – well, it's enough to say that he ended up with sufficient money to find his way to the university and home.

By his standards, all this was very efficiently managed. But what was he to do with the jogger's wallet, which was still in his breast pocket? Obviously, he must post it to poor Mr Mackintosh, adding the dollars he had spent but not revealing who he was. And he must do this as soon as possible. If there was a knock on the door, and British detectives came with a photofit that they had received from the American police, he would then be able to look innocent and invite them to search his house. That way, he would surely avoid what he feared: arrest, disgrace, extradition to New York, years behind bars or in one of those chain gangs where sadistic prison officers who looked like Clope didn't just put you in pink pyjamas but jabbed you on the bottom with electric cattle prods.

But it would be foolish to dispatch a parcel containing incriminating evidence from anywhere near the university. He would go to London, change some pounds into the $50 he now owed Mr Mackintosh, and post them and the wallet from somewhere in the city's centre. While he was about it, he could also buy himself a new wallet from one of the big stores. Simple! Pretty much foolproof! And that's why

Tristram was to be found setting off for London a few days later, complete with a moustache that was beginning to grow back and, covering his head, a woollen balaclava or ski-helmet that showed nothing but his eyes and mouth.

Why the ski-helmet? This was Tristram's latest blow against absentmindedness. If you had lost as many hats and scarves as he had over the years, you too would need something that was at once cheap, warm and, much of the time, not necessary to take off. In the past, he had tried attaching string to a trilby and tying it round his chin, so that he could politely remove the hat, push it backwards and be confident it was safely dangling just behind and below his shoulders. But that made him look like a hunchback and certainly seemed too eccentric for a young academic on the verge of international renown. Hence the black woolly balaclava.

The balaclava was particularly sensible, he thought, because it was particularly cold outside. Also, it was one of those days when he was sure to lose a hat, a scarf and anything else that wasn't firmly fixed to him. That dreaded vagueness had struck again.

Tristram bought a ticket for the London Underground by putting coins into a machine and found himself politely thanking it for its trouble in giving it to him. Then he walked to the escalator and, as he got on, was amazed to find people shooting up and at him. Why were these lunatics going the wrong way and trying to throw him back into the ticket hall? In fact, why were these moving stairs going the wrong way? 'Do you mind?' he said severely to a florid-faced city gent whose ascent seemed to be preventing his own descent, only to realise that, oh dear, oh Spooner, he had mistaken the up escalator for the down escalator.

'Oh dear, oh Spooner,' Tristram repeated to himself as glided down the correct escalator, walked to the platform that would take him to Oxford Circus, waited for the train and, when he saw it coming out of the tunnel, did what would-be passengers do at request stops for buses. He raised his left hand in the usual pleading but assertive way, not realising until the driver's surprised face flashed by that Tube trains made a practice of coming to a halt without anybody asking them to do so.

But a few minutes later he was in the street and, shortly afterwards, in a department store where he had a long if one-sided conversation with a fine-looking but oddly motionless young woman who was wearing a smart tweed suit. Could she please direct him to whatever department sold, er, um, I remember, wallets? She didn't answer, so he repeated his question more loudly, wondering why the store chose to employ assistants who seemed not only to be deaf but paralysed. But she just kept on staring at the top of Tristram's balaclava, a smile on her lips that he began to think a bit patronising. Then he realised. She was a very realistic mannequin showing off what a nearby sign described as suitable wear for the countryside.

It wasn't much better when Tristram finally found the department where they sold purses, wallets and so on. The mannequin in tweeds had made him think of shooting and other such countryside activities. So when a real-life shop assistant asked him what he wanted, he didn't say 'wallets' but 'bullets'. Why, he wondered, had the man stiffened? Why was he staring so nervously at him? Then he realised his error, laughed cheerily through his ski-mask, and said, 'Sorry, not bullets . . . wallets.'

'An easy mistake to make,' said the assistant quickly,

though Tristram thought he looked oddly relieved when he chose a new wallet, paid for it and, still chortling apologetically through his balaclava, left the store.

Out on the street again he kept noticing that people were pretending not to see him while giving him the same worried looks as the assistant in the department store. Why? Oh yes, it must be the ski-mask. Even though it was a cold February day, it was unusual to wear such a thing in London rather than on some snowy Swiss mountain. So he decided every now and then to raise the front of it and show the face beneath, smiling in his most pleasant manner as he did so. Yet even this didn't seem to stop the strange glances he was getting. Well, perhaps people were put off by the fact that his upper lip was getting furry as he regrew his moustache, giving his face an odd, unbalanced look.

Anyway, he lifted the mask for the tenth time and flashed a big, cheery, reassuring grin at a passing woman, who looked away and seemed to quicken her pace. Remembering the impertinent remark the security people had made at JFK Airport, Tristram found himself wishing he could buy something that helped moustaches grow faster.

'Fertiliser, that's what I want,' he said to himself as he walked down Regent Street, once again not realising he was talking aloud. 'Fertiliser – that would be just the ticket.'

He came to a big, posh bank, one that was sure to be able to exchange a few pounds for the dollars he needed to send to poor Mr Elwood G. Mackintosh. In he went, and joined the queue for the cashiers. Was it his imagination or were people looking at him almost more strangely than before? He moved his hand forward towards the ski-mask, meaning to lift or even remove it, smiling at everyone; but this movement seemed to worry the lady in front, for she nervously muttered, 'Oh dear,' and seemed to freeze. She was clearly the sort to be upset by a semi-demi-grown moustache. So Tristram kept the ski-mask in place, grinning benignly beneath it, thinking his own thoughts and muttering his own mutterings.

'Yes, fertiliser, that's what I need,' he said again, making the person just behind him, an elderly gent who was wearing a pink-and-green tie beneath an expensive-looking overcoat, start in what struck Tristram as an odd sort of way.

'GAS, that's what I definitely don't want,' he added to himself, thinking of the vagueness or Generalised Aphasia Syndrome that had been striking him since his arrival in London. 'That's quite enough GAS for one day.'

Anyway, he arrived at the cashiers' counter, behind which a young man with big saucer eyes was staring at him.

'Hello,' said Tristram in his friendliest voice, smiling with his mouth and eyes through the slits in the ski-mask, raising his hand in a matey sort of greeting and, without meaning to, showing the letters upon it. Yes, he had once again wondered if he might forget his own name when the time came to make a currency exchange, and so he had scrupulously scrawled TNT in red biro in a place where he could quickly see it.

'Hello,' answered the cashier in what struck Tristram as a strangely faint voice.

'I've come for some dollars,' began Tristram, reaching towards the breast pocket in which he'd placed both his new wallet and Mr Mackintosh's wallet. He meant to go on to say that he wanted to write a sterling cheque in order to pay for the dollars; but before he could get out the words a series of bewildering things happened.

First, the cashier dived beneath his counter. That struck Tristram as very eccentric. But even odder was the voice that then came from beneath the counter. 'Everybody down,' it yelled.

Then, even more surprisingly, there was a loud peal of electric bells, the door to the bank slammed shut, and from all around came the same shout: 'Everybody down!'

Like all the other customers in the bank, Tristram obeyed, for clearly something was not quite right. He found himself on the ground, head to head with the elderly man with the pink-and-green tie.

'Don't shoot,' quavered the man. But his voice was so frightened and faint that Tristram couldn't hear him through the balaclava or ski-mask that was keeping his ears nice and warm.

'Don't what?' he asked. 'Don't hoot? Why on earth should I hoot?'

'I'm sure they'll give you what you want,' stuttered the man, and this time Tristram heard him.

'Well, all I want are a few dollars,' said Tristram in an irritated voice. 'Do please tell me, what's the problem?'

'No problem,' panted the man, becoming inexplicably pale. 'No problem at all. I'd give you the dollars if I had them. Please forgive me for not having them.'

'But this is a bank,' said Tristram, by now thoroughly confused. 'You don't come into a bank to get money from the customers.'

'Thank you for that . . . thank you for that,' puffed the man.

Tristram was becoming even more bewildered. Why was he lying on the floor talking to an elderly man in a pink-and-green tie who was apologising for not offering him dollars and asking him not to hoot? Had everybody gone quite mad?

Then a thought struck him. 'Is there a fire?' he asked through the ski-mask.

'Fire?' palpitated the elderly man. 'Fire? No, don't fire. Or at least don't fire at me.'

Tristram looked round. As far as he could see, everybody was prone on the floor, some with their hands over heads that were facing downwards, some inexplicably staring at him as if expecting him to do something. Had he ventured into a fire drill? Or an exercise class? But who would hold exercise classes in a bank? And why did the faces of the people looking at him suggest that he would be leading the exercises? It was preposterous. He was an increasingly eminent academic, not a PT instructor or Pilates teacher. No, this was an example of mass hysteria, and he was having nothing to do with it.

So he stood up, only for the door to open with a crash and three policemen with machine guns to come rushing in and, believe it or not, crash into him and knock him over before he had time to say, 'Kindly look where you're going.'

'You're nicked, chum,' said one, pointing his gun at Tristram's head.

Tristram was too astonished to be frightened. 'Look,' he said. 'I only came in here to get some money.'

But the policeman was babbling something incoherent about whatever Tristram said being taken down and used in evidence against him. 'We know that,' he growled. 'Wait until I've finished reading you your rights.'

At the same time another policeman tore Tristram's balaclava off his head while yet another clapped handcuffs round his wrists. That struck him as outrageous but seemed to delight the elderly man with the pink-and-green tie.

'Well done, officer. This criminal was threatening to fire at us. But I remained calm throughout and kept him talking.'

'Threatening to fire, was he?' snarled one of the policemen, opening Tristram's breast pocket, searching it for a hidden weapon and, finding none, extracting both the jogger's wallet and the new wallet he had just bought for himself. And that was truly alarming. Tristram had assumed that this police attack was some weird case of mistaken identity, but now it occurred to him that the British police were acting on a tip-off from New York. They had followed him to London and to this bank, arranged with the staff to get him to lie down, and then pounced. This was arrest. Extradition to America, trial, pink pyjamas and the chain gang would surely follow.

'But it was all a mistake,' he cried.

'Tell that to the jury,' said the policeman, pulling him to his feet and, with the others, dragging him to the bank door.

'This is absurd,' wailed Tristram. 'And I want my balaclava and wallet back. They were quite expensive, you know.'

At that point the bank's customers started to stand up, some of them confusing Tristram still further by clapping. Were they applauding him or the police or what?

'And look at the robber's hand,' cried the elderly man. 'You'll find it has the name of an explosive written on it. And I'm sure I heard him talk about getting some fertiliser. And we all know that fertiliser can be used for bomb-making. And, yes, he was saying something about gas and having tried to use gas. I think,' he added excitedly, 'that together we have saved London from a terrorist attack.'

'Ho,' said several of the policemen as they pushed Tristram through the door and into a van. 'Ho.'

Robber? Terrorist? Suddenly Tristram realised what had been happening. The police were not arresting him because he had stolen the jogger's wallet, which was a relief, but because he was wearing a balaclava and they thought he was a bank robber, which was not a relief at all. In fact, it was outrageous. He was a British citizen and had the right to wear whatever he liked, wherever he liked. He was just as entitled to wear a ski-mask in a bank as he would be to wear a bowler hat on a ski slope.

'I'm a free man in a free country,' gurgled Tristram as, still handcuffed, he was forced down on to a seat in the police van.

'Ho,' said a policeman. 'Free to rob banks? Ho, ho. Think again.'

The first question Tristram had to answer at the police station, after he had been taken from a depressing little cell into an interview room, was one he especially feared, because it brought the jogger's name into the open. Who exactly was he?

'We think you're English and you're called Throstlethwaite,' said the taller, thinner and more senior of the two policemen who sat facing him, 'because you sound English and you are carrying credit cards with that name on them. Yet in your breast pocket there is another wallet and an American driving licence that says you are an Elwood Mackintosh. Which are you – or are you someone else altogether?'

Tristram's oppressed, flummoxed mind went completely blank. Yes, who was he? 'Um . . . er . . . um,' he stuttered.

'Let me think for a moment.' And he glanced down at the back of his hand, where the letters TNT were still imprinted.

This did not impress either of the policemen. 'There's no point trying to conceal your identity,' said the junior policeman, who was short and chunky. 'If we don't find out now we have plenty of ways of finding out later.'

Tristram didn't like the sound of that at all. Even an American chain gang and pink pyjamas would be better than an English torture chamber, which was what seemed to be on offer here. Would they take him to the Tower of London and place him on the rack? Surely that sort of thing had gone out years ago – but these days one never knew.

'No,' he said desperately. 'I'm not concealing my identity. As you can see, I'm wearing it on the back of my hand. I'm TNT, Tristram Nicholas Throstlethwaite, and Mackintosh . . . ' – here he paused, sensing that on his answer his whole future might hang – ' . . . Mackintosh is an acquaintance of mine whose wallet I picked up in mistake for my own when I was in New York for a big conference.'

'Conference?' asked the second policeman. 'What kind of conference?' His expression suggested that it must have been a conference for members of the Mafia.

'An academic conference,' said Tristram, still in a panicky, stuttery voice. 'I was giving a lecture on the Romantic poets. Kelly and Sheets . . . no, Shelley and Keats. That's it, Shelley and Keats. I'm an academic. I'm a lecturer. I teach at a university. And,' he finished with a moan, 'I'm a very absent-minded person.'

The policemen stared at him for a long time, until the tall, thin one said, 'Let's get this straight. You are a university lecturer but you don't know what you're lecturing about. You think your name is Throstlethwaite but you're not quite sure. You're in the process of growing a disguise in the form of a moustache. You're carrying someone else's wallet and you go into a bank wearing a balaclava with the name of an explosive written on your hand. You talk about getting fertiliser. You mention gas. Then you demand dollars from the cashier. Now, who and what do you think a judge and jury would think you really were?'

'An absentminded person who wanted to keep warm on a cold day,' replied Tristram. 'And I didn't demand dollars. I asked for them very politely. After queuing. In order to send them back to Elwood Mackintosh.'

The two policemen looked at each other. Either they had captured a lunatic or a most original bank robber or someone who was a bit of both.

'And,' said Tristram, trying to regain just a little bit of the initiative, 'I didn't wear gloves, did I? If I was a bank robber I'd have worn gloves, not gone into a bank with my initials on my bare hands.'

'Of course,' said the chunky policeman in what struck Tristram as an unnecessarily sarcastic way. 'Of course you could be an absentminded bank robber, couldn't you?'

'I can see that we're going to have to check you out very thoroughly,' added the tall policeman. 'We will phone your university or what you claim to be your university, and we will make contact with Mr Mackintosh in America. Meanwhile, I'm afraid I am going to have to ask you to remain here.'

Tristram sat shivering in the police cell, looking and feeling rather the way Fagin did in Phiz's famous drawing in *Oliver Twist*. He wasn't about to be hanged, like the old criminal, but something almost as bad was sure to follow. They would phone Clope and Clope, who had always hated him and wanted to sack him, would have his revenge in full for the misunderstandings over the dog and the mothballs. They would phone the jogger and the jogger would tell them about his mugging. Oh no, oh Spooner, oh dear.

Two hours later the two policemen unlocked the door and came into the cell, looking oddly disappointed.

'Well,' said the tall, thin one, 'you're a lucky man, Dr Throstlethwaite.'

'The Vice-Chancellor of your university certainly likes you,' said the short policeman bitterly. 'He says you're a bright young man and a credit to the college. And, of course, he's very friendly with influential people down here.'

'And,' added the thin policeman even more resentfully, 'he asked us to pass on a message to you: "Flinking Bunny".'

'Whatever that means,' said the short policeman in a voice that suggested 'Flinking Bunny' was probably a codeword for something unpleasant, probably illegal and possibly imported from Columbia.

'And I'm pleased to inform you,' said the thin policeman, seeming anything but pleased, 'that Mr Mackintosh in New York confirms everything you said.'

'Yes,' added the chunky officer with what sounded very much like a sneer. 'He said that whatever you said must be true. He also said not to bother to send back the dollars. He said please keep them all. He said he wishes he had more dollars to give you. You clearly have quite a gift for friendship.'

There was a long pause, during which Tristram tried to understand his sudden change of fortune. 'Can I, um, go then?' he asked.

'We could still prosecute you,' said the thin policeman, 'if only for causing a public nuisance and wasting police time. Anybody who goes into a bank wearing a balaclava should know the trouble he's going to cause.'

'And,' added the junior policeman, 'you should know we have had several phone calls from the public, including a Tube train driver and a woman pedestrian in Oxford Street, all informing us of a man in a balaclava behaving in a strange way.'

'Ah, um . . . sorry,' said Tristram. 'I'm a big friend of the police actually.'

'That's very nice,' replied the older officer stiffly. 'But I think that we would prefer to manage without your friendship.'

Back home, Tristram did a lot of thinking. He would give the remaining dollars in Mr Mackintosh's wallet to charity and the wallet itself to a charity shop, preferably one helping reformed criminals. That would appease his sense of guilt a little. But why had the jogger refused to take the money? Why had he stopped the British and, presumably, the American police pressing charges against him? Was Elwood Mackintosh a bit of a saint, like the bishop in *Les Misérables*, who gives the desperate Jean Valjean the silver he has stolen from him, thereby ensuring he doesn't go back to the chain gang and there spend years singing sad songs by Boublil and Schönberg, the authors of the musical version of Victor Hugo's novel?

Then Tristram realised: Mackintosh was still frightened of him. He was even afraid he could harm him from 3,000 miles away. After all, what had he, Tristram, said when he was robbing him? He had mentioned that, as well as the eminent professor from Michigan, he had a made a powerful friend in the New York police force. What were their names? Goon and Botty? No, Boon and Gotti. Suddenly he remembered: Gotti was the name of a renowned American mafioso who had died in prison after being convicted of several not-very-nice things, including 13 murders, but had presumably left behind quite a few members of his crime dynasty.

The spindly jogger hadn't only been mugged. He had been put into such a state of fear that he didn't dare protest about the robbery. And now he had heard from the British police that his attacker had been arrested for trying to rob a bank. Probably he suspected that Tristram belonged to a crime family too. He believed that he was a member of the Throstlethwaiti, an English-Italian clan with bushy moustaches and relatives in Sicily and New York. So the last thing Mackintosh wanted was to get involved.

Somehow this didn't make Tristram feel guilty. In fact, it made him feel pretty good. Maybe if he grew a really long, bristly pair of moustachios he, too, would look a bit like a mafioso. If he also put on a fierce, Palermo-style expression when one became necessary, he would surely silence the most exasperating students. Nobody would dare laugh at him for being absentminded or call him Flinking Bunny.

So all ended well. The Vice-Chancellor, so far from being upset that one of his best lecturers had been arrested, seemed to regard the whole affair as a bit of a lark, like snatching police helmets had been among the bright young things in the 1920s and 1930s. At any rate, he took to sighing nostalgically and giving Tristram complicit winks when he saw him, as if yearning for a time when he, too, had a life that didn't just consist of chairing committees with boring names and sleeping through lectures. As for Clope, who had presumably got some sort of wind of the events in London – well, he started to look at Tristram in an even more suspicious, wary way, giving the impression that he thought him not just a snake in the grass but a viper with poison fangs.

Yes, all ended well. There was no word from the Sherwood Forest Hotel about the damage Tristram had done to the drawer in which he had locked away his wallet. The Sheriff of Nottingham had presumably decided to let Robin Hood triumph this time. Tristram even found the key to that drawer. He had hidden it in what he thought was a safe place, which was inside one of the socks he had worn and then packed away in his suitcase among his other dirty clothes.

'Never put anything in a safe place again,' Tristram said sternly to himself as he came to a decision. He wouldn't send the key back to the New York hotel, thus reopening a can of worms he would prefer to consign to the garbage-dump of history. Instead, he would drop it in the local river. And so Tristram did, tossing it over the parapet and he repeated to himself the wise words that the helpful official in the American embassy in London had passed on to him on that ominous day a long lifetime ago: 'There's no safe place less safe than a safe place.'

Moments afterwards it occurred to him that he ought to have checked there was no traffic on the river below. So he peered over the parapet and saw, oh no, oh dear, a familiar face looking up at him. It was . . . it wasn't . . . it was. It was the Anonymous Hulk, the man-monster he had inadvertently insulted in the University Theatre, and the Anonymous Hulk was rubbing his beard. What on earth was an ogre of his size doing in what appeared to be a punt? And how had he managed to get his beard in the way of the key to a room in a New York hotel?

Tristram and Hulk stared at each other: Tristram disbelievingly and (he hoped) apologetically; Hulk disbelievingly and – but the punt was now too far away for Tristram to see anything of the Hulk's face except a vast, bulging blob coloured crimson.

## THE VAGUE BOOK 5

*Yes, I know I keep harping on about absentminded people sometimes being people of genius or, more accurately, people of genius often being absentminded. But how can I avoid making and remaking the point when I'm thinking of Albert Einstein or the almost equally brilliant Thomas Edison, inventor of the electric light bulb, the gramophone or phonograph and the electric typewriter, or of Gotthold Lessing, who was a major writer and philosopher back in the 18th century and regarded by many as the most learned person on the planet?*

*Whenever Einstein travelled he regularly left at home his nightshirt, toothbrush and umbrella and, it sometimes seemed, his common sense too. Back in 1933 he decided on impulse to leave London, where he was working, to pay a visit to King Albert and Queen Elisabeth of Belgium, whom he had met and liked four years earlier. But he had lost or given away most of his money and barely had enough to buy a third-class train and boat ticket. However, he got to Brussels, started looking for cheap lodgings and ended up in a slum district. There, he went into an inn and asked how he could phone Laeken, where the king and queen were living. 'Why?' asked the landlord. 'I want to reach Queen Elisabeth,' Einstein replied.*

*After directing Einstein to a phone booth, the landlord*

*and his customers decided this odd, unkempt, bedraggled violinist – for the great man was carrying his beloved instrument with him – was a lunatic or an anarchist plotting to assassinate the royal family, so they called the police. By the time Einstein finished telephoning he found himself surrounded by customers, headed by two Brussels policemen, who took him away for questioning. It was a wonder he eventually got to the royal castle at Laeken, but he did.*

*It was also a wonder, not least to him, that Einstein managed so much as to get to the country where he eventually settled. Once he lost his ticket on a German train, only for the conductor to reassure him that his face and reputation were ticket enough, to which Einstein replied, 'Thank you, but if I don't find my ticket I won't know where to get off the train.' And his archive apparently contains a summary of a page from his diary describing one of the occasions he departed by rail from Berlin: 'First he loses his wife, finds her again, and then he loses his tickets and finds them as well. Thus began Einstein's second trip to the US.'*

*Yes, and even on rainy winter days he would be found dreamily wandering without a coat around the American university town of Princeton, where he became an eminence grise – sometimes in slippers and sometimes in his shoes but invariably without the socks, he'd renounced years before, arguing that 'the big toe always ends up making a hole in them'; seldom with a hat to keep the rain from the great frizz of hair he seldom had cut and never brushed; AND sometimes adding to the impression of eccentricity by nibbling at an ice-cream. He would also get up in the middle of a meal and, even if there were*

guests, distractedly stroll into the kitchen and start
playing his violin.

Einstein wasn't too focused on his rewards either. Once
he received a cheque for the then significant sum of
$1,500 from the Rockefeller Foundation and proceeded to
use it as a bookmark and, months afterwards, lost the
book in which he'd placed it. Eventually, the foundation's
accounts department realised the cheque hadn't been
cashed and sent another. Einstein was bewildered.
'What's this for?' he wrote back.

Writing letters in a study whose floor was usually
chaotically crammed with papers and whose shelves were
filled with dusty books, he often used absently to sign off,
not with his own name but with that of the person he was
addressing. And on one occasion a caller phoned the
Princeton institute where he worked, asked to speak to
Einstein, and was told he was out. But could he please be
given the scientist's home address? No, that wouldn't be
possible. The caller's voice then dropped to a whisper:
'Please don't tell anybody but I am Dr Einstein. I'm on
my way home and I've forgotten where my home is.'

Distraction or abstraction took all sorts of forms with
Einstein. At a dinner held in his honour he started
scribbling equations in his notepad, only to notice that
everyone else was standing and applauding. Hastily he
stood up and politely joined in the ovation, seeming not to
realise that it was he himself who had just been
introduced.

Einstein also liked to go alone out to sea, abandoning
all sense of time as he drifted and meditated in the little
wooden boat he had bought and called Tinef, which is
Yiddish for a piece of junk. Once the coastguard was sent

*out to trace him, and did so, also discovering that, even though Einstein couldn't swim, he had forgotten his lifejacket. On a trip to Bermuda he was missing for so long, a full seven hours, that his wife decided he had been captured by Nazi agents; but, no, he was at the home of the German cook he had met at a local restaurant and accompanied on a sailing trip.*

*As for Edison, he used to get so lost in thought, usually about the problems thrown up by his inventions, that he would forget where or even who he was. When he was showing important people round his laboratory, he would simply disappear in the middle of a conversation without a word of apology. He supposedly spent his own wedding thinking over an idea about stock tickers that had just struck him and, when the ceremony was over, rushed straight off to his lab. A colleague found him there hours afterwards, his mind far from his waiting bride, Mary. 'What time is it?' asked Edison.*

*'Midnight,' came the reply.*

*'Midnight?' said Edison. 'I must go home then. I was married today.'*

*OK, I've heard it said that this story, like some attaching to Spooner, may not be true, but it fits with what we know of the first of Edison's two marriages. This started with his notably offhanded proposal to poor Mary, as she was called, when she was only 16 and one of the junior employees at his telegraph company. Looking up from the work in which he was absorbed, he simply told the astonished girl that he'd been thinking of her and 'if you are willing to have me I'd like to marry you'. The effect, it was said, was as if he was momentarily interrupting his normal business to conduct a brisk experiment in courtship. 'If you consent and your mother is willing we can be married by next Tuesday,' he added. And so they were, but none too happily, since he consistently neglected her for his work.*

*When Edison was developing the electric light bulb, he often worked through the night, ordering breakfast in the morning and then falling asleep before it arrived in his lab. One time, a colleague called Batchelor decided to play a trick on him, placing the remains of his own breakfast in front of Edison and then shaking him awake. The great inventor saw the mess of eggshells, crusts of bread, leavings of jam and smears of coffee and took out a cigar for his usual after-meal smoke, assuming he had just finished eating.*

*Another time, he went to pay taxes that were on the brink of becoming overdue, joining a queue in the tax office in his home town of Newark, New Jersey, in order to do so. When he reached the window, the cashier asked him his name. But by then Edison was so absorbed in his ideas that he couldn't remember what his name was. However, at that very moment a senior tax officer who happened to know him passed by, saying, 'Hello, Mr Edison.' So all ended well. 'But if my life had depended on my giving my correct name,' admitted Edison afterwards, 'I could not have done it.'*

*According to another version of this story, Edison gazed at the official at the window in total perplexity, was waved aside when he failed to give his name and, when he had recollected himself, found that he had passed the deadline for payment. As a result, he was forced to cough up an extra 12.5 per cent. I don't know which anecdote is true. What's certain, though, is that there were times when Thomas Edison had no idea that he was Thomas Edison.*

*Nor did Gotthold Lessing seem always to know he was Lessing. One murky night he arrived back in his house after an evening out and, finding he had no key, knocked on his own front door. His servant looked out of an upper-floor window, could not recognise Lessing in the darkness, and shouted down, 'The master's not home.' And did Lessing call him a dunderhead and demand instant entry, like any other master of the period? No, he did not. 'Very well, I'll call another time,' said Lessing, and went away.*

*Mistaking your own place for another person's place, or another person's place for your own, is quite common among the vague and gifted. That happened at least twice to Lord Dudley and Ward, a senior British politician during the Regency period and at one time Foreign Secretary. He imagined he was in his own house one evening and thought that his hostess, whom he supposed to be his guest, was outstaying her welcome. 'A very pretty woman,' he said, not realising he was speaking aloud, 'but she stays a devilish long time. I wish she'd go.' And on another occasion he apologised for the poor quality of a meal, blaming it on the illness of his cook, when he was in someone else's house and at someone else's table.*

*Again, a renowned 19th-century clergyman, Richard Chevenix Trench, was asked to dinner at his former palace by the cleric who had succeeded him as Archbishop of Dublin. Halfway through a dinner he was not particularly enjoying he looked up, saw his wife's face and a familiar-looking dining room and for a dreadful* moment assumed he was in his own home. 'This cook is one of our failures, my love,' he said. 'We will have to be rid of her.'

Like Trench, Spooner and William Bowles, clergymen have often made themselves notorious for vagueness. The 19th-century essayist Charles Lamb had a friend who was a Baptist minister and a fine scholar, the Rev George Dyer. He had an odd, jerky, hesitant way of speaking and sometimes rounded off an utterance with 'well, sir, but, however'. Like many other vague people – Beethoven, Edison, Coleridge, Landor, Newton and Einstein, among others – he was also careless about his appearance. 'His nankeen pantaloons were absolutely engraved with the accumulated dirt of ages,' wrote Lamb, adding that those 'nankeen pantaloons', meaning cotton trousers, were four times too big for him and had lots of tiny 'crevices, doors and windows' in them.

Dyer evidently lived in a pretty chaotic way, too. Lamb's sister Mary decided to mend his old armchair, which had scores of holes in it. But every time she prepared to sew up a hole she found that it contained a book that Dyer had placed in there and then forgotten, like a dog burying a bone.

Often Dyer was so abstracted that he would pass Lamb in the street and fail to recognise him. Once he left the writer's cottage in Islington in the middle of the day and, instead of turning right and walking along the path outside the front door, he marched straight forward. The fact that there was a deep stream in his way did not stop him. As Lamb wrote later, he kept walking until he totally disappeared under the water. He was rescued, given cognac at the suggestion of a one-eyed doctor who happened to be passing and firmly made to sit on a couch, where he babbled about his past misadventures and sang fragments of hymns.

At all events, Dyer recovered, as presumably did the woman whom he was said to have half-drowned whom he was baptising in the manner required by his church. He ensured she was totally immersed in the water, pronounced a blessing over her head, and simply left her there. When he was reminded of this by a mischievous friend, he became upset, muttering, 'No, no, it could not be,' for he was renowned not only for his vagueness but for his kindness of nature and an innocence verging on gullibility. One time Lamb, who enjoyed pranks, invited him to join him on Primrose Hill at dawn in order to watch the Persian ambassador worshipping the sun – and Dyer ambled up the slope to do just that.

Visiting other people's houses, though, seems to have made Dyer especially absentminded. Once he went to the London home of a Mr Montague and, told that he and his family were away in the country and wouldn't return for another week, signed his name in the guest book. Two hours later he returned to the same house, was given the identical news, again asked for pen and ink, and yet again signed his name, this time immediately below his earlier entry. And some time after he had said goodbye to another friend, the critic and essayist Leigh Hunt, Dyer reappeared at the door politely saying, 'I think, sir, I have left one of my shoes behind me.' He had walked halfway across Hampstead Heath before realising that one of his feet was covered only by a sock because he'd vaguely removed the missing shoe and placed it under Leigh Hunt's table.

*On another occasion, he mistook a coal scuttle for his hat and put it on his head as he left Lamb's house. After yet another visit to the Lambs he went away having somehow managed to replace his own hat with the brocaded headgear that footmen wore at that time. He then ran into a friend, who humorously sympathised with him for having become a servant. It was, I suppose, rather as if a diner at an expensive restaurant had somehow managed to exit with a chef's hat covering his hair.*

# Six

Was Tristram's mind in decline? Quite the opposite, or so he would have indignantly told you if you had been rude enough to ask. In many ways he felt sharper than ever and, despite Clope's continuing hostility, his academic career was on the rise. There had been a job offer from a major American university and requests for his essays from significant academic publications. He was already planning to extend his lecture on the contemporary relevance of Shelley and Keats into a full-length book, with added chapters on Byron, Wordsworth, Coleridge and others. He remained convinced that his absentmindedness was the flip side of a laser-like concentration that few of his generation could match and was neither more nor less pronounced than it had been five, ten or even fifteen years ago.

And that's true. Tristram's vagueness is far from being a sudden, ominous affliction. He has always been absent-minded, as his parents would have attested before they left Britain for foreign parts and his aunt, who lives a few streets away from his terraced house, will attest now. When last heard of, his father and mother, both of whom are biologists, were on a melting iceberg in distant Antarctica, studying penguins that, as they jokily but irritatingly wrote in their most recent letter, seem almost as confused by global warming as Tristram is by global everything else.

But now it's his Aunt Persephone who takes a positive delight in telling stories about his more abstracted behaviour and laughing in a way that makes him feel patronised, infantilised and rather smaller than his adult five-foot-nine.

'Why, Tristram used to try to eat his teddy bear,' she will tell her cronies with a particularly maddening smile.

'Don't be ridiculous,' Tristram will answer. 'All babies chew their teddy bears. It's what babies do.'

'Yes, but they don't usually kiss and cuddle their rusks at the same time,' Aunt Persephone will reply, enraging him by hee-hawing like a raucous old donkey at the supposed memory.

'Well, I don't do that now, do I?' Tristram will snap back, remembering that he's a distinguished lecturer with a high-flying future. But he'll quite likely be stirring salt into his coffee at the time.

The stories this good-humoured but outrageous aunt tells about his youth are often apocryphal. No, it's not true (or so one hopes) that, as an improbable but officious school prefect, he grabbed an admittedly undersized religious studies teacher by an ear, told him he was a cheeky little chap and ordered him to do 50 press-ups. No, it's not true (or is it?) that, while watching a production of *Macbeth* at the University Theatre in preparation for a school essay, he started to scrawl his thoughts, not in his notebook, but on the bald head of the man sitting in the seat immediately in front of him.

But it's certainly true that he often got the local shops confused, asking a surprised bookshop assistant for a tin of dog food and an astonished pet shop owner for a dictionary of quotations. It's true he began to feel hungry while queuing for a ticket at the University Theatre and asked the man at the box-office window for a hot dog with lots of mustard, realising afterwards that a poster advertising *Macbeth* had put Big Macs and other such fast food into his meandering mind. It's also true that because of his absentmindedness he ran into problems with his girlfriends or, as he rather pompously puts it, he had 'Woman Trouble'.

Things were more or less all right when Tristram was going out with Meryl, a hearty, buxom girl he had known from childhood. She knew about his vagueness and treated it with a sort of impatient amusement. 'They shouldn't let you out without a lead, Thross,' she used to say, cheerily using her nickname for him. 'Pull yourself together, or you'll be answerable to me.' And sometimes she'd give him a punch in the shoulder, which Tristram privately disliked but tolerated, because he realised it was playful and well meant. Meryl, you see, was keen on games and took a particular interest in boxing.

Anyway, he got quite a few punches from Meryl when he did something really vague, such as promising to take her to *Rocky II* or *Rocky III*, only to find that the two of them were watching something called *Rock Pool of Love*, which Meryl declared to be the soppiest film she'd ever seen. 'Thross, I think I'll streep you until you're black and blue,' she chortled after the heroine had run sobbing into the pool of the title and drowned herself. 'Streep', which was her word for her more robust behaviour, was of course derived from her actress namesake, Meryl Streep, whom she admired as a strong, self-sufficient woman who was also quite a looker. And, yes, that time poor Tristram Throstlethwaite got so thoroughly streeped he half-wondered if his shoulder hadn't been dislocated.

Not that Meryl wasn't feminine in her own way. From the start she insisted on what she called 'a goodnight streep', which was something she delivered with great panache, grabbing Tristram by the shoulder she might or might not have bruised and giving him the sort of smacking kiss Petruchio gives Kate during their marriage in *The Taming of the Shrew*, the one at which we're told 'all the church did echo'. But she was certainly very different from Beryl, whom Tristram met in a decidedly unconventional way.

He got on to a bus one afternoon feeling a bit tired and, without really looking, flopped down on what he thought was an empty seat. But it felt oddly uncomfortable, rather as if the stuffing had come out and turned out to be made of little bits of stick. Moreover, the sticks began to wiggle, which isn't at all usual even with badly made bus seats. They also seemed slightly to be squeaking, as if in need of oil. With an irritable snort, directed at the bus company, Tristram got to his feet, turned around and saw a thin, pale-faced young woman staring at him in a pained yet unsurprised manner. Surely he hadn't sat on her? Yes, clearly he had.

Tristram was appalled and, of course, deeply apologetic. But in reply to his earnest repetitions of 'sorry', the young woman said in a small voice, 'Please don't worry. It's the sort of thing that happens to me all the time.'

Tristram found this remark touching and, when the young woman stood up and pulled what looked like a heavy shopping basket from below her, he offered to get off the bus and help her carry it. She gave the shaggy moustache he had recently grown a resigned look, as if to say that, if he really was a crazed rapist, there wasn't much she could do about it. 'That would be very, very kind,' she murmured and handed him her basket.

Anyway, she learned that he was called Tristram and he learned that she was called Beryl, a name she said was 'very, very horrible, but I don't have any other and I don't know how to change it'. Apparently, she was a secretary at a local undertakers, a job that she didn't particularly like. 'I don't have to see the dead bodies,' she said. 'But I do see a lot of very, very sad people.'

'And you do your best to cheer them up?' asked Tristram.

Beryl looked at him reproachfully, clearly finding his question lacking in sensitivity. 'No,' she said. 'I talk to them and we are sad together.'

Again, Tristram thought this moving and, indeed, found her attractive in a fragile, wispy kind of way. And she was impressed to learn that he was an aspiring academic. 'You must be very, very clever,' she said. 'I wish I was clever, but I'm afraid I'm not. I'm not anything much, really.'

Yes, Beryl was certainly quite different from Meryl, who at that time was studying to be a PT teacher and taking a course in kickboxing. And Tristram found himself asking for her phone number when he left her at the door of the small terraced house where she apparently lived with her parents. Beryl stared at him in a way that seemed simultaneously doubtful and fatalistic. 'If you really, really want it, you can have it,' she said and, looking as if she knew she might be consigning herself and her fate to Bluebeard, she gave it to him.

Tristram was in a quandary. He had, he supposed, a regular girlfriend in Meryl, but he wasn't engaged to her or anything. And, apart from those big, smacking kisses, their relationship had so far remained disappointingly platonic. There was no reason why he shouldn't ask Beryl for a date. Indeed, he felt that after sitting on her, he probably owed her a trip to the cinema or a meal or something. On the other hand, Meryl might not like it if he did that and certainly wouldn't get on with Beryl. And Beryl would not appreciate Meryl, especially if Meryl decided to punch, kick or otherwise streep her. It would be in everyone's interest if he kept the two girls apart.

But something inside that strangely wired brain of his didn't seem wholly to agree. At any rate, he couldn't seem to stop calling each of them by the other's name. This didn't please Meryl at all, proud as she was of sharing a name with the great Streep.

'What?' she said when Tristram began a phone call by saying 'Hello, Beryl'. 'What? Are you taking the mickey, Thross? Why are you calling me Beryl? Beryl is a pathetic name. Do you think Meryl Streep would have had any success if she'd been called Beryl Streep? That's a name for a girly flop and, Thross, I'm not a girly flop.'

'No, you're not at all a girly flop, Beryl . . . I mean Meryl,' said Tristram hastily, knowing that he risked a pummelling if he wasn't careful.

'Watch it, Thross,' said Meryl. 'Don't Beryl me again.'

'OK, um, Meryl,' said Tristram.

'What?' said Beryl when he got her name wrong, 'What? I wish I was called Meryl, but I'm not. Beryl is a very, very pathetic name. It's a name for a flop, but then I'm afraid I am a flop.'

'No, you're not at all a flop, Meryl . . . I mean Beryl,' Tristram assured her.

'Well, you can call me Meryl if you like,' said Beryl. 'It's a much better name. There are even days when I feel like a Meryl and not a Beryl. Not many days, but a few.'

'No, I think it would be less confusing if I stuck to, um, Beryl,' said Tristram.

Anyway, Tristram remembered to call Beryl Beryl when they had their first date. He picked her up at six o'clock and, though he wasn't good at noticing what women were wearing, he realised that she had made quite an effort for the occasion. She wasn't wearing dungarees, as Meryl sometimes did, but a pink frilly number that he thought quite sweet.

'You look very nice, um, Beryl,' said Tristram.

'Almost like a Meryl, I hope,' said Beryl with a tiny, nervous smile.

'Well, not exactly,' said Tristram, 'but very nice.'

'Thank you, Tristy,' said Beryl, revealing for the first time what was to be her pet name for Tristram.

Off they went to the local Ritz, which was supposed to be showing a film about Cliff Richard going on a happy holiday but actually turned out to be screening a rerun of *The Longest Day*, which is not only very long but pretty bloody, since it involves the D-Day landings in 1944. This was rather embarrassing, since Tristram had promised Beryl he would take her to something soft and gentle but, all too characteristically, he had forgotten to double-check the name of the movie on offer. He had even said to her that he planned to give her a pleasant surprise, a film she would be able to identify with.

Should he have held her hand when she made tiny,

vomiting sounds at the scenes of mass slaughter on beaches that didn't appear to feature Cliff Richard at all? Perhaps, but he didn't feel he yet knew her well enough to do so. Yet when the film ended and the titles came up, he turned to her and saw that, though tears were streaming down cheeks that looked paler than ever, she had a gallant sort of look in her eyes.

'Well, I wouldn't call that film very, very soft and gentle,' said Beryl. 'But it was certainly a surprise and I'm very, very grateful for that. It shows you take me seriously.'

'Oh, I do, Meryl,' said Tristram with excessive and perhaps ill-advised emphasis. 'Very, very seriously.'

'You're right in thinking it's a film that a Meryl would identify with,' said Beryl. 'And it's probably good for a Beryl like me to see it. I think I may be able to look at the dead bodies in the mortuary now. Perhaps I'm turning from a Beryl into a Meryl.'

Meryl herself was less forgiving when he next misidentified her. It hadn't helped that his birthday present to her turned out to be a pink hot water bottle with a mauve bunny embossed on the cover. Tristram had bungled again, leaving in a cupboard the biography of Sugar Ray Robinson he had meant to give Meryl, all packaged and prepared to be dispatched to Beryl, whose birthday was a week or two later.

Meryl had done her best to be grateful, thinking that Tristram was trying to appeal to her feminine side, whatever that was. Nevertheless, she looked at the gift with an astonishment that wasn't alleviated when she inspected the accompanying card, which read: 'For Beryl, to ensure her little feet don't get cold.'

'OK, Thross,' said Meryl, 'that's one Beryl too many. You can't fool me. Who is this bloody Beryl with the ridiculous feet? A midget – or, more likely, some little fool of a tart who has given you the eye?'

'No,' said Tristram, 'just a stupid mistake. I don't know any tart called Beryl.' That was, he thought, not quite a lie, since Beryl was self-evidently a chaste and modest girl. It was, however, an evasion. He hoped he wouldn't live to regret it, because Meryl, as she often said herself, was as straight as a die and expected others to be the same.

'Good,' said Meryl, giving him a playful punch and a practice kick. 'Keep it that way.'

Some sort of awful denouement was bound to occur, and it did a few weeks later. George Macdonald, who would one day be Tristram's boss at the city's great university, and his wife Muriel, or the dear old dromedary as George called her, asked him to what they described as a very informal dinner. 'Oh, and let's also have your nice girlfriend,' said George. 'We'd like to get to know her better.'

Why did he say 'better' when he didn't know Beryl at all? The thought passed through Tristram's mind, but he dismissed it. Beryl was now his nice girlfriend. Meryl was also his girlfriend and not exactly nasty. She was vivid and vital and outspoken and fierce and, when she wanted to be, good fun. But it would demean a girl who thought Mike Tyson was a bit too soft to call her 'nice'.

Anyway, Beryl was initially thrilled when he asked her to accompany him to George's place. 'But what shall I wear?' she asked and asked again, with growing anxiety and dismay. 'They sound very, very important.'

'Well, he did say it was very formal,' answered Tristram. 'Why don't you wear that pink frilly thing that makes you look so good?'

'Oh Tristy, I'll have to do better than that,' replied Beryl.

And so she did. At any rate, she was wearing a red velvet evening gown when he picked her up. He couldn't quite understand why she was wearing something so formal when George had told him, and he thought he had told her, that it was an informal occasion. But she looked definitely attractive and he told her so, quelling her nervous enquiries about why he, Tristy, was wearing a crumpled tweed jacket and no tie.

'That's what they'll expect of me,' said Tristram in a self-deprecating way. 'I don't have much clothes sense.'

George lived a little way out of town, not a place it was easy to reach by bus or, Tristram felt, appropriate to do so. He didn't want to risk sitting on poor Beryl again. So he ushered her into the family car, which he sometimes borrowed from his parents now that he had at long, long last managed to pass his driving test. The modest bottle of wine he planned to give George was safely in the boot, Beryl was in the front seat, and all seemed well. But, oh dear, the car itself was almost out of fuel. So Tristram decided to repay his parents' generosity by filling up the tank and stopped at the nearest petrol station.

'Shan't be a moment, Tristy,' said Beryl as Tristram worked the petrol pump. Her nerves at meeting George had, it seemed, left her needing again to go to the loo, which was at the back of the garage.

'Hum,' said Tristram vaguely as he set his mind to the tiresome business of ensuring that the right petrol went into the right slot. He had once filled up the same car with diesel, an error that had almost destroyed its engine and upset his parents no end.

Anyway, Tristram finished paying for the petrol, returned to the car, jumped briskly in and drove off. He was well aware that it was necessary to concentrate hard when driving – hadn't he failed one driving test after going the wrong way round a roundabout, robustly cursing drivers who were actually going the right way? – and so he tended to go slowly, staring intensely over the steering wheel as he went. It was difficult to make conversation while doing this, but Tristram did his best, talking about his parents and his childhood and commiserating with Beryl about her own background, which had been a long series of sorrows and sadnesses.

'Poor Meryl, I mean poor Beryl,' said Tristram with all the sympathy he could muster.

But this wasn't an altogether wise topic, Tristram realised as he carefully engineered his way into a right-hand lane while signalling left and ignoring the hoots from a car that had been trying to overtake him. Beryl had been orphaned at an early age and brought up by cousins who apparently treated her like Jane Eyre or Cinderella, and the memory of those times was apt to reduce her to tearful silence. That had clearly happened now, for no word was to be heard from her. Also, she appeared to have relocated herself in the back seat, presumably to give her and her long red dress more room.

'I know it's a painful subject,' said Tristram. 'Let's talk of something cheerful. That'll get us into the mood for the dinner party.' But he must have depressed poor Beryl a lot, for still there was silence from the back. She didn't even respond to the jokes he proceeded to crack in hopes of restoring her spirits, but that was presumably because he couldn't remember all the punchlines.

As they approached George's house, just a few minutes late, Tristram glanced over his shoulder. What? What . . .

no Beryl! He stopped, got out, looked under the back seat and then, more in hope than belief, in the car boot. That contained nothing larger than the bottle of wine which he was taking to the Macdonalds and, small and slim though she was, certainly nothing Beryl-sized. The girl had inexplicably evaporated, which was to take smallness and thinness to an absurd extreme. 'Meryl,' he called, quickly amending this to a cry of 'Beryl'. But there was no answer from anywhere, in or out of the car.

Then he realised. He must have left her at the garage. And now he thought about it, he seemed to remember her saying something about visiting the loo. Oh no, oh dear, oh Spooner. He got back into the car, did a three-point turn, knocking over a bit of someone's garden hedge, and drove faster than safety permitted back to the garage. And, yes, Beryl was there. She was standing in her long, red dress beside the cash desk, tears streaming down her face.

'Oh Tristy,' she managed to gasp, 'how could you leave me when you know how nervous I am?'

The woman at the cash desk joined in, giving Tristram as hostile a frown as he could remember ever having received. 'Don't bring your quarrels in here,' she snapped. 'You settle your differences at home next time. Never mind, love,' she added, this time addressing Beryl, 'just remember that God made a big mistake when he created men.'

'I'm terribly sorry, Meryl . . . I mean Beryl,' said Tristram. 'I thought you were in the back seat. I should have looked.'

'Yes,' said the woman at the cash desk as Beryl continued to weep silently. 'And you should remember which of your girlfriends you're driving about. Men are swine.'

'I don't know if I'm strong enough to meet your friends,' said Beryl as he gently led her back to the car and ensured she was safely tucked in, complete with seat belt, in the front seat beside him.

'You are, you are,' said Tristram solicitously. 'And they're looking forward to meeting you. George specifically said he wanted to get to know you. Don't worry. I'll look after you. But we'll have to hurry because we're late.'

And he started up the car, and drove with his usual quiet intensity but this time saying nothing as he edged into a left lane while signalling right and ignoring the hoots of yet another car as he made as speedy a turn as he could, just about avoiding an old lady who had started to cross the road.

'Hooligans!' yelled the old lady in a surprisingly loud voice. 'Joyriders! Road hogs!'

'Oh Tristy,' squeaked Beryl, 'how I really, really did not like that.'

But at least Beryl was there beside him. He could clearly see her when he dared to glance her way, starting to mop up her face and replace her make-up with the help of the little mirror in her handbag.

They stopped outside a pleasant terraced house and rang the bell, which was answered by a George who looked the very opposite of formal. In fact, he was unshaven and wearing an old grey cardigan. He blinked at his visitors and then gave a hesitant grin. 'How nice to see you, Tristram,' he said.

'This is Beryl,' said Tristram with all the accuracy and pride he could muster.

'Hello, Beryl,' said George, again a bit hesitantly.

'Sorry we're so late,' said Tristram. 'A little misunderstanding. All my fault. Nothing to do with Meryl. Or, um, Beryl.'

'Oh,' said George in a worried sort of way, looking at Beryl's eyes, which were still red, and then at her dress, which was as red and long as ever. 'Oh.'

'Shan't be a second,' went on Tristram, remembering that he had left the wine in the boot. 'Just a small present. And I suppose an apology for keeping you waiting.' And he dashed back to the car and returned with the bottle, shoving it with a grin into George's hands.

'Well, thank you,' said George. 'I think you'd better come in.'

'Who is it?' came a woman's cry from somewhere deeper inside the house.

'It's Tristram and his friend Beryl,' said George. 'They've come bringing us a lovely bottle of wine.'

The woman appeared, wearing an apron over a casual top and jeans. It was George's wife, clearly in the middle of preparing dinner. Something stirred uneasily in Tristram's mind, but was soon superseded by two very different feelings. First, he was pleased to see George's wife, a cheerful, outgoing woman whom he had always liked but whose name he sometimes failed to remember. What was it? Margaret? Rachel?

Second, Tristram was worried about Beryl, who was standing in the hall looking completely lost. Perhaps she felt overdressed, thought Tristram. But there was no need to worry. These were nice people and would surely appreciate her having made so much effort.

'Well, thank you for the wine, Tristram and Beryl,' said George's still nameless wife. 'You shouldn't have gone to all that trouble. You'll stay to have a drink, won't you?'

This invitation struck Tristram as slightly odd under the circumstances, as did what followed from George. 'You must stay longer than that, now you're here. I'm sure we can stretch dinner to four.'

'Of course we can,' said George's wife. 'It will be a pleasure.'

Tristram still thought the conversation had taken a strange turn, but he didn't look remotely as flummoxed as Beryl. She hadn't said anything since mumbling 'It's a great, great pleasure to meet you' to George. Now she gave Tristram a stricken look and started mouthing wordless messages in his direction.

Yes, it was because she was embarrassed by her elaborate dress. He must find some way of putting poor, insecure Beryl at her ease.

'Doesn't she look terrific?' said Tristram in his heartiest, most upbeat voice.

'Terrific,' said George.

'Terrific,' added George's wife with a smile. 'You won't mind yesterday's meatballs, will you?'

That question seemed only to add to Beryl's distress. Was that because the evening was turning out to be even more informal than he had imagined, Tristram wondered. Oh no, it was because she was a vegetarian who sometimes ate a bit of fish but never touched red, brown or even beige meat. She had asked Tristram to tell George that, and he had forgotten to do so.

'*Mea culpa, mea maxima culpa*,' cried Tristram, doing his best to jolly things up by rubbing his hands cheerily together. 'I think meatballs are absolutely yum-yum and I can't wait to eat them. But I forgot to warn you. Meryl isn't a flesh-eater. If you've a bit of fish or vegetable, she'll be delighted, won't you darling?'

It wasn't the first time Tristram had called Beryl Meryl,

but it was the first time he had called her darling; but if he expected this to improve the increasingly awkward atmosphere, he was wrong. Beryl looked at him in the bewildered, helpless way a child might look at a trusted friend or parent who had decided to force castor oil down its throat while simultaneously giving it a cold bath – and was claiming that both atrocities were acts of love.

'Yes, of course,' said George's wife, again smiling. 'I'm sure I can rustle something up from the freezer.'

'You're very, very nice and very, very kind,' gulped Beryl.

'Not at all,' replied George's wife. 'And your name is Beryl and not Meryl, isn't it? I'm not sure I heard Tristram right.'

'Beryl,' whimpered Beryl. 'Unfortunately.'

'Not unfortunately,' said George genially. 'It's a nice name.'

'No, it's not,' quavered Beryl. 'It's a very, very horrible name. I wish I was called Meryl.'

'Oh,' said George, looking completely nonplussed, the more so because tears were beginning to fall down Beryl's cheeks.

'Time for a drink,' said George's wife. 'I'm pretty sure we've some white wine in the fridge.'

'That would be tremendous,' cried Tristram, clapping his hands together in what now looked more like desperation than good humour. And at that moment there was a ringing from the mobile phone which, though such things were rare, big and expensive in those days, he had bought himself and proudly kept in his pocket. Muttering a jaunty sort of apology, he took the call.

'Tristram, where the hell are you?' said a male voice.

'Here, about to have dinner,' replied Tristram, taken aback. 'Where should I be?'

'At George's.'

'But I am at George's. Who's that?'

'George.'

By now Tristram was completely confused. He was looking at George and yet George, who didn't appear to be on or near any phone, was speaking to him over the phone, though admittedly in a deeper voice. Was he bilocating in some strange way? Or was he, Tristram, dreaming? It was a bit like the sort of nightmare in which people keep changing faces and identities, and events spiral out of control. Perhaps Beryl, who was now openly sobbing, would change into Meryl. But Tristram did the traditional thing. He pinched himself and found that, yes, he was awake.

'Well, you can't be George,' he said definitively. 'George is George.'

'But I am George,' said the voice, sounding just a little irked. 'I'm George. George Macdonald. And the dear old dromedary and I are wondering if you are still coming to dinner. It's all ready and we have a pleasant surprise for you.'

Tristram gulped, thought, gulped again, thought again and, still gulping, answered, 'Oh my God, yes, awfully sorry. We're on our way. We're only a few minutes away.'

And that was true. Tristram was with George Wooster and, yes, his wife Rebecca. And, yes, they lived only half a mile or so from George and Muriel Macdonald. And Tristram realised that, in his fluster over leaving Beryl at the garage, he had mentally muddled one George with another George and the Macdonalds with the Woosters. They were all his friends. But it was the Macdonalds and not the Woosters who had invited him and his nice girlfriend to dinner.

Tristram turned off his mobile phone, put it down in the bowl of crisps that Rebecca Wooster had brought in and launched into an anguished explanation. The Woosters looked at him silently for a moment, then at each other, and began to laugh. And laughed and laughed. And, most surprisingly, Beryl stopped crying and began to laugh, too, though in a slightly hysterical way.

'Tristy's supposed to be very, very clever,' she said with a new clarity. 'But he isn't as clever as all that. Is he?'

'No, he isn't,' Rebecca replied, herself beginning to cry, but in her case with helpless laughter. 'I should keep an eye on him and an even bigger eye on yourself. And do come and visit us again, dear, won't you?'

'He also told me it was a very, very formal occasion,' said Beryl. 'And it isn't here and I bet it won't be at the Macdonalds or wherever we're going. Am I right, Tristy?'

Tristram thought, gulped, thought again, gulped again, and agreed she was right. At that, Beryl's face crumpled once more.

'You poor dear,' said Rebecca, her laughter abruptly stopped by what struck her as an awful revelation. 'I bet it isn't either. I'm about your height. Let me lend you something informal but nice.'

And, clucking like a mother hen with a dozen warm eggs in her nest she sought and found a simple frock that billowed slightly outwards and so didn't emphasise Beryl's thinness. And she gave the girl a big, warm kiss as she said goodbye and, addressing her but not Tristram, repeated her invitation.

Somehow Beryl seemed different as Tristram drove on to the Macdonalds. She didn't twitter or act apologetic. In fact, she didn't say anything at all as Tristram tried frantically to make up with her while avoiding pavements and pedestrians. She didn't even seem to want to talk about her unhappy childhood.

'Bloody bugger my bloody buggering childhood,' she suddenly said, astonishing Tristram into a silence that continued until he screeched up outside another terraced house.

'Better late than never,' cried George Macdonald. 'Or better never than late,' added Muriel Macdonald in a jokey way that wasn't altogether jokey. 'Yes, better...' began a familiar voice behind them, only to halt with alarming abruptness.

It was Meryl. She was the pleasant surprise George had mentioned. He must have invited her unilaterally. And as Tristram now half-recalled, with one of those strikingly sharp memories that always seemed to come too late, George had said, 'Let's have your nice girlfriend,' not 'Bring along your nice girlfriend'. And, like the Macdonalds, Meryl was registering the presence of Beryl as she stood just behind Tristram and his gaping mouth and quivering moustache.

'This is Meryl . . . I mean Beryl,' he managed to stutter. 'I, um, brought her along for the vegetables and the fish.'

Well, the people greeting the late arrivals were all well mannered. The Macdonalds seemed quickly to realise they'd have to lay another place at dinner, and Muriel and George scurried away quietly to do just that, and Meryl did nothing worse than stare balefully at Tristram as he and Beryl came into the sitting room. She looked at Beryl, clearly decided that so flimsy a thing could never be a serious rival, looked back at Tristram, clearly decided that she wouldn't care if such a man produced a rival in the form of Marilyn

Monroe or Helen of Troy, and, while addressing Beryl, continued to stare dangerously at him.

'You're Beryl,' said Meryl. 'I've heard a lot about you. Isn't Thross a stupid swine?'

'And you're Meryl,' replied Beryl. 'I've heard your name a lot too. Yes, he really, really is a swine. Quite stupid too.'

'What did the stupid, two-timing swine do to you?' asked Meryl, still eyeballing Tristram.

'He called me by the wrong name, made me dress in the wrong frock, left me at a garage, drove like a maniac, almost mowed down an old lady who screamed horrible words at us, took me to the wrong house, introduced me as you, and let them feed me meatballs, which are really, really wrong for me.'

'You poor little thing,' said Meryl. 'Later we'll punch the stupid, two-timing swine to death, turn him into bacon and eat him.'

'OK,' said Beryl, gratefully mustering something that sounded almost like a giggle. 'But we won't eat his moustache. That might make us sick.'

'Well said, Beryl,' said Meryl.

'Thank you, Meryl,' said Beryl.

The stupid, two-timing swine and prospective punchbag just stood there, trying and failing to rise above it all. He looked glazed and inane, a bit like the Tin Man in *The Wizard of Oz* before he gets his joints oiled. And when George came back in to summon them all to the table, genially crying, 'Hope you're having fun, children,' he didn't find he had much of an appetite.

'I hope everyone here likes fish,' said Muriel as she brought in a steaming dish and George poured out some white wine.

'Oh goody, goody,' squeaked Beryl, her spirits much

improved by her warm reception, the realisation she wouldn't have to eat meat of any kind, and, finally, the alcohol.

'Isn't Beryl sweet?' said Meryl.

'Isn't Meryl nice?' said Beryl.

Tristram likes to think of himself as basically a strong, resilient person, the worthy heir of those medieval warriors who went about bashing other people and sometimes each other with maces and broadswords. So he pulled himself together. It was time, he thought, for a bit of healing merriment. He owed that to the Macdonalds after being so late and bringing them an uninvited guest. He also owed it to the outraged Meryl and the upset Beryl. But he couldn't seem to get his funny stories straight.

'And so the Polish gentleman said . . . ' finished Tristram, turning pink, ' . . . oh dear, what did the Polish gentleman say? Something about the difference between pitfalls and pitbulls, I think. Or was it french polish? Or maybe he wasn't Polish or a gentleman. Anyway, whoever he was, he said something very amusing. Sorry, sorry.'

In his fluster Tristram had broken the prime rule of anecdote-telling, which is always to remember the last line before launching into the first. Anyway, nobody laughed or even looked particularly sympathetic, not even kindly George Macdonald, who was fond of Tristram and was enthusiastically monitoring his academic progress. Nor did they do so when Tristram, who had visited the Scottish highlands the previous year, tried to say something witty about a still painful subject, the massacre at Glencoe, forgetting that it was the Macdonalds who had been mass-murdered by the Campbells and not, as he announced to the table, the Macbeths by the Cadwalladers.

'It was the blackest day in our clan's long history,' said

George, looking a bit less than his usual ebullient self. 'We don't laugh about it a lot.'

But then people started to tell their own funny stories, and the odd thing was they were all about Tristram. He was the butt for the night or the scapegoat for the evening. So he had to put up with George remembering how he had almost failed his history O-level after misinterpreting a question about British naval power during the Elizabethan age. He had confused Elizabeth I with Elizabeth II and written an essay that somehow managed to mistake the Spanish Armada for the Falklands Campaign and Francis Drake for Margaret Thatcher.

'It's not true,' bleated Tristram.

Meryl pitched in, a mean smile on her face. 'OK, but what about the time you shoved some frozen sweet-and-sour pork through the catflap while trying to cram a cat into the microwave and, when it complained, asked your meal why it didn't seem to want to be eaten?'

'That's certainly not true,' wailed Tristram.

'I'll tell you what's true,' said Beryl, by now squealing with glee. 'He sat on me in a bus. He thought I was a seat and he squashed me.'

'*Et tu*, Beryl,' moaned Tristram, admitting that this story at least was perfectly true. 'But,' he added lamely, 'I like to think that it was only the flip side of my being...'

'Very, very clever,' chorused Beryl and Meryl in what struck him as not a particularly friendly way.

Soon it was the end of what had been an uproarious evening for everyone else but, sadly, not unadulterated fun for Tristram. 'Can I please take you both home?' Tristram asked Beryl and Meryl after they had said their goodbyes to the Macdonalds outside their front door.

It was, he thought, wise to face Beryl rather than Meryl when he made this offer, since he didn't particularly want a punch on the shoulder or a kick in the chest, still less to be turned into bacon and eaten.

So what next happened was a great surprise. With a jubilant cry of 'Bye, bye, Tristy,' Beryl gave him an almighty blow in the solar plexus. How could so frail-seeming a girl attain such power, he wondered as he sank half to his knees. It was as if she had the strength traditionally attributed to mad people or parents saving children who were trapped under cars. And it was so unfair. All along he had meant well.

'I think we'll go back together,' said Meryl. 'OK, Beryl?'

'OK, Meryl,' said Beryl – and off they went, laughing in a pleased way as they linked arms and put a puffing Tristram, his sagging moustache, his parents' car and the Macdonalds' house far behind them.

Tristram saw Meryl a few times after this, but she didn't speak to him. In fact, she next spoke to him about three years later. She affably called him 'a silly old pig of a Thross' at a party, which was her way of saying that a truce had been called between them. After all, they had known each other almost since childhood. And from time to time, he took her out to dinner or a theatre, though there were no more smacking kisses or, for that matter, any cheery punches or uproarious kicks. Though she still had a hearty way of talking, as if life was an extremely long game of lacrosse, Meryl seemed less aggressive and calmer.

As for Beryl, he never spoke to her again, though he saw her or, perhaps, imagined he saw her once or twice. Passing the funeral home, he thought he glimpsed her striding rather than just tripping out of the half-visible shed that lay behind the main office and was presumably a mortuary. Passing the place again, he could have sworn he saw her face through the office's slightly tinted glass and her arm suddenly rise and abruptly fall. Was she clapping a mourner on the back in an effort to make him less sad? Or striking an insubordinate undertaker? He could only guess.

However, he did know that Beryl was no longer frail, fragile or even thin because his next sighting of her was from the side of the street that lay opposite to what was, amazingly, a betting shop. She looked almost as well built as Meryl as she walked purposefully in, either to take bets from one side of the counter or make them from the other. What next, wondered Tristram – would she end up as a bouncer, throwing him out of a nightclub?

Anyway, there was a curious happening at a Christmas party not attended by Meryl or Beryl. He found himself in animated conversation with a pretty young woman. Her hair was golden, she had a sweet smile, and she seemed very keen on the Romantic poets. She had some particularly incisive things to say about Keats's 'Ode to a Grecian Urn', not a poem Tristram felt he had fully understood until then.

'More happy love, more happy happy love, for ever warm and still to be enjoyed, for ever panting and for ever young,' he proclaimed in a voice that radiated his enthusiasm for Keats and, perhaps, for this enchanting new friend.

'To what green altar, O mysterious priest, leadst thou that heifer lowing at the skies?' she replied in a way that struck him as, well, a bit flirtatious.

It was too early to talk or even think of having at last found a soulmate, but she seemed to like him and he was certainly attracted to her. She was, well, gorgeous. But what was her name?

'Cheryl,' she said with a particularly charming smile.

Tristram felt an unwanted lurch in his stomach. 'Could you please say that again?' he asked.

'Cheryl,' she repeated. 'And what's your name?'

'Um, Tristram,' said Tristram.

'Very nice to meet you, Tristram,' said Cheryl.

'Very nice to have met you, Cheryl,' said Tristram – and, flashing an apologetic but nervous grin, half-cantered, half-galloped to the other side of the room.

## THE VAGUE BOOK 6

*Franz Schubert, who died at the age of 31, provides yet more proof that you don't have to be old to be vague or abstracted. He often caused offence by forgetting important appointments. He usually omitted to take off his spectacles at night and slept with them on.*

*Desperately looking for socks to wear one day, he could find none that weren't disintegrating, leaving him wailing to a friend, 'I really do believe that whole socks are not knitted any more.' And when another friend, the baritone Johann Michael Vogl, sang a particularly beautiful song at a soirée, Schubert said, 'You know, that song isn't bad, who is it by?' The answer, of course, was himself. And the chronically absentminded Alexander Scriabin was still a young man when he appeared at a party in brand new boots, yet discovered on his return home he was wearing old boots which didn't match. Two of his fellow-guests had presumably been left with one boot each and a half-share in Scriabin's footwear.*

*But many of the great musicians, whether composers,*

*conductors or performers, have had the most wonderful
memories. Arturo Toscanini, for instance, hadn't only a
remarkable ear for detail but a power of recall that
verged on the phenomenal or photographic. Yet he was
apt not to notice when he indulged in his habit of singing
along with his orchestras. Indeed, he sometimes did this
so loudly that he once stopped a rehearsal to ask who was
making such an awful, distracting noise. The answer, of
course, was himself. Again, one of several reasons Otto
Klemperer had to sit down while conducting was that he
never fully recovered from the burns he suffered on the
night he set fire to his bed with a cigarette – and tried to
douse the flames with whisky.*

*And what about Fritz Kreisler, maybe the most
brilliant violinist who ever lived? He's said to have been
walking in New York with a friend when his attention
was grabbed by the fish in the window of a fish shop.
'Heavens,' the virtuoso reputedly cried, 'that reminds me.
I should be at a concert.' The rows of fish, staring out
with dead eyes and gaping mouths, had put him in mind
of the audience he was supposed at that moment to be
entertaining.*

*As for Beethoven, greatest of all, he never forgot a note
he had written, let alone a theme he had composed. Yet
the paradox we've so often noted applies to Beethoven
more than anybody else, for he was also notoriously
abstracted, especially when he was at work. And 'work'
often began with him walking for hours in the country
outside Vienna, sometimes humming to himself and
sometimes keeping up what a pupil and friend called
Ferdinand Ries described as 'a sort of howling, without
articulating any distinct sounds'.*

*After one such all-day walk he told Ries that he'd just thought of a subject for the last movement of a sonata and, on returning to his rooms, he rushed to the piano without removing his hat and started storming over the keys while his friend went and stood in a corner. Ages later, when the finale was more or less in shape, he looked up and seemed surprised to see Ries there. 'I cannot give you a lesson today,' he said. 'I must work.'*

*Some found him still more neglectful when the creative spirit seized him. A country organist called Gottlob Wiedebein had one ambition in life, which was to go to Vienna and meet Beethoven. He saved money, he went to the city and, as he hurried towards the composer's house, he received what initially struck him as an astonishing piece of luck. He found the street blocked by a corn-wagon and a passer-by helping to reload the sacks that had fallen off. It was Beethoven himself who, hearing Wiedebein's story, gave a loud guffaw, rubbed his hands with glee, invited him to stay at his house and, after handing him over to a servant with orders to attend to him most scrupulously, said goodnight and disappeared.*

*Disappeared and, as far as Wiedebein was concerned, never appeared again. Each morning the visitor got up early, only to discover that Beethoven had left even earlier. Worse, the composer returned home either not at all or very late, only to lock himself in his room. He was oblivious to the fact that he had a guest. This happened for 14 days running, whereupon poor Wiedebein gave up hopes of talking to the great man and forlornly returned to his house in Brunswick.*

*Beethoven was, of course, notoriously slovenly in his dress, omitting to change his shirt, remove his clothes at night or even take off the soap he'd put on before forgetting to shave, meaning that his face was swathed with congealed lather. He looked such a mess that, while he was composing one of his greatest pieces, he was arrested by a policeman who had seen him walking obliviously around looking like a beggar. 'But I am Beethoven,' he said. 'Yes, of course, why not?' the policeman is said to have cynically replied. And at home his untidiness was such that, while he was working on his Mass in D, he found one section – the Kyrie – was missing and in despair started to recompose it. As he later discovered, a maidservant had not unreasonably assumed the missing pages were rubbish, had taken them to the kitchen, and used them for wrapping up superannuated pots and greasy old pans.*

*But it was when Beethoven went into a raptus, as his friends called his bouts of creative abstraction, that he behaved most oddly. Once he wandered into an eating house and sat down. After an hour lost in thought he called to the waiter, 'What do I owe?'*

*'But the gentleman has not eaten anything yet,' came the reply. 'What shall I bring?'*

*'Bring anything you like,' said Beethoven in his blunt way, 'but let me alone.'*

*In a different version of this story, or perhaps on another occasion, he went to a restaurant with his head full of the Sixth Symphony that he was then composing, and ordered dinner. But when the waiter appeared with the food he yelled, 'I have dined,' placed on the table the money for the meal he hadn't eaten, and disappeared into the night.*

*With time and growing deafness, Beethoven's temper*

*became as notorious as his abstraction. While he was conducting his own Choral Fantasia, and accompanying the singers in a loud voice, he forgot a repeat. Part of the orchestra followed him, part followed the score, and the result was a horrible mess which left the composer yelling unrepeatable insults at the players and, in his rage, forcing them to begin the entire work again. And rather the same thing happened when he himself was playing one of his piano concertos at the Theatre an der Wien.*

*Early on, he forgot that he was the soloist and, springing up from his stool, began to conduct in his usual fierce and feverish manner, flinging his arms out so violently that he knocked both candles off the piano. The public started to laugh, so enraging Beethoven that he silenced the orchestra and made them restart the piece. This time, the manager placed a couple of boys near the composer to hold the candlesticks, only for Beethoven's right hand to give one of them such a blow on the face at a musical climax that he dropped the candlestick. At this the other boy, fearing he too would be struck, evaded the threatened boxes on the ear with odd jerks and quaint little jumps. The audience couldn't stop laughing, upon which a furious Beethoven tore sheets from the score, reducing his listeners to helpless mirth and causing him to abandon the movement. After this he adamantly refused ever to give another concert.*

*The composer so valued his privacy that he kept moving lodgings, which was good news for his landlords and the people living below him, since he had the habit of walking about splashing water on his face and arms and not noticing when it flooded the floor and started dripping through the ceiling. In his absence of mind and concentration on what mattered most, he also completely forgot that an admiring aristocrat had given him a horse and continued to make his journeys on foot or by coach, as if a steed was beyond his means. Suddenly he was presented with an enormous bill for fodder that he couldn't understand until it was revealed that his sharp-witted manservant had been expensively feeding the animal and then secretly hiring it out.*

# SEVEN

A dreadful thing happened. One July evening George Macdonald's wife Muriel suddenly died. She was a big, cheery woman and left the world in the way she probably would have wanted if she had been given a choice in the matter. She was in her living room chortling away at a rerun of an episode of *Fawlty Towers*, the one in which a crazed John Cleese tries to thrash his annoying car to death with a big bush, when her laughter became a sort of joyous sigh and she collapsed and expired, felled by a heart-attack.

Anyway, Tristram knew how much George adored his dear old dromedary, as he had inexplicably nicknamed Muriel, and was on the phone to his former boss the moment after one of his colleagues in the English Department, Hector O'Brien, told him the bad news. 'George,' he said to the answering machine, 'what can I say? It's a loss, an awful loss. I was so fond of her. Do let me know if there's anything I can do.'

Somehow Tristram managed mentally to return to the

matter that was supposed to be preoccupying him. Clope's latest idea was to ask his underlings to send him ideas for improving the English Department and then to present the letters and memos he'd received from them for discussion at faculty meetings. But Tristram knew that the touchy little professor would be likely to resist any proposal that he, Tristram, put forward. Hector and his other colleagues knew this too. That's why they had privately urged him to send Clope a letter suggesting that the teaching staff hold back on salary increases in the coming financial year and divert the money to good causes, like giving free books to worthy students. Clope, they said, would be sure to back an all-round raise if his least favourite underling proposed the opposite.

Anyway, Tristram started again to work on a letter that he knew all too well would anger Clope by making himself sound heroically self-sacrificing and uninterested in money. Then a thought struck him. Had he dialled the right number when he had offered George Macdonald his condolences? In his dismay had he erred, maybe placing his message on an answering machine belonging to George Wooster or some other George or some other Macdonald or even someone else altogether? So he checked and rechecked the number and very carefully dialled it again. 'I'm devastated,' he told the answering machine this time, 'and I feel so much for you. Muriel! Your dear, dear old dromedary. What a loss. Do call me if I can do anything at all.'

That done, Tristram felt better, though not a lot better. Memories of Muriel began to flood back and, finishing and putting down the missive to Clope, he launched into a letter of sympathy to George. 'What a loss,' he began, in his rush of emotion not even putting Macdonald's name or his own address at the top of the letter. 'Your wife, your dear wife, the dear old dromedary. How will you manage without her?' And he went on to recall some of the happy times they'd had together: the pub-crawl that ended with Muriel dancing along the street with a boater on her head; the picnic at which an argument about the respective merits of Shelley and Keats had led to her bombarding Tristram with prawn-and-avocado sandwiches; her hilarity when she heard the tale of the dog Henryson and the mothballs; and the exchange of other stories about Hamish Clope – or 'funny little Clope', as George's wife had called him.

As he signed the letter with a simple 'thinking of you, Tristram', adding 'XXX' to emphasise his devotion, the phone rang. It was George, sounding stricken. 'Thank you for your calls,' he said. 'Both of them.'

Ordinarily, George would have been amused by what must have been obvious to him – Tristram's fear of having sent the first of his phone messages to some surprised stranger – but not this time, not at all. He was sort of sandbagged.

'Can I do anything?' asked Tristram.

Was it his imagination that George was rather quick to thank him again but firmly refuse his offer? He clearly didn't want Tristram to give any sort of talk or address at the funeral, which, he explained, was likely to occur in a few days' time. Though George didn't say so, he couldn't risk some flinking bunny hopping about in a respectable church's pulpit during what would necessarily be a solemn occasion. 'It would be nice if you could be there,' he went on. 'Muriel was very fond of you too.'

Tristram said that of course he would come, then rang off, then realised that the afternoon post was about to go. Hastily, he shoved the letters into their respective

envelopes, addressed them, stamped them, took them to
the mailbox and put them in. Unhappy though he was, he
had a sense of achievement and relief at two difficult jobs
decently done. George would be pleased. Clope would very
likely decide that everyone's salary should get a satisfactory
increase – and, in all consistency, he'd have to include
Tristram among the beneficiaries.

Two days later he got another call from a George who
sounded marginally cheered up. 'Thank you for your letter,'
he said.

'I do hope it was OK,' replied Tristram. 'It's so hard to say
the right thing.'

'Well, I'm sure the right thing is for you and your
colleagues to forgo your salary increases,' said George. 'The
only problem is that I'm not the head of the department any
more, so I can't help you.'

Tristram was stunned, at first by what he saw as a particularly tactless example of his absentmindedness or manifes-
tation of that Generalised Aphasia Syndrome or GAS. His
moustache twitching in embarrassment, he began to
stammer out his apologies and explanations. He must have
put his letter of condolence in the wrong envelope. It was
stupid, stupid, stupid.

'Actually it made me feel a bit better,' said George. 'The
dear old dromedary would have been mightily amused. She
would,' he went on, 'have been even more amused if you'd
sent someone else the letter you must have meant for me.'

Tristram was silent for a moment, then gave a great
gurgle of anguished recognition, as if he'd looked into his
shaving mirror and seen a thin, malignant face staring out
and balefully mouthing the words 'Come back, Culloden'
and 'Death to all Throstlethwaites'.

'I must have sent it to Clope,' he stuttered. 'And I think I used your affectionate term for dear old Muriel. He'll think it awfully odd to hear her described as a dromedary. And he already thinks I'm a little eccentric. In fact, I don't think he likes me very much.'

'Oh well,' said George. 'If you can somehow retrieve the letter before it reaches him, I'd be very pleased to read it.' And, once again, Tristram thought he sounded a little happier or, at least, less miserable.

The undergraduates were on vacation, which was why Tristram had put the fatal letter in the post and not taken it personally into the English Department. But Clope, he knew, never stayed away from the department office for long and expected those of his staff who were in town to come in to meetings when he decided to convene them. And outside working hours that office was locked and inside them it was occupied by the secretary Clope had recently hired, a large, fierce lady whose first name nobody knew because she never revealed it. Her predecessor, a plump, motherly woman who had long worked for George Macdonald, was known to everyone simply as Mum or Mumps. But her replacement was Miss Gill or, to students and junior academics who had been frozen to their spines by her wintry gaze, The Big Chill or, because 'Gill' had a fishy ring, the Cod.

So what was he to do? Creep in at night and see if he could reclaim the letter, hoping that the door to Clope's office was unlocked or, since Miss Gill's undoubted competence made that unlikely, try to pick the lock? Or breeze in by day and improvise some sort of envelope rescue? Something of the sort had to be tried because a new worry had hit Tristram.

He had a horrible feeling he had scrawled his letter of condolence in a state of such intense, immediate emotion that he might have said something Clope wouldn't at all like if he read it. Oh yes, oh no, oh dear, oh Spooner, he had done just that. He had reminded George that Muriel wasn't at all impressed by her husband's successor. And he, Tristram, had more or less endorsed her view of the man. He had, he thought, even recalled Muriel's hilarity at the episode with Clope's Afghan hound, Henryson. That was provocative, could be dangerous, and might imperil what little remained of his standing in the department. This time even the Vice-Chancellor might not be able to prevent Clope sacking him.

But it was already Friday evening, too late to go into the English Department, which would anyway be closed for the weekend, but perhaps not too late to intercept the letter. As the whole department knew, since the professor wasn't reticent about such momentous matters, Clope had been out of town at some sort of conference, probably one at which senior academics discussed means of disciplining impudent junior lecturers, or delivered learned papers about medieval sermons, or, since he himself was in the chair, a bit of both – exemplary ways in which grim 14th-century preachers had scourged their inferiors with fearsome, leathery tawses. With luck he wouldn't be back until midday on Monday at the earliest.

Anyway, Saturday morning came, and Tristram went out and bought a black tie for Muriel's funeral, which was scheduled for the following Tuesday. Saturday evening came and he realised he had managed to mislay it. Monday came, and he set out to buy another tie. But first things first. The English Department would now have reopened. And therefore, far earlier than usual, Tristram breezed into the faculty office or, since he was inwardly feeling a lot less than breezy, strolled in forcing himself to give the sort of casually good-natured smile he thought that even the Cod might associate with gentle breezes.

'Fair laughs the morn and soft the zephyr blows,' he said as happily as he could, this time quoting a slightly earlier poet than his beloved Romantics, Thomas Gray. But if he thought this would help, he was mistaken. Miss Gill was not only Miss Gill, she was clearly in Monday mode, which meant a Big Chill or Cold Cod mood. No morn could do any fair laughing in her frosty presence. Nor was there any zephyr soft enough to blow its way through her snowbound defences. She looked as if she felt the way about morns and zephyrs the way she did about Throstlethwaites, which wasn't warm at all.

Would she perhaps thaw a little if she was called 'love', 'dear' or 'darling'? That was one of Tristram's new wheezes for battling forgetfulness. He knew that the actor and director Richard Attenborough had developed the habit of calling everyone on his film sets 'darling'. People assumed this was a theatrical affectation, but Tristram had read in the paper the other day that it was something very different. The great Attenborough called people both male and female, high and low, 'darling' because it allowed him to avoid the embarrassment of failing to remember their names.

But, no, calling Miss Gill 'darling' would be unlikely to endear him to her, especially as this morning she was looking grim in an unsettling new way. Certainly, there was something odd about her mouth. She had always had a thin-lipped look, but today those thin lips seemed to go inward, and when she spoke she seemed to be trying to keep them as tightly closed together as she could. At any rate, her voice sounded alarmingly blurry or slurry as well as menacing. If a cod had been given the power of sitting up and revealing its innermost feelings to the trawlermen trying to catch it, it would have looked and sounded like this. Truly Miss Gill resembled the cold fish people called her; or so Tristram thought.

'Yesh?' said the Cod or Big Chill. 'Yesh?'

'Yesh?' replied Tristram in a puzzled way, realising a moment too late that something in her mouth was affecting her speech, maybe an ice-cube that was unable to melt in so frigid an environment or a tongue that had contrived to defy physics by expanding in the cold. The Big Chill meant 'yes'.

'Yesh?' repeated Miss Gill in what was now an undeniably intimidating, accusing way.

'I was just wondering if the post had come,' said Tristram weakly.

'Yesh,' said Miss Gill. 'Sho what?'

'Well, I thought I could help you sort it,' replied Tristram, nervously flashing what he hoped was a comradely smile.

'You shought you could short she posht?' replied Miss Gill disbelievingly. 'But she posht is about to be shorted by me. I alwaysh short the posht.' And with a tiny sneer she pointed at the room beyond her own and, adding wearily, 'I'll shee if there'sh anyshing for Shroshtleshwaite, sho shtay there,' got up and stalked out of her office into the post or mail room.

What was Tristram to do? He simply sat and waited while the Big Chill presumably sorted that day's mail. Then his eye caught something on the other side of the room. It wasn't! It must be! Yes, it was! It was the small brown box that contained the black tie he had bought the other day for Muriel's funeral. He must have popped into the English Department and, all too characteristically, left it there. The Cod was nothing if not efficient and had clearly put it aside for whoever planned to wear it. So, rather than risk an offensive lecture about his carelessness, Tristram surreptitiously slipped the box into his pocket.

Back came Miss Gill. 'Noshing for Shroshtleshwaite,' she said with evident satisfaction.

'But plenty for Clope, I bet,' said Tristram with a supposedly disarming chuckle that, however, left Miss Gill pursing her lips in an even fishier way than before.

'Shat . . . ' she said, those pursed lips palpitating with a sort of blubbery importance, ' . . . shat'sh between the profeshor and hish shecretary. And hish shecretary ish me.'

'Of course,' said Tristram, wondering if he might wait until Miss Gill took a loo break and then make a dash for the mail room to see if he could locate his telltale letter to Clope. But that was a hopeless idea. To take loo breaks people had to be just a bit liquid, and Miss Gill was clearly as solid as a fish that had been left in a deep freeze. Tristram had no excuse for hanging around the office of a woman who clearly found him pretty resistible on the remote chance that nature might give her a rare call.

Well, perhaps he could return when Miss Gill went out to eat tadpoles or sedge or whatever people like her had for lunch. But that was also pretty hopeless. After all, the letter had most probably already been taken to the professor's own office and was now on his desk. Again Tristram toyed with the idea of breaking into the Clope lair – but how?

'Are you expecting the professor soon?' asked Tristram in what he hoped was an innocently enquiring voice.

'Shat'sh hish bushinesh, I shink,' replied Miss Gill in her usual unhelpful way.

'Yesh, I mean yes,' said Tristram, summoning up the courage to express the gratitude he had meant not to reveal. 'And, oh, thank you very much for the box.'

'Boksh? Boksh' answered the Big Chill, looking as if she wanted to box him round the ears as a punishment for mimicking the voice impediment she had inexplicably developed. And she added, perhaps to herself but just loudly enough for Tristram to hear, 'You'll get a boksh from me.'

'I know,' said Tristram politely, 'I did. I've got it. Sorry for my carelessness. And thank you again.' And he left the Cod poring over her papers and completely ignoring him, his remarks and his hasty exit.

By now Tristram was feeling very anxious indeed. More and more he was remembering what he had said in his letter of condolence to George. Dromedaries, dancing with boaters on the head, flying prawn-and-avocado sandwiches. Was that it? Yes, there were things in the letter that would make someone as serious as Clope think poor dead Muriel frivolous and him, Tristram, much more trivial than a university lecturer ought to be. But that wasn't the worst. Wasn't there also a reference to 'funny little Clope' and funny little Clope's dog Henryson? Whatever the precise details, they were clearly enough to put the spindly professor into the spikiest mood. The human needle, which is how Tristram still thought of him, would be more like a lance, pike or pointed cattle prod by the time he finished reading a letter that said he wasn't only little but funny.

Anyway, Tristram ambled up and down the department corridor, desperately mumbling extracts from the Romantic poets as he wondered what to do next. 'Oh, what can ail thee, knight at arms, alone and palely loitering?' he repeated as he paused outside Clope's closed door and, on a sudden impulse, surreptitiously tried the knob. It turned. The door opened. Clearly Clope or the Cod or both had been less efficient than Tristram had believed they were. He crept inside, closing the door after him. Risky though the endeavour might be, it was worth taking a quick look in case the killer letter had arrived on Friday rather than Monday; or so Tristram thought.

Very cautiously, he began to skim through the papers that had been neatly placed, presumably by the Big Chill, on Clope's desk. No, there was nothing. But wait. There seemed to be a small pile of – but, oh dear, oh God, oh no!

The knob on the door slowly turned. What could Tristram do? What lovers in French farces do when their mistresses' husbands arrive, that's what. He instinctively leapt for the nearest empty space, which was of course beneath Clope's unusually large and imposing desk. And as the door opened and someone came in, he was bunched there, trying to crunch himself into something as much like a compressed cricket ball as he could.

But who was the person above? All he could hear was the rustling of papers on the desk and all he could see was a pair of legs that ended in grey trousers, greyer socks and black boots. It could be Miss Gill the Big Chill, who seemed always to dress as much like a prison officer as she could but, more likely, it was Clope. And then there was a sound which made up Tristram's mind. That supercilious rustle was surely the Clope sniff. The professor had returned earlier than expected from his conference, no doubt with new ideas for disciplining his underlings or interpreting medieval Scottish sermons or both.

Trying not to panic, or at least not to panic more than he was panicking already, Tristram considered his options. What would someone caught in a similar situation in a farce decide to do? Leap out, perhaps, explaining in a barefaced way that he was a cleaner or a health-and-safety inspector or someone who needed to spend time under desks, perhaps on psychiatric advice as a way of confronting claustro-phobia. No, that wouldn't do. Or maybe he should simply stay there, trying hard not to cough or sneeze, as people in farces so often managed to do. That seemed a better idea altogether. So he crunched himself into an even tighter, smaller ball, thinking that this wasn't a very dignified position for a brilliant young academic on the brink of becoming a world authority on Shelley and Keats, not to mention Coleridge.

Then Tristram heard a noise that definitely wasn't the Clope sniff. It was a blend of a snort, a pant and a whimper. It was certainly a very odd sound to come from either the Big Chill or that human needle, Hamish Clope. He looked up, peered through his own crunched-up arms, and came face to face or nose to nose with the Afghan hound, Henryson. The noise was, he realised, the Henryson snuffle.

And the Henryson snuffle produced definitive proof that the boots and trouser ends did in fact lead on to the upward parts of Clope himself. 'Silence, Henryson,' came an unmis-takable voice. 'Unsatisfactory dog. There are no rabbits down there.'

Oh yes there are, thought Tristram. He hated the nickname 'Flinking Bunny', but not now. He would rather have been called Flinking Bunny a thousand times by insolent undergraduates than be stuck in the rabbit hole which was the space below the middle of Clope's desk. At last he knew what 'flinking' meant. It meant engaging in a sort of flustered shrinking. 'I'm flinking, I'm really flinking,' he whispered madly to himself as he tried to work out what to do next.

But Henryson wasn't flinking at all. For a long moment the dog and the man simply contemplated each other while Clope continued to rustle above them, and then the dog took the initiative, pushing forward his nose until it and Tristram's nose gently collided. Taking his cue, Tristram put a finger to his lips, making an almost inaudible hushing sound. Was it his imagination that Henryson gave a grave sort of nod? Perhaps. But when Tristram pointed to the door, the dog's complicity was clear. He removed his nose from the vicinity of Tristram, turned, trotted towards the door and again emitted the Henryson snuffle.

'Patience, Henryson,' said Clope. 'It is for me to decide when to leave. We will do so when I am ready and not before then.'

There was more rustling and then a noise that Tristram found more worrying than the Clope sniff. It could best be described as the Clope gurgle, and it was followed by words in the upraised Clope voice. 'What, what, what?' it said, 'what?'

Had Clope discovered the mortal epistle? There was no knowing. A bunny who was less flinking than Tristram at that moment might have brazened out the situation, emerging from beneath the desk and saying with a debonair smile, 'Ah, just what I was looking for down here, my letter of condolence to George Macdonald.' But, sadly, all the martial boldness of the great Throstlethwaite dynasty had drained out of Tristram. He could not have found the strength and courage to have picked up a battleaxe, let alone used it to bash in Clope's head. He just continued to crouch, cower and flink.

But then the boots and the trouser bottoms swivelled round and moved away from the desk. The upraised Clope voice said in a disturbingly angry way, 'Come, Henryson.' The door opened. 'Adequate dog,' said the voice, this time from a little further away. The door closed. But an alarming sound followed. It was the turning of a key. Clope had gone and very likely gone with the fatal letter in his hand. He had then locked Tristram in his office.

No pulling or pushing would open the door. Nor did the staple or the biro or the broken bit of old comb that Tristram successively poked into the lock have any effect. Banging was impossible, as that would bring the Big Chill into the office, complete with her wintry eyes, her sinister new lisp and her undoubted refusal to listen to any explanation for his presence there. So what was to be done now? Very quickly Tristram, who was at last thinking like a true Throstlethwaite, decided that there was only one possible means of exit and that was the window. The offices of the English Department were on the first floor, and the first floor was not scarily high. Tristram could lower himself down from there, or find his way to an adjoining room, or something, or anything.

He opened the window. Yes, the ledge was large enough to bear his weight and, yes, it was wide enough for it just about to be possible for him to step over to the adjoining ledge and, if necessary, from that to the ledge beyond it. Surely he'd find a window open and, if he didn't, he'd simply have to jump down. The height involved was about ten feet, but if he held tight to the ledge and gently lowered himself it would only be four or so from the soles of his feet to the ground. So he took off his spectacles and put them carefully down, gulped, opened the window and cautiously began to move through and on to the ledge.

Fortunately, the back of the block containing the English Department was pretty close to the back of another university building, creating a thin alleyway, which meant that, with good fortune, nobody would pass by and spot him. But not so fortunately, there was a young man walking below and, even more unfortunately, this was an undergraduate Tristram recognised. What was his name? Something beginning with a 'T'. No, an 'S' . . . Sparrow, perhaps, or Swallow.

Sparrow or Swallow inevitably looked up and saw Tristram as he edged out of the window and on to the ledge. 'Hello, Dr Throstlethwaite,' he said in a surprised way.

'Hello,' said Tristram, deciding it would be inappropriate to compensate for his uncertainty about Sparrow or Swallow's name by calling him 'darling'. 'You're probably wondering why I'm up here.'

'Well, yes,' said Sparrow or Swallow.

It was time for inspiration and Tristram found it. 'I am doing a little experiment,' he said. 'I wanted to know how Wordsworth and Coleridge felt as they clambered around the mountains in the Lake District.'

'Oh,' said Sparrow or Swallow, who was, as Tristram remembered, one of the brighter, more inquisitive English students. 'I thought they had hills and not mountains in the Lake District.'

'The hills can be very steep,' replied Tristram in as superior a tone as a man could reasonably muster under the circumstances; that's to say, while he was teetering on a ledge and trying not to fall off it as he swivelled round to shut the window behind him. 'There are places where you have to be very careful not to tumble into the lakes.'

'I see,' said Sparrow/Swallow in a voice that suggested he didn't see at all. 'Do be careful,' he added as a lurching Tristram's hand went to his jacket pocket. He wanted to check that it still contained the little box that he had found in the Big Chill's office. If he had managed to leave it in Clope's office it might incriminate him as an intruder. Besides, he needed the black tie packed inside the box for Muriel's funeral, didn't he?

Yes, what seemed to be a box was there. It was in a pocket that was already jammed with bits and pieces of this and that. But as he pulled it out to check its identity, the inevitable happened. He swayed and grabbed at the window he had been trying to close and the box fell, breaking open as it landed on the paving stones below. Tristram couldn't see what had fallen out but Sparrow/Swallow could and did.

'Oh dear,' said Sparrow/Swallow, 'I think there may have been a bit of a breakage.'

'Don't be ridiculous,' said Tristram, rediscovering some of the sharpness of tone he liked to display to undergraduates who irritated him. 'It's soft and it hangs around the neck. How can it break?'

By now three or four other young passers-by, noticing something odd was happening at the back of the English Department, had made the detour that took them beneath Clope's window. They clustered round Sparrow/Swallow, inspecting the box with him. And together, they looked up at Tristram as if he wasn't just an eccentric ledge-walker but had gone crazy.

'Er, I thought you would probably want to put it in your mouth, not round your neck,' said Sparrow/Swallow. The other students nodded in half-nervous, half-amused agreement.

'Who would want to put a tie in his mouth?' scoffed Tristram, by now thoroughly annoyed.

'Tie?' asked Sparrow/Swallow.

'What do you think? It's for a funeral, for God sake.'

'Funeral?' repeated Sparrow/Swallow. And others joined him and the other students, who were beginning to giggle in the sort of way that particularly exasperated Tristram.

'Yes, funeral,' he snapped. 'Funeral! It's what considerate men put round their necks at funerals. To show respect for the dead, for Heaven's sake!'

'Oh,' said Sparrow/Swallow in what was now a humouring-the-mad sort of voice. 'I didn't know that.' And he held up a small pink-and-white object that Tristram could without his specs only just identify. It couldn't be. It was. It was a pair of dentures.

'I'm afraid they're a bit broken, and if you want to tie them round your neck, you'll anyway have to attach them to a bit of string,' went on Sparrow/Swallow, who was, as it happened, taking a course in anthropology. Maybe there were tribes that hung teeth round their necks at funerals and maybe Dr Throstlethwaite belonged to one of them. Or maybe its origins were some ritual burial that Coleridge and Wordsworth had attended while clambering round the Lake District. Maybe Throstlethwaite wasn't as deranged as he seemed.

'Ah,' said Tristram, feeling thoroughly abashed and not a little worried as he swayed and teetered on the ledge. 'I think there must have been a mistake.'

And he realised at once what that mistake was. How could he have thought he had left the box containing his new black tie in the Big Chill's office when he had bought it on Saturday, which was a day the Big Chill's office wasn't even open? He had picked up a box that looked rather the same but contained false teeth that were en route to or from the dentist. They were obviously Miss Gill's false teeth. And it was because she had taken them out, or was waiting to put them in, that she had been speaking like, well, like a cod that had somehow acquired a semi-human voice.

'Ah,' repeated Tristram. 'Perhaps you would be good enough to put them back in the box and toss it back up here.'

Sparrow/Swallow did just that. Tristram caught the box, opened it, and saw at once that a false tooth or two had left their moorings in their false gums. He knew he should take them back to the Cod, but somehow he couldn't bring himself to do so. He didn't at all like the idea of enduring her unforgiving gaze, her thin yet blubbery lips and her ferocious lisp. The Throstlethwaite valour was of course legendary, but there were times when the better part of valour was discretion. It was time for the canny manoeuvre that had so often surprised and outwitted enemies during the Wars of the Roses – the Throstlethwaite retreat or, more accurately, the wise Throstlethwaite withdrawal.

So Tristram turned round, reopened the window, and tossed the box containing the broken dentures back through. It would, he mused, be perfectly safe in Clope's office and would soon be discovered there. But as he told himself later, a man as vague as him should never be allowed to muse and move at the same time. Tristram closed the window, turned, teetered, tottered, stumbled and fell. Luckily Sparrow/Swallow broke his fall, but he still twisted his ankle as he landed, not badly, but painfully enough to leave him hopping about and muttering, 'Ow, ow, ow.'

'Are you all right?' asked Sparrow/Swallow, rubbing his shoulder, which had caught the impact of the tumbling Tristram.

'Fine,' gasped Tristram. 'Fine. And I'm very grateful to you, Mr Sparrow, I mean Swallow.'

'It's Mr Thrush, actually,' said Sparrow/Swallow or, rather Sparrow/Swallow/Thrush in his pleasant, humouring voice. 'I hope your trip through the window helped you understand the Lake poets better.'

Tristram didn't know what to say, so he just gave what he hoped was a friendly grin and walked away, or rather hobbled off, doggedly reciting lines from Wordsworth's 'Written in London, September, 1802': 'O Friend! I know not which way I must look for comfort, being, as I am, opprest.' The only problem was that, though his mind and foot were feeling pretty oppressed, there seemed to be no comforting friend or Friend anywhere about.

The next morning Tristram overslept. He had set his alarm clock – a replacement for the one that had burst open so spectacularly during his lecture on Shelley and Keats – very carefully indeed, knowing that there was a big, sad event to attend. Unfortunately, he had set it for nine o'clock in the evening when he should have set it for nine o'clock in the morning. So he had to hurry to be in time for Muriel's funeral, which was occurring at noon in a church about half a mile away. What was he to wear? Yes, a dark suit. And there it was on the floor of his bedroom, with both the trousers and the jacket disastrously, hopelessly creased.

They would clearly need to be pressed. Tristram limped downstairs – the ankle twisted by his fall from Clope's office was still bothering him – and began to iron the jacket while simultaneously swallowing some coffee and brushing his teeth. Unluckily, his chest chose that very moment to let him down. He coughed, swivelled as he coughed and (sorry for the repulsive details) spluttered out his toothpaste, some coffee and a large amount of toothpaste-packed and caffeine-filled saliva on to the suit's trousers. Immediately he rushed over to the cold tap, half-filled a sponge with water and used it to rub away at a stain which, toothpaste being toothpaste, didn't appear to want to come out. In fact, it seemed to go further in. And at that very moment another thought struck him. The tie! The black tie! Somehow he had managed to confuse it with Miss Gill's dentures and, after his adventures under Clope's desk and on and below Clope's window ledge, he had felt a lot less like going shopping for a replacement than like slowly, very slowly, hobbling home.

So he limped upstairs to inspect his cupboard, only to find that the ties he possessed but seldom wore were not exactly suitable. Perhaps it was old-fashioned of him to think he had to wear a black one. A darkish tie would surely do. But what about a green, red or purple one, especially as most of them were plastered with dots of an equally jolly hue? No, that wouldn't be right at all. And then the smell hit him, and, yes, it was the smell of burning.

Down Tristram tottered, back into the kitchen, to discover a fresh disaster. He had not only left on the iron. He had left it lying on the lapel of his jacket, and the lapel was more or less on fire. He whisked the iron off the lapel, grabbed the watery sponge and squeezed it over what was, oh dear, oh no, oh Spooner, a large smouldering hole. What was he to do?

Not panic, he told himself. Throstlethwaites seldom if

ever panicked. There was a family story of how at the very height of the Wars of the Roses a Throstlethwaite actually called Sir Tristram had smiled and serenely uttered the family motto, '*nihil timeo praeter timorem ipsum*' or 'I have nothing to fear but fear itself', just before a raging Lancastrian bashed his head in and his brains out. The answer was obvious: Tristram would continue to press his suit, wear it, but conceal both the damaged lapel and the toothpaste-stained trousers by wearing his sturdy old brown overcoat above them. True, that might look odd, since it was July and promised to be a hot day; but what was the alternative, the time to Muriel's funeral now being so very short?

But what about the tie? That was a necessary accoutrement. Then Tristram had a moment of inspiration. He had a black tie already. Agreed, it was a bow-tie that went with his trusty dinner jacket. But so what? It would still signal the sadness and the respect for Muriel and George that he felt. And then came another flash of inspiration. Why not wear both his dinner jacket and the trousers that went with them? Both were black as black, and his overcoat would conceal them. Moreover, any part of them that wasn't concealed would at least not be stained with toothpaste. All would be well.

Except all wasn't quite well, as Tristram discovered when he went again to his clothes cupboard, and found the dinner jacket hanging in the right place but, as had been the case with his dark suit, the trousers lying hopelessly crumpled on the floor. He swivelled round in exasperation, and the result was yet another moment of inspiration. His eyes lit upon his shiny, non-crease pyjamas. And those pyjamas weren't just shiny and non-crease – they were smart, sophisticated and black as black as black. So, with time running out, he decided there and then on his funeral costume: white shirt, black bow-tie, dinner jacket, pyjama bottoms and, covering them all, his trusty brown overcoat. Who could now dare say, as his aunt still sometimes presumed to say, that he wasn't clothes conscious?

But it was still July, still a hot day, and Tristram was red-faced and sweating when, almost but not quite late, he half-limped, half-sprinted into the church, hurried halfway up the aisle, tripped and fell. 'Sorry, sorry,' he muttered as he got up and hastily grabbed the nearest empty place, which, he was horrified to discover, was right next to Professor and Mrs Hamish Clope.

Tristram had never met Clope's wife before. He didn't even know her first name, assuming she had one. The rumour in the department was that the professor kept her closely shut up, conceivably in a kennel beside his dog Henryson. Whatever her precise abode, she was a small, thin woman, even smaller and thinner than Clope himself. Her expression was melancholy, which was unsurprising since she was at a funeral, but also meek and strangely wistful. And her body was bowed, indeed oddly and disturbingly bowed. It couldn't be true, Tristram told himself as, panting and flashing Mrs Clope a dazed smile, he settled down beside her. But, yes, it was true. Mrs Clope was a hunchback.

Hot, perspiring, uncomfortable and embarrassed as he already was, Tristram felt a new anxiety. Wasn't there a reference in that fatal letter to 'the dear old dromedary'? Nobody knew why George called Muriel that rather than rhino or hippo, which had apparently been his first pet name for her. Nobody liked to ask, assuming it referred to a private joke or maybe a game they had played in their early days. But Muriel had always seemed to like the nickname. However, Clope had no sense of fun or even of humour, and would surely think it criminally tactless of him, Tristram, to refer to a woman, especially a dead woman, in such a way. Hadn't he circulated memos ordering his underlings not to use words females might find offensive, such as 'lady' or 'miss'? On the face of it, 'dear old dromedary' was rather more disturbing than that. Indeed, any reference to a primitive desert animal with a hump would be especially offensive to a man whose poor unfortunate wife had a serious problem with her back.

As these thoughts flitted through his head, Tristram glanced beyond Mrs Clope, who was shrinking away from him. He looked at Clope himself and found that the professor was staring at him with an intensity – how could he describe it? He was used to the man's looks, which had become more wary and suspicious but also more hostile since that embarrassing incident involving the balaclava, the bank and the police. He had become accustomed to the Clope squint, the Clope sniff, the suppressed Clope snarl and undisguised Clope glare. He was even used to the Clope mutter of 'Come back, Culloden'. But this was something else. This was loathing. This was murderous hatred. If Clope could have opened the coffin that was only a few yards away, he would undoubtedly have done so, bodily extracting poor dead Muriel and jamming poor live Tristram inside in her place.

Was it the intensity of the death-ray coming from Clope or the July heat that was the problem? Both probably, but either way Tristram began to feel very peculiar, in fact so peculiar that he barely registered the funeral service as it proceeded. Certainly, he felt that if he didn't shed his overcoat he might faint, victim of the double grilling that, like a steak in an over-efficient oven, he seemed to be receiving.

Somewhere in the distance, one of Muriel's oldest friends was paying tribute to her famous sense of fun. Somewhere in the distance a psalm was sung, a prayer was said. Tristram stumbled up to his feet and down again as the ritual demanded. But increasingly he felt even worse than grilled meat. He felt the way a lobster might feel if it was being cooked, not in boiling water, but in the fires of Hell themselves. And finally he had to admit defeat. He took off his big, brown overcoat, inevitably revealing the mix of clothes beneath. Mrs Clope winced still further away. Clope seemed barely to acknowledge the service, so fixated was he on his subordinate and, most of all, on the pyjama bottoms that the wretched young man had assumed would pass for trousers.

For it had to be admitted that Tristram wasn't exactly his own best friend. With his black bow-tie and pyjama bottoms, he looked like a waiter caught halfway through the process of going to bed. As Tristram would have admitted if he had been *compos mentis*, it wasn't the most conventional dress for a funeral. An unfriendly boss, which Clope undoubtedly was, might even have said that he was letting down the university department he was helping to represent.

Eventually Tristram stumbled from the church, giving what he hoped was a big, friendly grin at Mrs Clope as he left the pew and, feeling he had to say something to a woman who still looked shocked and alarmed, muttered, 'Nice to see you, Mrs, um, Mrs, um . . . darling.'

Tristram stood outside for a moment, blinking and

sweating and not fully taking in what was happening around him. A colleague or two came up to him and shook their heads in disbelief. George Macdonald clapped him on the back and, ignoring his unusual dress, thanked him warmly for coming. His friend Hector O'Brien asked him if he was quite well. And, yes, Clope appeared from nowhere and spoke.

'Why were you smiling at Mrs Clope?' asked the fierce little professor, looking more than ever like a miniaturised caber. It was as if he wanted to fling himself at Tristram's head. 'Why did you call her "darling"? And worse, much worse . . . much, much worse.'

'Your wife?' gasped Tristram, not quite knowing what he was saying. 'God bless her. Please give her my warmest good wishes. And tell her Richard Attenborough says "darling" too. And my best wishes to your other pet. Darling Dunbar, I mean Henryson.'

'Come and see me tomorrow,' said Clope in a voice that wasn't merely dark but would have made midnight at the winter equinox in Lapland seem like Barbados in high summer.

All Tristram could do was nod feebly. But then an old gentleman, presumably someone who had passed through Muriel's life years ago but still remembered her well enough to want to pay homage to her corpse, came up and bristled at him.

'Your medals are showing,' hissed the old gent.

'What? I don't have any medals,' replied Tristram, thinking that the world was going as mad as he felt.

'Yes you do, and they're showing,' said the bristling old gent.

That little show of hostility made Tristram feel better. He

and his moustache bristled back in what he hoped was the traditional Throstlethwaite style. This was the way his ancestors had reacted to Lancastrians when they had met them in battle. With or without moustaches, they had sometimes bristled so effectively they had managed to get their foes to surrender, so preventing the Throstlethwaites having to go through the nuisance of killing them or, of course, getting killed themselves.

'I haven't even fought in a war,' he said. 'So how can I have any medals?'

'I'm not arguing with you, I just want you to stop showing your medals,' replied the old gent, pointedly staring just south of Tristram's midriff, turning on his heels and going.

Tristram looked down at his lower self and remembered something his father had told him. 'Showing your medals' was a euphemism that had disappeared with the coming of the trouser zip. It meant showing the buttons that ought to be so safely done up that nothing embarrassing behind them was sufficiently visible to dismay other people, especially suggestible women. But, oh dear, there were buttons on his pyjama bottoms, and, oh dear, oh Spooner, those buttons were indeed undone. Had Clope thought he was flashing at his wife as well as grinning at her? And in church too? Surely not.

Feeling as worried by that thought as he was annoyed by the bristling old gent, Tristram did up his buttons, draped his overcoat over his shoulders and left the graveyard for home. He had been invited back to George's house for a bit of a wake, but he knew his old friend would understand if he didn't make it. He wasn't dressed in absolutely the right way and his feet were giving him too much pain; or so he decided. The prospect of tomorrow was enough. Tomorrow would clearly be difficult, but, as he half-remembered someone saying somewhere, tomorrow was another day.

## THE VAGUE BOOK 7

*The Scottish moral philosopher Adam Smith changed our view of economics, but would he have done so if he hadn't regularly disappeared into a kind of waking coma? His great contemporary, Thomas Carlyle, called him 'the most absent man in company that I ever saw, moving his lips and talking to himself and smiling in the midst of large companies', yet when he was awoken he would talk ably and unstoppably on the subjects that interested him. He used to go out of his Kirkcaldy house into the street in his dressing gown and start to walk, once continuing for 15 miles before the church bells of Dumferline abruptly woke him from his abstraction.*

*There's a story of him showing men round a Glasgow tannery and, while discoursing on the division of labour, walking into a tanning pit and having to be dragged out of what was 'a noisome pool containing fat from hides, lime and the gas generated by the mixture'. There's another of him taking a piece of bread and butter, rolling it around, then putting it into a teapot, pouring water on it and, when he'd tasted the result, declaring in injured tones that it was the worst cup of tea he'd ever drunk. Other stories involve his habit of absentmindedly imitating others, which was embarrassing when he became a Customs House commissioner and, instead of signing his own name on official documents, regularly signed the name of whomever had signed above him.*

*Smith's mind was so often on higher things that he*

*neglected lower ones, which was even more the case of Isaac Newton, whose brain encompassed the air, the sky, the universe beyond. Is it true that he was found in the kitchen in front of a saucepan of boiling water, an egg in his hand, observing his watch as it bubbled away? Perhaps. But there are many well authenticated examples of his absentmindedness. When he was a young man and had to manage the family farm after the death of his stepfather, he would sometimes be found sitting under a hedge, absorbed in his calculations while the sheep strayed and the cattle broke fences and trampled on the corn. Later, he led what he assumed was his horse to a hill two-and-a-half miles from his Lincolnshire house, only to realise when he reached his destination that the animal had slipped away and he was simply dragging a bridle.*

*Often Newton forgot to eat, drink or even sleep. He would go out to dine in the hall of Trinity College, Cambridge, take the wrong turning and, realising he'd done so, return straight back to his chamber. He would go into his study to fetch a bottle of wine for guests and simply not reappear. On one occasion he came downstairs to find that a friend had waited so long to see him that he'd eaten the boiled chicken that had been left for the great physicist's supper. 'See what we studious people are,' said Newton, lifting the cover and seeing a plateful of bones. 'I forgot that I had dined.'*

*With Einstein, he's probably the most famous example of that justly celebrated but unjustly derided figure, the absentminded professor; but people like him traverse the centuries and even the millennia. Didn't the world's first great philosopher, Thales, have his head so far in the*

*clouds of 550 BC or thereabouts that he fell into a well?*
*Three centuries later, didn't Archimedes forget to put his*
*clothes on and ran into the street shouting 'Eureka' after*
*a dip in the bath had shown him the significance of the*
*water his body had displaced and so the amount of base*
*metal that had been introduced into a king of Syracuse's*
*golden crown? And didn't he effectively die of abstraction,*
*being too absorbed in a mathematical problem to pay*
*attention to one of the Roman soldiers who had conquered*
*his city – and getting stabbed to death for the supposed*
*insult?*

*Cut to the 19th century AD, and we've Louis Pasteur,*
*who was so obsessive about cleanliness he tried never to*
*shake hands. At the dinner table he would wipe his glass*
*and plate and minutely inspect his food, on one occasion*
*extracting the nasty bits from a loaf of bread, putting*
*them in a glass of water, then vaguely picking it up and*
*drinking it. We've André-Marie Ampère, Pasteur's*
*compatriot, the prime discoverer of electromagnetism and*
*the physicist commemorated in those units of electric*
*current or 'amps' so dangerous to absentminded people*
*changing plugs. Not only did he cause a scandal by*
*forgetting a dinner appointment with the Emperor*
*Napoleon; on another occasion, he was seen feverishly*
*scribbling calculations on the side of a horse-drawn*
*delivery van that proceeded to move on, forcing him to*
*run beside it as he continued to write and use his cloak as*
*an eraser. And over in America, we've a pioneering*
*botanist called Thomas Nuttall who had a knack of*
*wandering off and getting lost in perilous places. On one*
*occasion he fled from a search party for three days,*
*assuming his pursuers were Indians, and on another he*

*lay down in exhaustion and despair at ever being
discovered, only to be rescued, carried and paddled home
by, yes, a Native American or Indian.*

*A bit later the German mathematician David Hilbert
is said to have put on a guest's hat and led his wife out of
his own house saying they had troubled their visitor long
enough, and another time to have turned to a colleague at
a conference and asked, 'What are Hilbert spaces?'
forgetting that they were geometrical constructs he
himself had famously discovered. A similar story is told of
James Sylvester, an Englishman who became a professor
at Johns Hopkins University in Baltimore and founded
the* American Journal of Mathematics. *He forgot one of
his own proofs, declaring it couldn't be true. He also once
handed a student an ink bottle, asking him to drop it in a
letter box, as he needed a quick answer.*

*But Hilbert and Sylvester were mere amateurs in the
vague stakes beside Norbert Wiener, a brilliant American
mathematician who spent most of his career at the
Massachusetts Institute of Technology, dying in 1964.
Once he accosted a student in the street, had a long
question-and-answer session with him, and ended asking
in a confused voice, 'Do you recall, when we met, in
which direction I was headed?' Another time he was
observed studying a paper with immense concentration,
then getting up and anxiously pacing about before
returning to do battle with what everyone assumed was a
profound mathematical problem. Once again he got up,
only to collide with a student who said, 'Good afternoon,
Professor Wiener.'*

*'Wiener, that's the word,' cried Wiener, clapping
himself in the forehead – and ran triumphantly back to*

his table to fill his name in what was actually a crossword puzzle.

In the classroom he was reputedly a lively, entertaining lecturer, but sometimes a bit inscrutable. When his students asked him how to do a certain problem, he paused, thought, then wrote the answer on the blackboard. The class was nonplussed but tactful. 'Is there any other way to do the problem?' he was asked. Wiener paused again, thought again, brightened and said, 'Yes, there is another way.' Then he simply wrote the same answer on the blackboard.

Off campus he wasn't less abstracted, especially when his car was involved. He drove to New Haven for a meeting at Yale University, forgot how he'd got there, and took a bus back to Cambridge. Next morning he went to his garage, found his car was missing, and called the police to report it stolen. And one day he parked his car in a large lot full of other vehicles, and went into the adjoining building to attend a conference, but when he came out couldn't remember where he'd left the car or even what it looked like. So he waited and waited until all the other cars had gone but one, which he rightly deduced was his own.

But the best-known Wiener anecdote comes from the time he and his family moved to a new house in the same Cambridge neighbourhood where they had long lived. Inevitably, he forgot his new address and lost the written instructions his long-suffering wife had given him, so he set off in the direction of his old place, encountering a young child standing outside. 'Little girl,' he said, 'can you tell me where the Wieners have moved to?'

'Yes, Daddy,' replied his daughter. 'Mommy said you'd probably be here, so she sent me over to show you the way home.'

# EIGHT

But tomorrow did come. Tomorrow suddenly became today, bringing Tristram the sort of headache that comes with a bad hangover. And that was inexplicable, since the previous day he had drunk nothing alcoholic, yet perhaps also explicable, since he had absorbed nothing but trouble, disaster and ominous events. At some stage today he had to brave the outrage of his boss, who would very likely bring up the subject of that misdirected letter. He would accuse him, Tristram, both of calling him, Clope, 'funny' and 'little' and of madly smiling and possibly even flashing at his, Clope's, wife. Anyway, he blundered downstairs in his smart, black pyjamas, his feet still bare and his ankle still hurting, and started to bring the day and himself to life.

Except that today was obviously one of those days. How could he be anything but distracted, given what lay ahead? He switched on the electric kettle, not quite sure if he would make himself a cup of coffee or tea. He then filled a saucepan with a pan of water, meaning to boil an egg, and lit the gas underneath it. Then it became clearer and clearer he would need a pill for his worsening headache and painful ankle. But where were the pills? Oh, upstairs. So he half-dashed, half-hobbled up the stairs and into his bedroom. What was it he wanted? Oh, a shirt. He must find and iron a clean, white one to wear for his meeting with Clope. It wouldn't help his cause to look a mess when he confronted the evil needle or killer-pencil or crazed caber or whatever the pointy professor resembled. Yes, and where had he left his spectacles? He looked on, beside and under his bed but, no, no specs were there.

The kettle began to whistle at the same time as the phone rang. Who could be calling him? Grabbing a shirt, Tristram hurried downstairs into his living room and picked up the receiver. It was his Aunt Persephone, wanting to chat and, it seemed, invite him to lunch the following Sunday. 'Hold on,' panted Tristram. 'I can't hear you properly. I'll have to turn off the kettle.'

So he put down the phone, limped as fast as he could from the living room back into the kitchen, and turned off the kettle. Now, why had he put it on? Because he wanted tea or coffee. But which? Tristram paused and considered, then realised he was still holding his crumpled though clean shirt. He would need the iron and the ironing board, but he would have to be very, very careful. He didn't want to ruin another piece of clothing, did he? He stood quietly for a moment, mourning the burned lapel of his jacket, put his shirt on to a kitchen counter and started to pull the ironing board from its cupboard. But then he heard an odd whistling sound. He lurched back to the kettle but, no, he had switched it off, so the sound couldn't be coming from there. It seemed to be coming from the living room.

His aunt! He had forgotten that he had left her waiting on the phone and, not for the first time, she was trying to attract his attention by whistling in as loud and high-pitched a way as she could manage. He picked up the phone and started to apologise, only to be interrupted by a familiar but somewhat exasperated voice.

'Shut up,' said Aunt Persephone. 'Just tell me if you can come to lunch on Sunday or not.'

'I'll have to check my diary,' said Tristram, put down the phone and rushed as fast as he could to his study. But where was his diary? He must have put it somewhere. But where? Oh, and while he was about it, where had he left those spectacles? He couldn't go half-blind into Clope's lair, could he? He looked on, beside and under his desk, but no, they weren't there. Then his eye caught a paper on Keats which had been given him by one of his best students and which he had, in fact, managed to read. He tucked it just under his armpit, telling himself that he mustn't forget to take it into the English Department when he went there to meet his doom.

Doom! Clope! The very thought transfixed him. How could he explain himself to the spindly ogre? Then he smelled a troubling smell. Something was burning in the kitchen. It couldn't be the iron because he hadn't yet put it on. What was it? The saucepan for his breakfast egg! He tottered back to the kitchen and, yes, the saucepan had not only boiled dry but had an ugly brown mark on the bottom. He would have to put on another pan, because he knew he couldn't face Clope without eating something beforehand. And then he heard that high-pitched whistling again.

Oh, his aunt! Why did she have to bother him when he needed to get himself ready? He half-ran, half-hopped back to the living room and picked up the phone. A curt voice said, 'So where the hell is your bloody diary?' Tristram was shocked, but not too shocked to reply.

'I have it here,' he said primly. And he took what he supposed to be his diary from under his armpit and prepared to read it. Supposed! It was actually a paper on Keats. What was that doing there? Keats had died in 1821, and the essay had been delivered to him two weeks ago, so it certainly wouldn't help him discover what he was doing this coming Sunday.

'Sorry, Aunt Persephone,' he said. 'What I thought was my diary was actually a rather good essay on Keats. Be back in a moment.' And he put down the phone before his aunt could reply and, cursing his sore ankle, hurried back towards his study, stopping off in the kitchen to turn on the cold tap as high as he could, put the burned saucepan under it and grab an egg out of the refrigerator. Yes, and where had he left those damned elusive specs? Holding the egg, he speedily looked on, beside and under the stove, the shelves, the counters and the draining board but, no, they weren't there. In any case, what he mostly noticed was his intensifying headache.

He half-dashed, half-stumbled upstairs and began to rummage through the bedside drawer in which he was supposed to keep his pills. Supposed! No pills were there. Where were they? He needed them too badly to stop looking now. They must be in one of his kitchen drawers. And so, putting the egg down on his bed, he teetered back downstairs and into the kitchen, almost tripping over the ironing board that was still sticking halfway out of its cupboard. And that reminded him: he had to iron his shirt and, yes, his shirt was waiting for him on a kitchen counter.

Tristram pulled out the ironing board, set it up, turned on the iron and told himself that under no circumstances must he leave the room without making sure he had turned it off. Then he picked up his shirt and was about to put hot steel to rumpled cotton when he heard a gushing sound. What was that? His aunt! Oh God, she must be trying to attract him back to the phone with a desperate new noise. Instead of whistling she was whooshing. So he did a sort of one-man polka back to the living room and picked up the phone, only to find she had rung off. That, he thought, was rude, annoying and worrying, since he still hadn't found time fully to search for his specs. He looked on, beside and beneath the sofa, the chairs and the little table but, no, they weren't there. Then he sat down for a bit, muttering, 'Ow, ow,' as he rubbed his ankle, which had been left aching by all that searching and rushing. But, no, the gushing sound hadn't stopped.

He hurried back to the kitchen and, as he entered, found himself slithering across a floor that was now thinly covered with water. What had happened? Oh, the cold tap had filled the saucepan and spurted out of the sink on to the tiled floor, making it not only slithery but, he thought, dangerous for another reason. Fool that he was, he had done what he swore he wouldn't. He had forgotten to turn off an iron that was now sitting and steaming on its board, all ready to tackle the shirt nestling beside it.

But that was precisely the danger. Suppose the iron gave him a shock while he was turning it off and simultaneously standing bare-footed in water. Tristram had read of the death of the priest and philosopher, Thomas Merton, who had been electrocuted when a heater fell into the bath he was taking. Such a shock would save him from his encounter with Clope, which would be a good thing, but might leave him dead, which would be a not-so-good thing. So Tristram slowly and carefully heaved himself up on to the kitchen counter, crawled slowly and carefully along it, and carefully but quickly turned off the iron at the switch.

But the counter began to creak, and so, fearful he might be about to break it, Tristram leapt off on to the floor, fortunately landing on his good foot. However, he slithered, slipped and banged into the ironing board, causing the iron itself to fall immediately beside his head and, as he lay there wondering what to do next and where the hell his specs were, to scorch his hair rather badly. And at that very moment there was a bang on the door.

The postman! Leaping up, angrily kicking the iron across the kitchen floor with his bare, good foot, shouting, 'Ow, ow,' as he tried to ignore his frazzled head, his burnt toe and his aching ankle, Tristram slid, slithered, tottered and tumbled to the door. But it wasn't the postman. It was, he realised, a pair of Jehovah's Witnesses. He stared at them. They stared at him and, especially, at his hair, which was giving off a little smoke. One of them gave a squawk, perhaps thinking that those bare feet, those jet-black pyjamas, that bristling moustache and those smouldering locks betokened a creature lately arrived from the fiery depths of Hell.

At any rate, they didn't launch into their usual patter, but turned and hurried away, leaving Tristram puzzled but grateful. Now he could find the pills to cure a headache that, unsurprisingly, was worse than ever. Now he could iron his shirt and dress. Now he could cook himself that egg and make that coffee or tea. Now he could find his spectacles, wherever they were. Now he could gather together his papers and his head and go off to encounter Clope. Now he might even find time to telephone his aunt. He had everything in hand.

Or did he? He started to mop up the floor, squeezing the water into the sink, when he remembered he hadn't yet had the warming drink he had promised himself. So he picked up the kettle and poured hot water into a cup, in his confusion forgetting to put either a teabag or instant coffee into it. Oh no! That was no good. He emptied the cup, which he noticed was looking a bit dirty, and remembered the danger of ironing while he was standing on tiles that were still pretty wet. He needed to put some rubber between his feet and the floor. Wellington boots, they would make things safe! And so, his mind on the possibility of electrocution, he dropped some washing-up powder into the cup, filled it with water from the kettle, dashed to the front hall, and crammed the boots on to his bare feet.

But his headache was more painful than ever. How could he have forgotten the pills that were, he now believed, in a kitchen drawer? However, the morning newspaper had just been delivered and had fallen on to the doormat. He picked it up, only for his attention to be grabbed by the headline, which warned of yet more trouble to come at Britain's big banks. Had he opened the deposit account his manager had thought sensible? If so, what was its number? He must check both that and the rate of interest he was being offered. But first he must dress and face the dreaded Clope.

So he trundled upstairs in his Wellington boots and, thinking it would be a wise precaution to leave them on, somehow managed to pull his pyjama bottoms off over them and replace them with his underpants and everyday trousers. But where was the clean shirt he wanted to wear? Oh yes, waiting to be ironed downstairs. So he stumbled and bumbled back downstairs, picked the iron up from the floor and began to run it across a shirt which, however, refused to become smooth. Why? But as he was reminding himself that the iron was now switched off, and so had probably gone cold, he remembered the pills and stumbled and slipped to the kitchen drawer. And, yes, they were there!

Thank God. His headache was now head-splitting and his ankle, the one he had twisted the day before with that bold Throstlethwaite leap from Clope's ledge, was continuing to play him up. He crammed a couple of heavy-duty aspirins into his mouth, grabbed the cup and swallowed them. But, oh dear, that wasn't the best cup of tea or coffee he had ever made, was it? It was sort of transparent, kind of bubbly, tepid going on cold and, well, soapy. Some sort of cleaning material had clearly managed to find its way into the cup. That was ridiculous. It was also queasy-making. Had he swallowed something noxious, even poisonous? But if he fell ill or even dead, that would save him from his crunch meeting with ghastly Clope; or so Tristram again told himself.

Never mind. It was time to brush his teeth and shave. So he scampered up to the bathroom and, in his haste, smeared toothpaste all over his chin and lower cheeks with one hand while spurting shaving foam on to his toothbrush. Then he stopped. Something was wrong. What was it? He must obviously pause and think. Shouldn't he have a pee? And where had he put those bloody specs? And why hadn't he managed to iron his shirt? And mustn't he choose a tie? He wandered into his bedroom for a moment of patient reflection and, all too inevitably, sat down on the egg he had left on his bed. He had squashed his breakfast.

It couldn't go on, but it did, this way and that or that way and this, until Tristram realised that enough was enough, He decided to break the chain by leaving the house. He had eaten nothing; he had drunk nothing except a small amount of washing-up liquid. He hadn't phoned his aunt back. He had a sticky, yellow patch on the seat of his trousers. His teeth tasted of shaving foam and, though he had scraped most of the toothpaste off his face and run a razor over his chin, tiny white sticky patches were visible on his cheeks. But he had put on his shirt and a red-spotted tie which, with his jacket, did much to hide any crumples. But, sadly, he had not found those damned, elusive spectacles, even though he had emptied all his pockets in a desperate attempt to see if they were lurking there. Oh, well, never mind. He could still see, if not as well as he would like. Yes, he could still see, even if it meant he would sometimes have to peer. So off he set, to the university.

'I must remember to do one thing at a time and finish it,' Tristram said to himself as he slammed the door and repeated the mantra as, still limping slightly, he walked down the street, trying and failing to think of a quote from Keats or Coleridge about the perils of multi-tasking. But what was that squelching? It was coming from him. He looked down and saw that he was still wearing his Wellington boots. They would look odd, he thought, especially since it was a warm and cloudless July day. So he would have to return home and replace them with socks and shoes. But then he remembered: he had emptied his trouser pockets and failed to put back their contents, which meant he had no change and, of course, no key to his front door.

Oh well, said Tristram to himself. He would have to pick

up a spare key from his aunt, who kept a largish stock in readiness for occasions such as this. Oh well, oh well. There was now no choice. He would have to go on. It was time to confront destiny.

Clope stared at Tristram for a full minute, his mouth tight shut, making him look rather like a very thin counterpart of a postbox whose opening slit had been barred with a strip of steel. Then he spoke in a frighteningly quiet but rather hoarse voice.

'I'll come straight to the point,' he said. 'Are you having an affair with my wife?'

Tristram was almost more amazed than aghast. He had been dreading this interview. He had meant to come to it better dressed and certainly not wearing Wellington boots. He had tried to hide these by pulling his trousers as low as they would go, so that only the shiny rubber at the bottom would show. Unluckily, this served to expose more of his ineptly ironed shirt. So it was a case of either being messy in the stomach area or rubbery in the foot department. His solution was to make a compromise between the two sartorial choices, which meant that he half-limped, half-squelched into the English Department looking a bit crumpled above and, in what was undeniably an odd choice for a hot July day, as if he was wearing galoshes below. He had feared the professor would take that as an insult – but, if so, it was as nothing beside the injury he was now claiming to have suffered.

'I'll repeat my question,' went on Clope, sounding even more as if he had been gargling with gravel. 'Are you having an affair with Mrs Clope and do you plan to abscond with her?'

'What a terrible idea,' gasped Tristram.

The Clope squint and the Clope sniff were now reinforcing the Clope growl. Moreover, his face was getting redder and redder. 'A terrible idea, is it?' said Clope. 'I suppose it might seem so given the fact that you are pleased to make offensive remarks about her bodily affliction. But I repeat my question yet again. Are you having an affair with my wife, Mrs Clope?'

'No, of course not. Certainly not.'

'Then would you kindly explain why you have sent me a letter gloating and boasting of your intimacy with the woman you call your 'dear old dromedary' in what I assume to be a crude and callous reference to Mrs Clope's congenital deformity? And then asking me, her husband, how I will manage without her? And as if that were not insult enough, you taunt me by writing 'thinking of you' and adding what I assume to be three kisses after your signature?'

'It was all a mistake,' stuttered Tristram, in his desperation remembering the Throstlethwaite who had acted so bravely when the House of York was defeated at Bosworth Field by the part-Lancastrian and renegade Yorkist Henry VII back in 1485. Couldn't he reproduce the same valour now?

But Clope had already produced the telltale letter, the one intended for George Macdonald and, lifting it into the air, he was fixing or (rather) riveting Tristram with the steely Clope gaze.

'A mistake indeed,' growled Clope. 'And I would like some answers. Have you organised a picnic at which Mrs Clope ran around singing in the inappropriate hat you call a . . . ' – and here a sneer found its way into the accusation – ' . . . a boater?'

'No, no,' gasped Tristram.

'And have you and she thrown, what, prawn-and-avocado sandwiches at each other?' If such a thing were possible, the professor sounded even more outraged, though Tristram couldn't tell if this was because prawns were more effete than avocados or because avocados were more contemptible than prawns. If Clope had been gargling, it would surely have been not just with gravel but with rocks or maybe lumps of concrete.

'Prawn-and-avocado sandwiches?' stammered Tristram, in his escalating panic forgetting he had ever shared such food with poor, dead Muriel Macdonald. 'I don't think I eat them very often. Really I prefer . . . ' – and he desperately reached for a substance that just might appease the crazed man opposite – ' . . . yes, I prefer good old Scottish beef.'

Clope glared at him, this time as if he was one of those English raiders and rustlers who had ridden across the border in medieval times and stolen innocent cattle from hard-working Scottish farmers.

'So you and Mrs Clope have been throwing beef sandwiches at each other,' said Clope.

'Never, never,' panted Tristram, trying to collect himself as he added, 'I have far too much respect for Mrs Clope to throw beef sandwiches at her.'

'I see,' said Clope. 'So what sort of sandwiches did you throw at her?'

'No sandwiches,' said Tristram.

'I see,' said Clope. 'So what did you throw at her? Cake? Biscuits? I am her husband and it is my right to know.'

'Let me explain,' wailed Tristram, 'please let me explain.'

'There is no explanation,' answered Clope. 'I am often away on academic business at major conferences and vitally important meetings. So Mrs Clope is often left alone. She is a well-conducted woman with whom I have had few problems in the past. But it is clear to me that her naturally acquiescent nature has been exploited by a ruthless predator. By you, Throstlethwaite, by you.'

Tristram had, of course, been called many things in his time, such as a four-eyed prat and brain-dead git. But 'ruthless predator' was new and, as Tristram thought for a mad moment, not wholly unwelcome. As happens to many people during crises, and certainly as has often happened to him, his mind briefly drifted to another subject. Once again it picked on Bosworth Field. What was it his ancestor had done when the much-misunderstood Richard III cried out 'a horse, a horse, my kingdom for a horse' in the heat of battle? He had hurried loyally away to track down a spare horse, that's what, only to find nothing more suitable than a donkey.

'And now,' went on Clope, 'and now we come to the very heart of the matter. You and Mrs Clope have apparently been using the term 'funny little Clope' during your assignations. To whom are you referring?'

Tristram didn't have an answer. Though he had obviously never discussed Clope with Mrs Clope, there was only one funny little Clope. That was Hamish Clope. In his confusion, his mind again flashed back to the battle of Bosworth Field. According to family legend, the Yorkist Throstlethwaite had loyally brought the stricken Richard III that donkey, only to run into a ferocious Lancastrian, who had cut off his head and, later, placed it on a spike above the walls of the city of York itself. And now Tristram knew how that head felt as it stared helplessly down at the scarlet face and bulging eyes of the enemy.

'Um,' said Tristram. 'Um.'

'I should say at this point that Mrs Clope denies every one of your accusations,' said Clope. 'And she is usually a truthful woman who naturally respects me. I can say with confidence that she has never called me "funny".'

'No, of course not,' interrupted Tristram. 'You aren't funny at all. Or, of course, only when you want to be.'

'But even the best women can have their heads turned by unscrupulous men,' continued Clope, ignoring that still feebler attempt to curry favour. 'And you, Throstlethwaite, are an unscrupulous scoundrel. And that brings us even deeper into the heart of the matter.'

'But I didn't do anything with Mrs Clope,' burst out Tristram. 'I don't even know her.'

'You don't know the woman beside whom you had elected to sit at Mrs Macdonald's funeral? You don't know the woman you proceeded to call "darling"?'

'No, no, it was Richard Attenborough who called her "darling",' blurted Tristram.

Clope's face turned a still deeper red and his eyes bulged still further outwards as he reacted to what sounded like yet another example of English perfidy.

'So Richard Attenborough is having an affair with my wife too,' he hissed.

'No, no,' wailed Tristram. 'I don't think he knows Mrs Clope either.'

'And you,' went on Clope, 'you are telling me you don't know Mrs Clope when I, her husband, saw you slither and nestle beside her in your pyjamas?'

'No, no,' wailed Tristram. 'It's all a mistake. My letter wasn't about Mrs Clope. It was about Muriel, I mean Mrs Macdonald.'

'You mean the woman in the coffin?' said Clope, his face

reddening a shade or two even more. 'Are you telling me you put on pyjamas and, let me add, failed to do up its buttons for the sake of the dead wife of a former head of the English Department?'

There was a long silence, after which Clope asked, or rather snarled, a new question. 'And I observe that you have come into the English Department and my office in Wellington boots. Is this yet another insult to me or, how can I put this, another expression of your perverted mind?'

This interview wasn't going as well as Tristram had hoped. He had to admit that. Moreover, the professor's accusations were not merely mad but inexplicable. He blinked and peered, wishing he was wearing the spectacles that would at least let him read Clope's expression more accurately. But all he could do was stare myopically at the professor, who stared back at the young man who had tried to subject his dog to water torture, poison him with moth-balls, use every ruse to oust him from his post as department head, carry on a blazing love-affair with his wife which had culminated in the pair of them throwing prawn-and-avocado sandwiches at each other while chorusing 'funny little Clope', plot to remove a corpse from its coffin, publicly seduce it in an orgiastic black mass involving rubber boots, and then taunt him with a letter that ended with three large kisses. Nothing in Scotland had prepared him for this. Such things simply did not happen in Dundee. Action, firm action had to be taken and taken now.

Again, there was a long, long silence in which Clope went on glaring at Tristram and Tristram went on gulping and peering at Clope. What on earth was the professor on about? But gradually, very gradually, a possible explanation began to surface in Tristram's seething brain. He had dashed off his letter of condolence to George Macdonald in a mental tumult, hadn't he? And perhaps in such a tumult, such an intensity of feeling, such a hurry, that he hadn't opened with the conventional 'Dear George'? And now he remembered with awful clarity. He hadn't written anyone's name at the top of the letter, and he had then sent it to Clope. And that had convinced the already paranoid professor that he was writing, not about Muriel at all, but about Mrs Clope. 'How will you manage to live without her?' – which was more or less what he recalled writing to George about Muriel – had been wrongly interpreted as a mix of threat, boast and vindictive sneer. But how could he possibly explain this to a face that was scarlet with indignation and eyes that bored into him like a pair of white-hot pokers.

As had happened a few moments ago, Tristram's mind drifted self-protectively off into a half-irrelevant direction. It wasn't just the missing spectacles that were a problem. Why were his feet feeling almost as odd and embattled as his brain? Oh yes, he was wearing those controversial Wellington boots and, in the heat of the office, they were beginning to get clammy. If they hadn't been on his feet, he thought, maybe he would have been more alert, Clope a little less touchy, and the interview less distressing. He must, he really must remember to change them.

Indeed, his nerves and the heat were making him feel clammy all over. He would have to change his vest when he got home. He would have to change all his undergarments. Undergarments! Was Clope really implying that he, Tristram, had sat in that church next to a respectable lady, with nothing beneath his pyjama bottoms? That wasn't true. In his vaguest mood he would never, could never, have done something so indecent.

'Underpants,' groaned Tristram, 'I was wearing underpants all the time.'

But did this reassure or calm the seething Clope? No, he
was looking not just daggers and white-hot pokers but
lances, cattle prods and long, thin cabers when a surprising
thing happened. The silence was broken by the door being
violently thrown open. Miss Gill stood there, the little
brown box in one hand, her broken dentures in the other.
And she stared, too, but not with contempt at Tristram but
with simmering rage at Clope.

'Kindly explain thish,' hissed the Cod, waving the
dentures at Clope.

'What?' asked Clope. 'What?'

'I looked and looked for theshe,' went on Miss Gill, 'and
then I found them. Found them in your offish. Your offish,
Profeshor.' And she waved her dentures again, this time
with a venom that made them open and shut. The false
teeth snapped and, so it seemed, snapped at Clope as if they
belonged to a hungry alligator.

'What?' said Clope again, adding as he tried to recover
his customary superiority, 'Woman, you are interrupting a
meeting.'

This achieved what Tristram later decided was a paradox.
The Big Chill was heated up; the Cod was inflamed. 'Don't
you "woman" me,' she yelled. 'I'm not your woman. I'm
nobody'sh woman.'

Tristram had assumed that, though the Cod was cold
and rude to everybody else, she would be loyal and perhaps
even friendly to the professor who employed her. Clearly
he had underestimated her. She was a very angry person,
period, too angry for it to be safe to offer her a place on an
anger management course. But perhaps her anger would

now work for him by distracting Clope; or so Tristram began to hope.

'Kindly go away,' said Clope in what, for him, was a slightly unsettled, nervous voice.

'Go away?' screeched Miss Gill. 'I'm not going away until I have had a full and proper ekshplanashion. Only you could have taken the denturesh I have jusht had repaired at great expensh and wash waiting to take home to fiksh them to my gumsh. Only you could have broken them. Only you could have thrown them on to the floor of your offish. Your offish, your locked offish, Profeshor Clope.'

'My offish?' said Clope, sounding even less in command of things. 'What offish?'

Suddenly the blood of the Throstlethwaites came surging back into Tristram's veins. It was time to take advantage of an unexpected turn of events, as so many members of his great family had done before him. Why, there was even an ancestor who, noticing the Lancastrian who had captured him was looking for his Thermos or whatever it was that medieval warriors used for drinks in battle, had managed to sneak away or, rather, clank off to safety as fast as his armour would let him. Tristram decided to do much the same.

So he addressed Clope with a new firmness: 'First of all, I am wearing Wellington boots because I didn't want to be electrocuted. And the letter that worries you so much was not meant for you; it was meant for George Macdonald. It was about his wife Muriel. If you look at it again I think you will find there's no name at the head. It was sent to you in error.

'And,' added Tristram defiantly, 'and please reassure Mrs Clope about the pyjamas. The pyjamas and the underpants.

And be reassured yourself that I have no plans, no plans at all to run away with your wife.'

At that Miss Gill, who until then had totally ignored Tristram, turned her gaze from Clope and looked at him. And there was a sort of relish in her eyes. As Tristram decided later, she sniffed scandal. But at the time he simply rose and made as dignified yet brisk an exit from his office as was possible, given that he was wearing armour of his own in the form of those Wellington boots. At the door he turned, gave a slight bow to Clope and, with a squelch of his footwear, began to trudge homewards, this time reciting an extract from Coleridge's 'The Rime of the Ancient Mariner': 'Alone, alone, all all alone, alone on a wide, wide sea! And never a saint took pity on my soul in agony.'

Well, perhaps 'agony' was overstating the case and 'wide, wide sea' a bit inaccurate, especially as the streets in the vicinity of the university were rather narrow. But Tristram did feel pretty alone and somewhat in need of a compassionate saint or two.

That wasn't the end of the day's troubles, of course, since Tristram had forgotten that he had forgotten something forgetful people often forget: his house key. Even though he rang his bell and knocked hard, somehow failing to remember that he lived alone, he couldn't get through his front door. Oh well, it had happened before and would doubtless happen again. He began to tramp, trudge, limp and squelch towards his aunt's house in search of a replacement key.

On he went, down a street that took him past one of the larger, local supermarkets. Did he want anything there, he asked himself. Strolling or, rather, squelching up and down an aisle or two would give him the feeling of normality he badly needed after that somewhat tricky conversation with Clope. Really, the man was quite mad. How could he possibly think he, Tristram, was having an affair with his wife? How could he think his wife would have an affair with anybody? That small, bent, cowed figure looked more likely to hide with the other mice in the hay than roll about in it with a formidable young lecturer, like him.

Brooding about this crazy misunderstanding, and feeling increasingly angry at his lunatic boss as he did so, Tristram shunted his trolley down an aisle, picking up milk, juice and yoghurt as he went. Then he added a jar of instant coffee. What next? Over he went to the delicatessen.

'What can I get for you?' asked the young woman at the counter.

'Oh,' said Tristram, remembering where he was but not quite remembering what he wanted. 'Six slices of smoked Clope, please.'

'What?' said the girl. 'I don't think we have that. What is it, some kind of fish?'

'No, no,' said Tristram. 'Clope is a person. Clope is a professor at the university.'

It was clearly the first time the young woman had been asked to serve someone who admitted to being a cannibal. 'Oh,' she said, looking worried.

Tristram decided to make a joke of it. 'So not Clope,' he said with what he thought was a light laugh. 'He'd be too stringy to eat anyway. Even if we smoked him.'

'What?' said the girl again, looking even more anxious.

'I don't want indigestion,' chortled Tristram in a fresh attempt to put her at her ease. 'So no Clope for supper today.'

The girl looked at him as, still without his spectacles, he peered at her over the counter. Who was he, this person with the messy moustache? And why was he wearing Wellington boots? And why was he laughing in that weird way? She'd read something about that German who had gone around advertising for people to eat and had, in fact, eaten bits of someone who replied to his ad. Well, she wasn't going to co-operate with this man's horrible schemes.

'I think I'd better get my supervisor,' she said, and disappeared.

Tristram was puzzled and irritated. All he wanted was some smoked mackerel to help with one of his two latest health wheezes. One of these was to swallow plenty of choline pills, which were supposed to sharpen the mind and memory. The other was to eat as much fish as possible in imitation of P.G. Wodehouse's Jeeves, who consumed just such a diet. That kept Jeeves's brain cells alert. That ensured that, clever as Jeeves was, he never succumbed to the absentmindedness to which he, Tristram, had to confess he was occasionally prone.

But why did the girl need a supervisor to get him smoked fish? Really, bureaucracy in this supermarket had gone mad. Next thing, they'd be asking him to sign some paper before allowing him to buy a bottle of milk. Come to that, why was everyone, starting with Clope, behaving in such a strange way today? With a sigh he left the delicatessen, parking the trolley beside the counter as he went in search of a few other items: some aspirins, some disposable razors and, oh yes, a bottle of decent red wine. And a few moments later he was back with them all and, his mind still on the oddness of everyone and his eyes still imploring him to find them some specs, dropped them all into the wrong super-market trolley.

'I wandered lonely as a cloud that floats on high o'er

vales and hills,' Tristram said to himself, quoting
Wordsworth as he slowly pushed the trolley up and down
a couple of aisles before landing up in front of the supermarket's collection of flowers. 'When all at once I saw a
crowd, a host, of golden daffodils,' he went on. Ho, hum
. . . ho, hum. There were no daffodils today, since it was
July, but there were plenty of other choices. He really
should take a bunch of something to his aunt as an apology
both for asking her for yet another spare house key and for
failing to respond to her invitation to Sunday lunch. But
which? What? He stood, his hand on the trolley, and
pondered the blooms stacked before him.

Suddenly a voice came over the supermarket Tannoy,
rudely interrupting Tristram's poetic reverie. 'Would the
customer who took the wrong trolley from the delicatessen
counter please return it there at once,' it said.

Really, thought Tristram, how careless some people
were. He had known undergraduates as inconsiderate as
that and reproached them severely. Then he looked down
at the contents of the trolley he was pushing. Wine, yes.
Razors, yes. But why was there an enormous bunch of
bananas below them and, yes, mangoes, melons, pears and
kiwi fruit below them? Oh dear, oh Spooner, he was the
villain and must return the trolley at once. But as he turned
the corner that would have brought him back to the delicatessen counter he saw something, or rather someone, that
stopped him and the trolley dead in their tracks.

It wasn't. It couldn't be. His eyes, being without spectacles, were surely betraying him. But it was, it was. It was
evidently the man whose trolley he had taken instead of his
own, and that man was the man Tristram thought of as the
Anonymous Hulk. And the Anonymous Hulk was the big,

red-faced monster he had mortally offended by persistently mistaking him for his friend or, now, his ex-friend Valentine. He had seen him in the University Theatre a few times since their last, near-fatal encounter there, usually in the foyer or near the bar, but had never felt able to carry out his good intention, which was to explain his error and apologise for it. Instead, he had hurried off in the opposite direction. Was now the time to make up for this omission?

Er, probably not. As he seemed dimly to remember, there had been another encounter with the Hulk. He had disposed of a key to a drawer in a New York hotel by hurling it over a parapet and into the face of the Hulk, who happened to be boating in the river underneath. And, no, the Hulk didn't look as if he would be especially receptive to his, Tristram's, charms right now. In fact, he looked like an ogre that needed a lot more than bananas, melons, pears and kiwi fruit to slake his hunger. He looked like the sort of ogre who would be only too glad to grind up a promising young lecturer's bones, mix them with his flesh and slurp down the lot. And this ogre was growling something at the young shop assistant, who was making what looked like moustache gestures at a tall, thin man in a white coat, presumably the supervisor she had inexplicably gone to see, and he was nodding in reply.

Well, it was clearly no time for the renowned Throstlethwaite valour, especially as Tristram had spotted what was, yes, surely his own trolley tucked a few yards away. Rather, it was time for the almost equally famous Throstlethwaite strategic withdrawal. So Tristram took the wine, disposable razors and aspirins out of the Hulk's trolley, slipped them as inconspicuously as he could into his own trolley, pushed it as quickly as possible to the check-out counter and began to unload it. His aunt would just have to do without flowers, he said to himself, as he removed wine, razors, aspirins and – what, disposable nappies?

Once again, his trolley just wasn't his trolley. In his fluster and his shortsightedness he had taken another, this time one evidently belonging to a young mother. He put down the nappies on the shelf opposite the till and pushed away the trolley.

'Just take for these, can you?' he whispered to the check-out girl, who nodded in a weary way and rang up the money for the wine, razors and aspirins.

'Thanks, thanks a lot,' muttered Tristram, shoving the wine, razors and aspirins into a plastic bag, whipping out his wallet, giving the girl a tenner, shoving the change into his pocket, remembering to retrieve the wallet but, in his anxiety to leave, not remembering that he didn't want any nappies. Without thinking, he shot out a hand and picked them back up. And so it was that he ended up outside the supermarket, one of those hands carrying the bag containing what remained of his shopping and the other, oh dear, oh Spooner, holding disposable nappies he hadn't paid for.

What a day! He had locked himself out of his house, been accused of adultery by his boss and was now a shop-lifter. What was he to do? Take the nappies back into the supermarket, of course, and secretly dump them some-where. But then a thought struck him. Suppose he was stopped by the security man he had just blithely passed and the security man asked him to explain himself. Wasn't there a risk of misunderstanding? He had already been in trouble with the police, over that unfortunate business in the London bank. Very likely he was on some computer list as a one-time suspect. This time, the police might decide that, though one instance of theft or attempted theft was forgivable, a second was beyond the pale.

Then another thought hit him, this time even harder. Nappies implied the existence of a baby. Had one been secreted somewhere in the trolley he had just left behind? He hadn't noticed any infants of any size, but then he hadn't been looking for one or, indeed, wearing his trusty specs. Moreover, babies were very small, often asleep and therefore easy to overlook, even by sharp-eyed people. It could have been tucked half-visibly under or near the shopping that, as he seemed to recall, had surprised him with its bulk. If so, would its mother be anxiously looking for it? Would she think it had been kidnapped? Indeed, would the baby itself be safe in the trolley that he remembered shunting aside at the check-out?

Tristram stood a few yards from the entrance to the super-market, holding the plastic bag with the wine, razors and aspirins in one hand and the nappies in the other, quite unable to decide what to do next. And then, to his conster-nation, he noticed figures assembling just behind the entrance door. Who were they? Tristram stood and peered, wishing he hadn't mislaid those specs. Yes, they were the girl from the delicatessen, her thin, tall supervisor, the security man and, oh no, oh dear, that scary ogre, the Anonymous Hulk. They stood and stared at him. He stood and stared at them. A minute passed. Nobody made a move, at least until Tristram decided it was time that his inner Throstlethwaite once again became his outer Throstlethwaite.

He flourished the nappies apologetically. He put down the plastic bag and jokily pointed a couple of fingers, pistol style, at his head. He shook that head, again apologetically and, still jokily, hit himself on it with the nappies. Then, mouthing the words 'mea culpa, mea culpa', he stepped up towards the supermarket's door and tossed the nappies back in.

'All a mistake,' he called as he did so. 'And sorry about the baby. If there is a baby. Hope it's happy after its ordeal. If there was an ordeal.'

Nobody in the line of figures moved except the Hulk, who caught the nappies. And did he roar with rage? Did he threaten bloody vengeance? No. Like the others, he seemed oddly intimidated.

'I'm very fond of babies,' added Tristram loudly and in the cheeriest, most reassuring voice he could muster. But the Hulk just stood and stared at Tristram. He didn't seem angry. He didn't seem hostile. He didn't seem particularly red, let alone scarlet, let alone purple. He just seemed motionless and speechless.

Was this an opportunity to right a wrong by apologising for the errors in the theatre and at the parapets? Perhaps; but as often with Tristram, the words didn't come out as tactfully as he might have hoped.

'Sorry for mistaking you for an ogre,' he cried. 'I've nothing against ogres. There are days when I can be a bit of an ogre myself.'

The Hulk didn't react at all. He continued to stand and stare as if transfixed. But the girl from the delicatessen counter made a movement. One of her hands moved up to her mouth, as if she was suppressing a gasp of disbelief and horror, and then slid back down to her side.

'Goodbye then,' cried Tristram brightly, picking up what was left of his shopping. 'Good eating,' he added, rubbing his stomach with what he hoped was the sort of gesture that would be regarded as friendly in a foodstore. And he went his way, vowing never again to visit that confusing supermarket.

## THE VAGUE BOOK 8

*Remember Sir Frank Benson, the great actor-manager, who once entered the stage of the Lyric Theatre in Hammersmith as Richard II trailing a lead to which he'd forgotten to attach the king's pet dog? The British, American and I daresay every nation's theatre continue to give rise to many tales of forgetfulness, but with Ralph Richardson, whose Hamlet actually inspired Benson to become an actor, he was surely in a league of his own. Playing the monster Caliban in* The Tempest *– and a particularly wild and primitive Caliban, who spent part of the production hanging upside down with a fish in his mouth – Benson sometimes forgot to remove his pince-nez before coming onstage. Playing Shylock, he would omit to bring on props absolutely vital to his last scene – the bond he'd made with Antonio; the knife with which he planned to scoop out that merchant's flesh; and the scales in which he hoped to weigh that flesh – and so had to sneak into the wings and get them from a panicky stage manager. Playing Hamlet one evening, he spent the interval reading a newspaper in his dressing room and, when the call came for him to resume his performance, he absently asked, 'But what's the play?'*

*'Hamlet, sir,' came the reply. Benson looked down at the black costume that the Prince of Denmark traditionally wears. 'Ah,' he said. 'Sables. I should have known . . . ' – and went out and, it's said, acted immaculately.*

*Another time he prepared to perform the raging
Caliban in the sober suit he wore for Malvolio in* Twelfth
Night, *and seemed very surprised to learn that the play
that night was* The Tempest. *And it was in that same
suit that he committed what was, I suppose, a topsy-turvy
Spoonerism in York's Theatre Royal. There had been
trouble with the lights. Glimmering bicycle lamps on
stepladders were substituted, but a man in the audience
wasn't happy. 'I paid two shillings to come and I can't see
a thing,' he cried. And, still dressed as the puritan
Malvolio, Benson came into the stalls to investigate.*

*'In that case,' he told the complaining spectator, 'give
me your money back.' Sheepishly, the man handed over
the two shillings the ticket had cost to this stern and
forbidding figure and, clutching the money, Benson
returned to the stage.*

*Wherever he and his touring company went, he took
letters he had received and divided them into 'urgent' and
'very urgent' but didn't always answer them, despite his
habit of rigging up criss-crossing ropes in his hotel room
and hanging them off it, like handkerchiefs on a clothes
line. In North America, where he enjoyed far less success
than in his native England, Benson's problems seemed to
increase. One freezing night in Canada he disappeared
just before the company was due to catch a train, only to
be found by an aide-de-camp on a stool at a quick-lunch
counter drinking milk and lecturing an uncomprehending
fellow-customer on 'the song of Shakespeare'. Another
time he appeared only moments before he was due to
play Hamlet with a grazed face and swollen nose,
convincing an already distraught theatre manager that
the performance had finally to be cancelled. Benson had*

dived into what he thought was a pool but turned out only
to be a few inches deep – and, patched up by a local
doctor, insisted on carrying on with the play.

His performances reputedly veered unpredictably from
the brilliant to the awful, and his grasp of his words could
be uneven too. But he compensated by inventing lines that
he managed to make sound authentically rhythmic and
Shakespearian. Where in the tragedies, comedies or
histories can one find 'the strucken casement of chop-
fallen age'? That was Benson, not Shakespeare. When he
played the pretend-mad Edgar in King Lear, he
improvised an entire crazed speech, quietly remarking 'or
something like that' to an astonished prompter as he left
the stage. He was also prone to shift lines from one play
to another, so that Benson's Henry V suddenly became
Benson's Theseus from A Midsummer Night's Dream,
telling his troops 'joy, gentle friends, joy and fresh days of
love accompany your hearts'.

His vagueness could be catching too. Many examples
of Spoonerisms perpetrated by the Bensonians, as his
troupe liked to call itself, have come down to us. 'Have
you inserted the paragraphs, Mr Snake?' – Lady
Sneerwell's words to the scandal-mongering Snake at the
beginning of Sheridan's School for Scandal – became
'Have you inserted the snakes, Mr Paragraph?' Rosalind's
'men have died from time to time and worms have eaten
them but not for love . . . ' in As You Like It became
'worms have died and men have eaten them but not for
love'. And Macduff's anguish when he hears of the
murder of his wife and children, 'What, all my pretty
chickens and their dam at one fell swoop . . . ' didn't
exactly throb with the usual horror when the actor turned

*it into 'all my chitty dickens and their pram at one swell foop'.*

*Time for just one more theatrical Spoonerism, this time one from Broadway, where John Van Druten's I Remember Mama, a comedy about Norwegian immigrants that also became a film and a musical, ran for two years after its opening in 1944. Mady Christians, playing the mother of the family, gathered her children round her, among them a boy played by Marlon Brando, and promised them a reading from a Dickens novel that unfortunately she changed into* The Sale of Two Titties.

*But most theatrical anecdotes involve plain forgetfulness, sometimes from the most unlikely people. That superb actress and flawless professional Sarah Bernhardt was performing in London in a play by Alexandre Dumas called* L'Etrangère *or* The Foreigner *when she came to a speech in which her character, a lady eccentric called Mrs Clarkson, had to describe her improbable adventures to the Duchesse de Septmonts. Her mind went blank, and wasn't reactivated when Sophie Croizette's Duchess whispered to her the first words she was supposed to say. 'I wanted to tell you my reasons for behaving as I have done,' Bernhardt declared, paused and, to Croizette's horror, finished with 'but I have thought it over and decided not to tell you them today.' Some 200 lines had gone missing but, according to Bernhardt's memoirs, the audience didn't notice.*

*Have you noticed something very odd? Aside from a very brief guest appearance by Beryl Bainbridge in my first chapter, Bernhardt is the first woman to have featured in my Vague Book, and the divine Sarah's vague moments were not habitual. Is the reason that tales of*

male absentmindedness are so much more common than
those involving women that until recently men hogged the
public limelight and so inspired more anecdotes? Or that
women are much better at multi-tasking, meaning that
they don't so often focus on one matter to the exclusion of
others? To put it another way, do female right hands and
right brains tend more frequently to know what female
left hands and brains are doing? Or what? But the
American theatre has thrown up an example or two of
chronic vagueness among women: Carol Channing being
one example, Jean Kerr another.

Is it really true that Channing had a long and pleasant
conversation with a man who came up to her table in a
restaurant, asked her companions afterwards who he was,
and got the answer 'Your first husband'? Perhaps. But she
indisputably took the hand of the British actor Peter Bull,
pressed it to her heart and said, 'For years your name has
been a legend to me, John Bull.' As for Mrs Kerr,
successful dramatist and author of the long-running
Broadway comedy Mary, Mary, she wrote about her habit
of confusing her children's names with each other,
sometimes her children with their pets, and sometimes her
dog Frosty with her cat Kitty. It was she who collided with
the famous feminist Betty Friedan in a theatre foyer,
stretched out her hand and said, 'How do you do? We've
never been introduced – but I'm Betty Friedan.'

Keith Waterhouse, the author of Billy Liar and Jeffrey
Bernard Is Unwell, is probably the only modern British
playwright who could compete with that. He, too, wrote
often about his chronic and sometimes debilitating
absentmindedness. Though he could remember the
eight-digit number he'd been given when he served in the

RAF in his youth, and even the number his mother used as a regular shopper at the Co-op, he couldn't remember his phone number or sometimes even his address. Stopped by the police, he was able to tell them the number of the car he'd owned a quarter-of-a-century before but not the car he was driving.

As the working journalist he also was, Waterhouse found himself driving from London towards Portsmouth but quite unable to remember the town he was visiting or the person he was supposed to be seeing. And more or less the same thing happened when he went to Los Angeles to interview Charlton Heston. The moment his plane touched down, the actor's name was expunged from his memory bank and, as he wrote later, he began to fear that he'd have to go to the relevant studio and ask for 'that tall fellow who was in Ben Hur', except he couldn't remember the name of Ben Hur either. He was still racking his brains when he ran into a famous British actor in a hotel lobby. 'Hello, Peter,' said Keith, 'perhaps you can help me . . . ' And 'Peter', who was actually Michael Caine, did so.

Yet the old paradox applies. Up to his death at the age of 80, Waterhouse was one of the most able and reliable writers in Britain, always on time and on length with the famously incisive columns he wrote for the Daily Mail. Yet he admitted to being unable to remember anyone's name for more than ten minutes. Once he ran into a man on the street, who said, 'Hello, Keith, fancy meeting you.'

'Well, well, well, well,' replied Waterhouse. 'Fancy meeting you.'

'You don't know who I am, do you?' said this familiar-looking man.

'Of course I do,' fibbed Waterhouse.

'No you don't. What's my name then?'

'If you don't know I'm certainly not going to tell you,' answered Waterhouse.

And that's surely a moment of inspiration to delight all vague people. Why go the trouble of using the ruses recommended by those who would make us less absentminded? For instance, why hold someone's hand and repeat his or her name again and again and again? Yes, Beryl . . . no, Beryl . . . yes, Professor Clope . . . no, Professor Clope . . . my big toe, Professor Clope. In our hearts, we know that we can biff, beat and hammer a name into our heads and it will still go missing. Somehow Meryl will always slip past those fizzing brain cells and become Beryl. People should know their own names. Why should we, too, have to remember them?

# NINE

Eventually Tristram got home not only with his key but with a double portion of smoked mackerel. This had meant confronting Aunt Persephone, who greeted him with a huge sigh and a big silent shake of the head, though he didn't know or very much care whether these were aimed at his squelching wellies, his earlier failure to respond to her invitation to lunch, or his overall forgetfulness. What mattered was that he now had a key to his house, albeit one with an irritating and somewhat insulting attachment. His aunt had fixed an enormous label to the thing, reading: 'I AM A KEY. PLEASE DO NOT LOSE ME'. Oh well, thought Tristram, I have more important matters on my mind than a relative who decides to treat her favourite nephew, a man who happens to be an internationally admired scholar with a distinguished and possibly stellar future, as a small, stuffed animal in *Winnie the Pooh*.

One of these major concerns was obviously Hamish Clope and his, Tristram's, future in the university's English

Department. But another was that damned absentmindedness. He really had to deal seriously with it. He had to
draw on the legendary resourcefulness and tenacity of the
Throstlethwaites. He had to follow the example of the
ancestor who had climbed up an oak tree to escape some
over-excited Lancastrians and stayed there for four days,
catching rainwater in the leaves and eating acorns, slimy
medieval insects and a very surprised owl. He had boldly to
confront the problem. And that was why he had looked for
and found a fishmonger as he loped and limped back home
from his aunt and managed to buy what he had been inexplicably denied in that awful, confusing supermarket: a
pound of smoked mackerel.

But was the occasional oily fish, combined with the odd
choline tablet, enough to deal with the problem? Tristram's
voluminous reading and occasional blundering through the
Internet hadn't managed to uncover anything that seemed
more helpful. He knew that rats did better in mazes if they
were fed piracetam nootropil, but then he wasn't a rat and
couldn't anyway imagine his doctor prescribing either that
sinister-sounding substance or, indeed, strychnine sulfate,
which was also supposed to improve the memory. He could
imagine the conversation.

Tristram: 'Please could I have some strychnine?'

Dear old Doctor Fotheringay, who had been the family
physician for aeons: 'Strychnine? Why?'

Tristram: 'Don't worry, it's only for me.'

Fotheringay: 'Shouldn't you try some counselling before
taking a step as radical as that?'

Again, chicks apparently learn more quickly to distin-
guish beads from grain if they're injected with testosterone,
but Tristram didn't think dear old Fotheringay would think

bead identification or its human equivalent a sufficient reason for shooting extra male hormones into his biceps. Besides, he wasn't a chick, chicken or any sort of fowl and was, he thought, perfectly capable of picking any stray jewellery out of his breakfast cereal.

No, decided Tristram, as he continued these whimsical musings; choline was the answer. It was a natural ingredient in egg yolks and pulses, both of which he often ate. He would double, treble, maybe even quadruple the dose of choline pills he was taking. And the side-effects seemed to be minimal. Indeed, the only obvious one appeared to be that you might begin to smell a bit fishy; fishy and presumably even fishier if you were already eating lots of oily fish, as Tristram had already started to do. That might not endear him to another Meryl, Beryl or Cheryl, were his life to take a romantic turn. But for now the Clope crisis mattered more than any possible emotional entanglement. Love could wait. Clarity of mind was the priority. So choline and more choline was the overriding need. And, by way of reinforcing his determination, he then and there pulled out the choline bottle he had bought from the local health-food shop and swallowed four pills.

Not that this helped to solve the immediate problem, which was, of course, his lost spectacles. He had mislaid them all too often before, but had always managed to find them in the end, though sometimes in unexpected places. At various times he'd misplaced them in the fridge, beside the video recorder, once even in the microwave, which hadn't been a disaster, since they had steel frames which had begun to draw attention to themselves by crackling and then cracking when he had absentmindedly switched on the machine. That had happened because he'd done something all too typical of vague people: his fingers had gone on to automatic pilot. While his head was peering down and his brain was thinking of something else, his hand had gone its own way, unthinkingly removing those damned glasses from his nose and abstractedly putting them down in the little oven where he meant to place a carton of soup. He was, he ruefully thought, lucky not to have tried to eat the specs while wearing a dollop of mulligatawny.

But he had searched every possible and, he thought, impossible place in the house and still those specs seemed determined to elude him. Their absence had so confused him that he turned to the telephone in a forlorn attempt to trace them. The result was a ringing upstairs, a sound that filled Tristram with relief. But up in the bedroom he found that he had simply managed to call the mobile phone he kept in his jacket pocket. The moral was clear, and Tristram repeated it to himself several times: one cannot telephone one's spectacles . . . one cannot telephone one's spectacles . . . one cannot telephone one's spectacles even in desperation and panic . . . one cannot telephone one's spectacles and expect a reply.

But if his glasses weren't in the house, where were they? Tristram mentally retraced the steps he'd made in the last few days, but couldn't remember when he'd last had the spectacles on his nose and so where he might have left them. It was, he decided, time to go out and start asking for help from shopkeepers or the staff of other places he had visited. Yes, he had visited that annoying butcher, the one he feared had cut up the dog Henryson, in order to buy himself half a pound of steak. But the butcher bloke had, as usual, seen his request as a chance to exercise his celebrated sense of humour. 'Well, I've got a couple of sharks in the back room,' he had chortled. 'Shall I see if they've any spectacles in their stomachs?'

'No,' replied Tristram primly. 'I thought I might have left them on your counter.'

'Perhaps I swallowed them myself,' cried the butcher bloke in an ecstasy of mirth. 'Perhaps I'd better slice myself open and cut up myself. Ho, ho, ho, ho.'

'Ho, ho,' said Tristram, privately thinking that a pretty good idea, and left.

A visit to the corner shop, which sold newspapers and sweets and oddments, proved no more rewarding. The shopkeeper seemed unaccountably to feel accused. 'Why would I want your glasses?' he said. 'I have glasses of my own.'

'No, no,' said Tristram. 'It's just I thought I might have dropped them on the floor.'

'And you think I swept them up and threw them into the dustbin?' asked the shopkeeper.

'No, no,' said Tristram, feeling that, with Clope as his boss, he didn't need another paranoid person in his life. Again, he left.

The chemist, where he had recently added to his very necessary store of aspirins, proved equally frustrating. The woman at the counter seemed to assume he wanted to order and buy a pair of spectacles and wouldn't be put off, showing him frame after frame. 'No, no,' said Tristram. 'I'm looking for mine, mine.'

'Well, when you've bought new ones they will be yours, won't they?' she replied.

'No, no, thank you, thank you,' said Tristram, more testily than he intended and went his way, in a moment of grim exasperation recalling the church services of his childhood and muttering an extract from one of the psalms: 'Eyes have they and see not, they have ears and hear not, noses have they and smell not...'

At that point he stopped. Yes, he had eyes and wasn't seeing too well and, yes, the annoying chemist had ears but wasn't hearing what he said. But his nose was undoubtedly smelling, and what it smelt was a distinct aroma of fish. And, yes, the smell of fish did seem to be coming from him. And then his ears heard something odd. It was a miaow. And when he turned round his eyes were strong enough to see that he was being followed by a cat, a large, ginger cat with a hungry look in its eyes and, he suspected, a taste for fish.

'Scat,' said Tristram irritably. 'I'm not a fish. So beat it.' But the ginger cat didn't seem put off. It kept its distance but continued to follow him, presumably hoping that a cod or a dolphin or something would fall out of his, Tristram's, pocket and provide it with a seafood banquet.

A few minutes later Tristram was outside the University Theatre. He'd been there pretty recently, seeing Ibsen's *Ghosts*, which ends with a young artist called Oswald going mad from inherited syphilis and shouting, 'Give me the sun, give me the sun,' to his understandably concerned mother. Well, Tristram is the sort of person who, were he given the sun, would probably manage to mislay it and, perhaps as a result, he had been much moved by Oswald's cry. So maybe he had absentmindedly taken off his specs. Maybe he had put them on his lap. Maybe they had fallen off as he got up to leave the stalls. That sort of thing had happened before, so it was worthwhile venturing into the theatre to see if anyone had picked up those damned, elusive glasses.

'Try the stage door, dear,' said the helpful woman at the

box-office, so Tristram walked a few yards round the corner and, indeed, there was a musty old sign marked 'Stage Door' and, just inside, a grumpy-looking doorkeeper. 'No cats,' this old man said, 'absolutely no cats.' Tristram looked around and, yes, there was the same ginger moggy, this time with a mangy black-and-white cat just behind it. Both sat and stared at him.

'Scat, scat,' he said. Then, turning to the grumpy door-keeper, who seemed a lot less interested in the young lecturer than in the crossword puzzle he was doing, Tristram went on, 'I've come about my spectacles, I think I may have left them...'

'I know why you're here,' interrupted the grumpy door-keeper. 'Upstairs, second on the right.' And he returned to his puzzle.

'Thank you very much, very kind,' said Tristram in his most sarcastic voice, went upstairs, took the second door on the right and found himself – but where?

He was on a stage, presumably the theatre's main stage, looking down on two figures in the stalls. One was a long, thin, languid young man who was resting his feet on the back of the seat in front of him. The other was a small, scrawny woman nestled beside him.

'Oh God, another one,' said the young man. 'I thought we were finished for the day. But at least this chap looks the part. Plump and hairy and weird.'

Tristram was puzzled and offended. 'I'm looking for my spectacles,' he said in an even more irritated voice than he had used on the doorkeeper. The young man in the stalls looked at him with an odd mixture of contempt and interest.

'I didn't ask you to speak,' he said, 'but now you're doing so you might as well go on.'

'What?' said Tristram. 'What?'

'That's not bad,' said the young man, turning to the young woman. 'Let's ask him to say "What, what" again, but this time in a higher register.'

'What?' half-screeched Tristram, 'what?'

'Good,' said the young woman. 'And we love the moustache, don't we, Julian?'

'It could be bushier and the hair could be longer,' said Julian. 'But what's really necessary are some big, round spectacles.'

By now Tristram was too exasperated to do anything but answer, 'But I've come for my spectacles. That's why I'm here. I'm looking for my spectacles.'

'Good,' said Julian. 'Good. Say that again but more shrilly.'

Tristram lost his temper, becoming undeniably shrill in the process. 'Give me my bloody spectacles if you have them.'

'Better,' said Julian, 'but we'd better leave out the "bloody". That wouldn't please the bloody children or their bloody parents, would it, Julia?'

Julia agreed it wouldn't. Tristram just stood there and blinked. Children? Parents? Bloody children and bloody parents? All he wanted was his spectacles and somehow he had wandered into a kind of crazed kindergarten.

'Please could you say "to-whit, to-whoo",' said Julia.

'Let me repeat myself,' said Tristram very slowly, in a voice that contrived to be both outraged and humouring, 'Do you have my spectacles? Does anyone have my spectacles?'

'We've done that,' said Julian. 'It's time to move on. What we really want to see is you jumping about flapping your arms and shouting "to-whit, to-whoo . . . to-whit, to-whoo".'

Tristram prepared himself to declare, first, that he was a distinguished academic and was certainly not about to do or say anything of the sort; and second, that it was a very strange sort of place that required people seeking lost property to flap their arms and shout 'to-whit, to-whoo'. To the best of his knowledge – and his knowledge was based on far too much personal experience – such behaviour was not expected if one had left an umbrella on a train or a bus. But then he heard a surprising noise, a miaow from somewhere behind him. The ginger cat had clearly managed to sneak past the grumpy doorkeeper and his crossword and find its way on to the stage.

'What's that?' asked Julian.

'Appears to be a cat,' said Julia.

'Aha, a Method actor,' said Julian. 'But while I'm impressed to find you bringing your own pussycat to an audition for our Christmas show, I really think you can rely on us to provide one. If you're going to be our owl it would look pretty strange if we didn't have another actor as your cat, don't you think?'

'But I'm not here for any audition,' yelled Tristram. 'And I'm not a bloody owl.'

'You don't want to be in *The Owl and the Pussycat*?' asked Julian.

'No, I do not.'

'Then why are you wasting our time? Don't you know it's our audition day? Don't you know we have to find a cast for our Christmas show before the summer ends? Don't you know anything?' said Julian.

'It's just not professional,' added Julia, filling the word 'professional' with the sort of reverence a nun might bring to a mention of a particularly great and holy pope.

'And I've got to tell you, old chap,' went on Julian nastily. 'You smell. In fact, you pong. You pong of fish. I can smell you across the footlights. And whoever heard of an owl that ponged of fish?'

'Even seagulls don't smell of fish,' added Julia. 'They smell of birds. And sea.'

'Just so you know,' said Julian. 'Goodbye.'

Tristram didn't answer, but turned and stalked off the stage with all the dignity he could muster and, turning right instead of left, opened a door and found himself in a cupboard filled with fire-fighting equipment. 'I'm not an owl,' he cried to the bucket of sand on the floor. 'I'm not a bloody owl,' he repeated to the hose dangling above it. 'I am not a bloody owl.' The hose and the bucket naturally made no reply but, Tristram thought afterwards, looked as sympathetic as a hose and a bucket could reasonably look.

Anyway, it was several moments before, still seething with affronted dignity, he found himself walking past the rude doorkeeper and into the street. He snorted. He growled. He said aloud, 'And I still haven't found my spectacles.' What he didn't notice, in his affronted yet still dignified state, was that he was being followed by no less than three cats, a small, grey one having joined the ginger tom and the mangy black-and-white moggy.

They followed Tristram home too, and followed him when, still not having found those missing spectacles, he emerged from his house to do what he knew he must do. Clope had called a meeting of those of his subordinates who were in town. After his extraordinary encounter with the paranoid professor the other day, he longed, he positively yearned to give the occasion a miss. He had even telephoned Miss Gill, planning to say he had fallen ill, but changed his mind when he heard her strange, slurred voice and even stranger question.

'Howsh Mishush Clope?' she asked in a less hostile way than usual.

'Mrs Clope? Fine as far as I know,' a surprised Tristram replied.

'And you should know,' said the Cod, emitting the sort of frosty gurgle that, Tristram supposed, passed for laughter in Big Chill territory.

Tristram decided to ignore that. 'Well,' he said, 'I'm feeling a little under the weather today and thought I might miss the professor's faculty meeting...'

The gurgle interrupted him. 'While the catsh away, the mishe will play,' interrupted Miss Gill, and gave yet another weird, wintry gurgle. 'No shmoke without fire, thatsh what I shay.'

Suddenly the truth hit Tristram. This madwoman thought that he was missing a meeting with Clope in order to carry on his affair with the professor's poor, cowed wife. He had to put a stop to any such gossip, so he swiftly changed his mind about the meeting. 'No,' he said stiffly. 'I will be at the meeting after all.'

'Shuit yourself,' said the Cod with what sounded like a disapproving sniff.

For a moment Tristram thought Miss Gill was telling him to shoot himself, which struck him as a bit vindictive even for her. But, no, she was clearly still waiting for her dentures to be repaired and still perhaps hoped that the rake Throstlethwaite would take revenge on Clope, whom she blamed for the breakage. So 'suit yourself' was just an expression of disappointment, containing the hope that one day Tristram would grab Mrs Clope by the hair and whisk her off to the Throstlethwaite lair, giving her, the Cod, the opportunity to spread even more scandalous gossip round the university than she had clearly spread already.

And that was presumably on Miss Gill's mind, since she became unwontedly communicative. 'Can't be eashy, being Mishush Clope,' she said.

'No?' replied Tristram cautiously.

'Imagine being married to the short of man who goesh about shtealing denshures, breaking them and then lying about it,' said the Big Chill. 'It doeshn't bear thinking about, doesh it?'

For a moment, Tristram was tempted to do the brave, righteous thing and confess his own involvement in the beastly business, but then he remembered the fate of Sir Roger Throstlethwaite of Upper Throstlethwaite in the County of Yorkshire back in the 1480s. It had happened like this: The Duke of Buckingham had incurred Richard III's wrath by failing to agree to the murder of the little princes in the Tower of London, had then unwisely rebelled against the king, been defeated, and so got himself sentenced to death. This troubled Tristram's ancestor, who felt he had been instrumental in persuading the duke after a game of real tennis that killing a couple of socially presentable children might not be a terrific public relations move. So, bold and upright knight that he was, he had gone to Richard III to admit his part in the fiasco. Sadly, his reward, like the duke's, had been to have his head cut off. So, no, it wouldn't be wise to make a confession to Miss Gill. It wouldn't serve the English Department or the university if it resulted in her biting off his head with her half-broken dentures, would it?

So Tristram simply said, 'No, you're right, it doesn't bear thinking of,' and rang off.

So off he went to Clope's meeting, and Clope's meeting turned out to be as difficult and unnerving as he had feared. For that, there were several reasons, starting with the fact that once again he had made an error with his pills. Reaching into his bedside drawer for his choline tablets, he had thoughtlessly grabbed and swallowed a handful of what was, oh dear, oh Spooner, rather radically the wrong tablets.

They were the same shape and the same size and came in a same-looking bottle but, no, they were not choline tablets at all. They were the strong sleeping pills Fotheringay had prescribed for him when he'd gone to that dear old doctor complaining about Clope-induced stress and insomnia. As we've so often noted, Tristram comes from a long line of valiant warriors, but that doesn't mean he's insensitive. And who wouldn't wake in the night and find it hard to get back to sleep if he had made a mortal foe of a boss who looked like a human needle that wanted to stab him or, at other times, an upright cattle prod that yearned to electrocute him?

The obvious answer was to correct the effect of the sleeping pills with a lot of coffee, but sadly that couldn't be considered, not after the effect that an excess of caffeine had so embarrassingly had on Tristram when he had delivered the Fanny Carter lecture. So there was little to do but try his best to stay awake during the Clope confab. And there were ruses for doing so, or so he had read. One was to chew gum. It was apparently impossible to fall asleep while doing so. Another was to get up and walk around from time to time. That gingered up the circulation. And a third was surreptitiously to stick a biro into one's hand. A man who was more or less simultaneously chewing, walking and piercing his palm with a pen, would surely not succumb to sleep, however boring the occasion.

Also, there was choline, which aided memory and attentiveness and might help in such a situation. So Tristram found the correct bottle in his bedroom drawer and swallowed a few pills and, bracing himself as best he could, set out for the English Department. He noticed but, abstracted as he was, didn't fully notice that he was once again being followed by cats, becoming a sort of Pied Piper for the moggy classes. The little, grey one had disappeared, but it had been replaced by a large and rather fierce-looking, black creature, which in turn was being warily pursued by the same ginger tom and the same mangy black-and-white feline. And, again without Tristram realising it, the three-cat parade managed to find its way through the door and up the stairs that led to the English Department, where for reasons best known to itself it stopped and waited.

Miss Gill was in her usual office and her usual seat but, as far as Tristram was concerned, she was a very different Miss Gill. There was no frosty Cod, not even a sniff of a Big Chill. In fact, Miss Gill gave what Tristram assumed was a smile, though her missing dentures meant that it was more a twisted gape somewhat reminiscent of the entry to a dank, old cave. And then she did something really odd. She winked. It was as if she was saying, 'I've always underrated you, you rogue, you.' Tristram didn't know how to respond, so he gave what he hoped was a quick friendly nod.

'He'sh got hish dog with him, and I hate dogsh,' said Miss Gill.

'Oh,' said Tristram, again delivering that friendly nod.

'Nashty, shmelly thingsh,' went on Miss Gill, 'and they have fleash. Fleash. Ugh!'

'Oh,' repeated Tristram and, bracing himself for the fray, walked the few steps down the corridor and into Clope's office.

Clope was in his office. So were several of Tristram's colleagues – friendly Hector O'Brien; earnest Helen Taylor; big, muscular Rhys Jones; tubby Vincent Button; and suave Sholto Sinclair – all of them looking as solemn as they invariably did when the professor was presiding over a faculty meeting. There, too, was Henryson, tethered by his lead to a leg of his master's chair. The Afghan hound seemed to recognise Tristram as he slank into the office a few minutes late. At any rate, he wagged his long tail in a forlorn, hopeless sort of way. 'I mustn't call him Dunbar, I mustn't call him Dunbar,' said Tristram to himself, remembering the mistake he had made when he had been looking after Henryson. 'And, above all, I mustn't fall asleep.'

'So Dr Throstlethwaite is with us,' said Clope, pointedly looking at his watch. 'Then we can begin.'

'Sorry for that,' said Tristram in his most appeasing voice, but Clope ignored the apology and turned to the first of the questions that his subordinates had suggested in their letters needed to be raised.

'The curriculum,' said Clope. 'Should we be thinking of adjusting it? This is Dr Button's interesting suggestion. Are we encouraging levity? Are we asking our undergraduates to spend too much time on too many of the less weighty writers?'

Tristram feared that this meant that an attack on his beloved Romantic poets was coming. So, clearly, did his colleagues, for the discussion soon turned to the merits of Keats and Shelley, Coleridge and Byron. Tubby Vincent

Button, who was always trying to ingratiate himself with Clope and was therefore as near to a favourite as the balky professor possessed, contrived to suggest that Keats was immature, Coleridge uneven, and Shelley and Byron shallow and immoral. Friendly Hector O'Brien and suave Sholto Sinclair voiced their disagreement. But both were clearly waiting for Tristram, as a specialist in the Romantic poets, to intervene.

But for several reasons he was finding it difficult to do so. One was, of course, the obvious hostility of Clope. If he defended his beloved poets, it would only incite the professor to take the opposite view. Another was that, oh dear, oh Spooner, Tristram was feeling the effect of the sleeping pills. What was he to say? He tried to focus his mind. He opened his mouth, but before he could speak the professor leaned forward, looked at him, gave the Clope squint, leaned still further towards Tristram, then gave what everyone recognised as the Clope sniff, only a Clope sniff that was even longer and louder than usual.

This struck Tristram as so openly aggressive, so stunningly rude that his mouth stayed soundlessly opened. He sat and gawped at Clope. However, the professor's next words weren't what he expected: 'Has anybody brought a fish into my office?' asked Clope.

There was a long silence during which Tristram became aware that his colleagues were looking at him. Indeed, he realised that one or two of them had already edged their chairs away from him. Was it true? Had the choline pills had even more effect on him than he had already realised? The lunatics in the theatre had accused him of, well, ponging. It was, wasn't it, so difficult fully to smell one's own smell. But, again, what was he say? If he admitted that he was taking choline tablets he would, in effect, be admitting that he didn't trust his own memory, which wasn't an idea he wanted to put into Clope's head. And thanks to those sleeping pills, his own head was beginning to feel more and more woozy.

'Oh dear, forgive me,' said Tristram, after he had closed his mouth and opened it again. 'It must be the oily Clope I tried to buy at the supermarket. No, sorry, the smoked Clope I didn't buy. No, sorry, sorry, the smoked and oily mackerel I got from the fishmonger. I ate it last night – and, well, you know how it is...'

The Clope stare became the Clope glare. Again, there was a silence, this time punctuated by a half-suppressed giggle from friendly Hector O'Brien. But the professor obviously felt he had to maintain control of the meeting as well as of himself. So after a further loaded silence he changed the subject.

'Perhaps Dr Throstlethwaite has something useful to say about the point at issue,' he said in a voice so steely it was clear he didn't think Dr Throstlethwaite had anything useful to say about any point whatsoever, whether it concerned fish, Clopes or Romantic poetry.

It's a curious fact, observed of soldiers in the trenches in the First World War, that men about to go into battle can find themselves yawning. And the combination of danger and those damned sleeping pills had exactly that effect on Tristram. He blinked. He tried not to yawn, but yawn he did. And his attempt to stifle the yawn made it sound hoarse, throaty and, as a yawn, even more pronounced.

'The topic seems to bore you,' snapped Clope. 'Perhaps that reaction should guide us when we reach a decision on the future of the curriculum.'

'No, no,' said Tristram. 'I think the Romantic poets are jolly . . . ' – and he reached in his anxious but woozy, snoozy, half-anaesthetised way for the right word – ' . . . jolly . . . jolly. Jolly, jolly jolly.'

Again there was a silence, again punctuated by a giggle that friendly Hector O'Brien tried to pass off as a snuffle.

'Jolly jolly,' hissed Clope. 'I think we must ask ourselves whether it's the purpose of a university to inculcate jollity in its undergraduates.'

'Hear, hear,' said tubby Vincent Button, wincing away from Tristram as the young lecturer made a new attempt to stay awake and alert. He stood up, walked or (rather) tottered towards tubby Vincent Button but, so far from attacking him, walked or (rather) half-stumbled round the room and sat or (rather) slumped down again.

'Let us return to this matter later in the meeting and pass on to the subject raised by Miss Taylor,' said Clope, ignoring Tristram's little walkabout. 'Are we becoming too lax when we are adjudicating the quality of the work given to us by our undergraduates? Are we mistaking B work for A work and C work for B work?'

And earnest Helen Taylor launched into her spiel, in her conscientious but verbose way, offering arguments on each side of the question. Tristram desperately tried to follow what she was saying but found it more and more difficult. He blinked, blinked again and did his best to ensure that blinking did not end in complete ocular shutdown. Recalling those ruses for staying awake, he pulled a biro out of his pocket and began to jab it into his palm. What else? Oh yes, chew. He hadn't anything to put in his mouth, so he began to chew the air between his teeth.

On and on earnest Helen Taylor droned, emphasising

the importance of fairness, the danger of discouraging undergraduates, and so forth and so forth. Again Tristram drove the biro into his hand. Again he chewed and chewed, not realising that sometimes this meant that tooth hit tooth, creating a weird, percussive sound, like drumsticks clashing together or ivory castanets. Earnest Helen Taylor paused for a moment, looked at him reproachfully, then carried on and on and on.

But were his attempts to stem sleeplessness actually working? Tristram didn't know. He still couldn't stop blinking and, occasionally, yawning. He felt himself beginning to pitch forward but managed to stop himself before he tumbled on to the floor and fell asleep there. He jabbed the biro into his palm, tried and failed to stop himself emitting an ouch of pain, then dropped the biro and, still chewing and clicking frantically away, he gripped the sides of his chair. He liked earnest Helen Taylor and didn't want to spoil her spiel, but why wouldn't she come to a close? Why couldn't she shut up? Her words were like chloroform or ether and she herself was becoming a bit misty. And she was still mistier because Tristram wasn't wearing those damned spectacles, the ones he'd lost, the ones he couldn't find, the ones that had sent him into that crazy theatre, the ones that had ended up with him being mistaken for an owl, of all things.

'The Owl and the Pussycat!' murmured Tristram, failing to realise he was expostulating aloud. At that, earnest Helen Taylor stopped speaking and everyone turned and looked at him. Even Henryson, who had been dolefully lying on the floor, gave an interested start at 'pussycat', a word that clearly meant something to him. However, Tristram didn't register any of this, but continued to blink and yawn and chew and click his teeth and grip his chair and peer myopically forward in his befuddled eagerness to stay awake.

'You have some contribution to make to the debate, Dr Throstlethwaite?' inquired Clope, eyes glinting as he stared at his least favourite underling.

'Um? No, no,' replied Tristram, staring back in his mentally mazy and now slightly cross-eyed way. Suddenly he felt he was in a dream. Suddenly he felt sorry for Clope or 'funny little Clope', as Muriel Macdonald had called him. After all, fancy having to spend one's life with a name like that. He'd double-checked 'Clope' on the Internet and found that what George Macdonald had told him all those months ago was right. In France, it was a word for a cigarette. And, in truth, the small, thin professor did indeed look a bit like a cigarette. Fancy resembling a cigarette. Poor Clope, having to be called Professor Cigarette. Poor Mrs Clope, having to be married to a cigarette and being called Mrs Cigarette. In fact, it was worse than that, since 'clope' in France was street slang. Fancy being called Professor and Mrs Ciggie, Fag, Snout, Reefer or Weed. Poor dear Clope. Poor dear Mrs Clope. Poor darlings, as the great Richard Attenborough would have called them.

These thoughts swirled around the jumbled casserole that was Tristram's brain and, unfortunately, came out in another murmur. 'Poor darling Mrs Clope,' he said, giving what was half a smile, half another enormous yawn.

Tristram couldn't see the rest of Clope too clearly, but the waves of hate emanating from him were unmissable. His eyes were like – what was the word? In his disoriented state, Tristram couldn't remember it. Gobbets? Gibbets? Globules? Giblets? No, gimlets, gimlets. They were gimlet enough to penetrate iron, let alone a young lecturer's frazzled brain.

But Clope had already made a promise to himself. This Throstlethwaite might be a proven scoundrel and a probable seducer but, whatever the provocation, he wasn't going to lose his temper in front of the demonic Casanova's colleagues and his own subordinates. That would play into the evil-doer's hands, because the evil-doer's little game was all too evident. Throstlethwaite was taunting, teasing and generally provoking him in the hope that he, Professor Clope, would explode with rage. That would allow Throstlethwaite, spawn of Satan that he was, to pretend he was a moderate, balanced person. It was all a plot to discredit him, Clope, and then take his place at the head of the department.

What was the next subject for discussion? Tristram hardly knew. Friendly Hector O'Brien seemed to be putting forward some ideas for change. Words like 'English' and 'teach' and 'undergraduate' were coming out of his mouth and, since Tristram knew that they were good words and Hector a good person, he gave what he hoped was a nod each time he heard them. But it isn't easy to try to chew, nod, smile encouragingly, peer myopically forward, and grip on to your chair all at the same time. Or it isn't easy to do so without looking like some sort of puppet only part of whose apparatus is working, which is pretty much the way Tristram looked.

'You wish to add something to the discussion, Dr Throstlethwaite?' Clope asked, or rather hissed, after Tristram had given a particularly emphatic nod, though he hadn't the faintest clue what statement or argument he was agreeing with.

'Um, no, not really,' replied Tristram with a big nod, followed by a gigantic click of the teeth, followed by a throaty yawn that just wouldn't be suppressed, followed by a lowering of the eyelids, followed by a snore that did, however, have the effect of jerking him back awake.

Clope sensed an opening or at least a chance to make Tristram look more foolish than he was already making himself look, while creating a division between him and his colleagues. 'We are clearly boring you,' he said. 'Dr O'Brien is boring you. Miss Taylor is boring you. Perhaps even I am boring you.'

Confused as he still was, Tristram realised that he had to try to explain himself to Clope and Clope's giblet, sorry gimlet, mind. 'No, no,' he managed to say. 'It's the medicine, it's the medicine. I swallowed the wrong medicine.'

'I see,' replied Clope in a voice which implied the medicine was alcoholic and he didn't see at all. 'In that case perhaps we should take advantage of you while your medicine has not put you completely to sleep. Perhaps we should ask you to put forward the proposal that you so signally, so very signally failed to send me by . . . ' – and here Clope paused in a particularly menacing way before cracking out the final word of the sentence like a gunshot – ' . . . letter.'

Proposal? Letter? What was this hazy cigarette of a person trying to say? But then something stirred in what was now the muddled mush, the uncooked pudding of Tristram's head. Yes, all Clope's underlings had been asked to submit suggestions by letter. Yes, he had tried to do so himself, but unfortunately had sent Clope the wrong letter. Yes, that had caused a lot of confusion. And, yes, he had formulated a proposal, and that proposal had to do with salaries. His colleagues wanted him to say – but, what, what?

'We are waiting, Dr Throstlethwaite,' said the hazy cigarette.

Tristram blinked, clicked his teeth with as much wake-up power as he could muster, stood up, turned around twice, and spoke. 'Thank you, darling,' he said. 'We should all get salary increases.'

Even in his muzzy, woozy, half-asleep state Tristram sensed that this had caused a stir, and not a good one. Another half-suppressed giggle from friendly Hector O'Brien had become an unsuppressed snort. Indeed, all his colleagues were leaning forward in something like consternation. As for Clope, he seemed oddly pleased, despite being called darling by the monster Throstlethwaite.

'I see,' said Clope. 'You think it is more important for yourself and your colleagues to receive rewards rather than, let us say, give extra money for books to needy and deserving undergraduates studying serious subjects?'

Was that what Tristram thought? He really didn't know. 'Is that what I think?' he somehow contrived to say.

'That is what you said you thought,' replied Clope crisply. 'And I am sure I speak for everybody here when I say that it seems a strikingly selfish idea.'

Something like a collective moan rose from Clope's underlings, a noise which the professor chose to interpret as the sound of self-sacrifice and therefore consent.

'Let us agree that there will be no salary increase this year,' went on Clope. 'It is a time of financial difficulty. It is also a time for generosity. Generosity to others and not to ourselves.' And he gave Tristram a look that somehow combined hatred with triumph.

'Hear, hear,' said tubby Vincent Button, but in a voice that was noticeably weak, wan and unconvincing.

'Traitor,' whispered big, muscular Rhys Jones, but in the direction of Tristram, not Clope.

'Idiot,' added suave Sholto Sinclair quietly.

Again, something stirred in Tristram's befogged mind. Yes, he had agreed with his colleagues to put forward a suggestion about salaries, but one that was different from the proposal Clope had just rejected. Oh dear, oh no, it wasn't just different. It was the very opposite. The idea was – and now an awful clarity began to penetrate the mushy pudding that sat, or rather wobbled, on top of Tristram's shoulders and passed for a brain – the plan was to manipulate the professor into giving everybody a salary rise by suggesting nobody should receive a salary rise. That was what he had written in the letter he had meant to send Clope but had sent in error to poor George Macdonald. The spirit of Spooner had resurfaced, condemning friendly Hector O'Brien, big, muscular Rhys Jones, suave Sholto Sinclair and Tristram himself to what was, in effect, a salary cut.

'Um,' Tristram said. 'I think I may have made an error.' And in his confusion and embarrassment he stood up and tottered towards the door. Anything, he thought in his muzzy way, was better than to remain in the company of a professor who loathed him and colleagues who were clearly turning against him.

'Would you excuse me . . . ' he began to say, stopping as his half-awake eyes caught something surprising. Surely those were his lost specs, perched on the windowsill. What were they were doing there? Could he have left them there when he escaped from Clope's office? Could they have remained undiscovered on the edge of the sill while he searched for them all over town? But it was too deep a mystery for a man in Tristram's bleary, wonky state to penetrate, so he simply blundered towards them and picked them up, mumbling something apologetic but impenetrable about Generalised Aphasia Syndrome.

'It's the GAS, it's the GAS, I swallowed the wrong GAS,' he said as he perched the glasses precariously on his nose, returned to the door, opened it, then turned round to face his old foe and newly alienated friends. 'Would you please excuse me, darlings?'

'Indeed we will excuse you,' Clope was already replying when something odd happened. The three cats which had followed Tristram into the English Department appeared at the door, presumably assuming that at long last this was fish time. They peered hopefully in and, like everybody else, got the shock of their lives.

The dog Henryson saw the cats and, though they were respectively black, black-and-white and marmalade, the dog clearly saw red. He gave a bark, leapt up and made for the door, forgetting or ignoring the fact that his lead was tied round Clope's chair. So the chair went with him and Clope went with the chair. The chair tilted as it went and so did Clope.

'Unsatisfactory dog,' screeched Clope, grabbing the arms of the chair in a desperate effort not to be thrown on to the floor. 'Highly unsatisfactory dog. Sit, sit.'

Tristram was appalled. But how could he help? 'Sit, Dunbar, sit,' he yelled.

Dunbar, or rather Henryson, came to a sudden halt, stopping the chair and giving Clope a mighty jolt, but not because he had been called unsatisfactory, misnamed Dunbar or ordered to sit. The black cat, bolder than the other two, had stayed at the door, arched its back and started to hiss. There was a momentary dog-cat standoff, in which the chair swayed, as did the raging, bawling Clope, who was still precariously perched on it. But then the black cat clearly decided that the chance of fish wasn't worth the risk of a battle. He sped after his moggy colleagues and Henryson sped after him, pulling the chair as he went. And as the cats, the dog, the chair and the professor raced, slid, juddered and crazily teetered down the corridor and past the open door of Miss Gill's office, the inevitable occurred. Clope lost his grip on the arms of the chair and landed with a thump on the floor.

Out came Miss Gill, to see Clope on all fours, staring up at her and a still frantically barking Henryson and the chair disappearing down the corridor in hot pursuit of the three cats.

Her reaction was instantaneous and not that of a loyal secretary. 'Firsht my denturesh and now your dog,' she cried. 'It'sh no ushe coming crawling to me. You won't get round me that say. I reshign . . . I'm having nothing more to do with you, your shmelly dog or itsh filthy fleash.'

Clope clambered to his feet, not so much sniffing as panting and his face not so much red as purple, and his eyes not so much squinting as madly bulging. And, as Tristram mused in the tranquillity that eventually followed the storm, who could blame him?

This Throstlethwaite had not only attempted to poison him, Clope, with highly toxic mothballs and take his job. He had not only fed dog food to his, Clope's, wife and then tried to seduce her. He had not only done his best to drown his dog Henryson in a perverted ritual in a public convenience. He had not only come to church in pyjamas and rubber boots in hopes of leading the congregation in another devilish ritual, this time involving Mrs Clope and a corpse. He had not only called him 'funny little Clope' in a letter, come drunk to a faculty meeting, and yawned and slept and blundered about and thrown a biro to the floor and made strange percussive noises with his teeth. He had not only done those and many, many other things. He had devised a fiendish new plot, which was to cover himself with a sort of fish perfume, lure an army of cats into his, Clope's, office in order to excite the dog Henryson and embarrass and enrage him, Clope, in front of his subordinates.

And now this Throstlethwaite was standing there, wringing his hands in a fake display of contrition and muttering something incomprehensible but provocative about Dunbar and giblets and gas and spectacles and dears and darlings.

So Clope ignored Miss Gill. He ignored tubby Vincent Button, who had helped him to his feet. He ignored all his gawping subordinates but one, and that one was, of course, the malignant Throstlethwaite. Clope uttered a noise that was part hiss, part pant, part growl, part hoarse screech. He stumbled up to his enemy, stretched out his arms as far upwards and outwards as they would go, and began to do something none of those present could or would ever forget. He began to strangle Tristram.


'Poor chap,' said the Vice-Chancellor. 'But then he was never really one of us, was he?'

Tristram looked at the Vice-Chancellor through the spectacles he had at long last found and even managed to keep. 'I suppose not,' he replied uncertainly.

'No sense of humour,' went on the Vice-Chancellor. 'Too many sermons. I don't think I ever saw him laugh or even smile. Did you?'

'I suppose not,' said Tristram.

'And I'm told his last act was to deny his subordinates a salary increase. Can't have that, can we? Not when the cost of eating and drinking is going up.'

'I suppose not,' said Tristram, still a bit lamely.

'No sense of fun, that was Clope's problem. Don't you agree?'

'I suppose not.'

'But that doesn't really excuse him trying to murder you, does it?'

'I suppose not,' answered Tristram.

'Still, I don't know why they had to use a strait-jacket,' said the Vice-Chancellor. 'Not the dignified exit one expects of a head of a major department at a great university, was it?'

'I suppose not,' agreed Tristram.

'The question is, how are we to replace him?' went on the Vice-Chancellor. 'Give the wrong impression if we hang about. Suggest we think the whole faculty has gone mad. Can't have that, can we?'

'I suppose not,' said Tristram.

'Well, I have a candidate,' said the Vice-Chancellor. 'Young, bright, vigorous, growing reputation, international quality, decent sort, not a prig, good scholar, popular area of expertise, sense of fun, likes a joke, reminds me of myself 40 years ago, nothing to do with sermons, great future. Ring any bells?'

'Oh,' said Tristram. 'Who?'

'You,' said the Vice-Chancellor. 'What do you think?'

'Um,' said Tristram. 'Um.'

'Of course, we all know you're a modest young chap. We all remember how you ended the Fanny Carter lecture. If only every speaker would get as quickly off the stage rather than hanging about for applause or completely unnecessary questions. That way, one could always get to lunch on time. Or dinner. Or a glass of port or brandy before turning in.'

'Um,' repeated Tristram.

'I've spoken to some of your colleagues,' continued the Vice-Chancellor. 'I've even spoken to that woman with the strange speech defect. Always,' he added solemnly, 'always talk to secretaries and other menials. They see things other people don't.'

'Ah,' said Tristram, wondering what on earth Miss Gill, who until just a day or so ago had despised him, could have said in his favour.

'She didn't say much, I suppose because of those teeth,' said the Vice-Chancellor. 'But she gave me the impression that you had the warmth of character and approachability that is so necessary in high office. She said you had been especially kind to Clope's wife.'

'Ah,' repeated Tristram.

'Might be helpful to everyone if you took Mrs Clope under your wing,' continued the Vice-Chancellor. 'I only met her once or twice. She seemed to me rather a sad and lonely person. Refused to drink anything but water. Would give a good impression if the department and especially if you were taking an interest in her during her husband's absence. Might comfort poor Clope too. Might help to restore him to sanity.'

'I suppose so,' lied Tristram.

'As for your colleagues, I think they would welcome your appointment. They almost all smiled with anticipation and one or two even chuckled with pleasure when I put the idea to them. But they did,' and here the Vice-Chancellor paused for a moment, 'they did have one reservation.'

'Ah,' said Tristram.

'They said you could be a trifle absentminded.'

'Ah.'

'But I told them there's an answer to that. If you forget something make sure there's someone who does the remembering for you. Rely on well-trained menials. Don't get bogged down in detail. Look at the large picture and always leave time for yourself. Delegate, delegate and delegate again. That's my motto and it's never done me any harm.'

'Ah.'

'So if we're agreed, I think we can allow ourselves a little celebration. A toast to you and the department. And,' went on the Vice-Chancellor with a smile, 'it happens that I have some vintage champagne that I reserve for the most special of special occasions.'

And the Vice-Chancellor stood up and went to the corner of his magnificently furnished office. There, on a mahogany table, was a silver bucket from which the top of a fine and clearly very expensive green bottle was protruding. Gingerly, lovingly, almost reverentially, he plucked it out and handed it to Tristram.

'Never forget that the first duty of an eminent man is to keep a good cellar and use it well,' he said. 'You open the bottle.'

So many confused thoughts and feelings – excitement at this wholly unexpected promotion, guilt at the fate of Clope, worry about Mrs Clope, surprise at Miss Gill, grateful feelings towards the Vice-Chancellor, a slight pain in the neck that Clope had tried to twist right off – were whirling round Tristram's head that he didn't know what to do next. The cold of the bottle reminded him of the orange juice 'with bits' that he drank every morning at breakfast. The sight of the champagne put him in mind of those racing drivers one sometimes saw on television, celebrating their successes on their podia. So he removed the wire round the cork and, his mind a mad mix of triumphant Formula One drivers and orange juice that needed to be stirred, Tristram gave the bottle a violent shaking.

The cork flew off like a tiny cannon ball, grazing the Vice-Chancellor's right ear as it sped towards the mantelpiece, hitting what was clearly a very valuable china shepherd, and sending it to the floor, where it broke into a dozen pieces. Meanwhile, the champagne spurted, foamed and flooded out, splashing on to the Vice-Chancellor's head. Both men stood there transfixed, not knowing what to do.

It was Tristram who finally spoke. 'Oh no, oh dear,' he said. 'Oh dear, oh Spooner.

## THE VAGUE BOOK 9

*Oh dear, oh Spooner indeed. I'm not at all sure this journaling is helping me as much as Furtbattler – remember him, the plump shrink with the beard, the endless questions and the strange, purring manner? – once told me it would. But let's go bravely on in the tradition of my ancestors, the indomitable Throstlethwaites. Let's say farewell to the theatre with a tale about Wilfred Lawson, a well-known actor in the earlier 20th century. He was apt to forget and muddle his lines, with the result in one live television play a fellow-actor had to turn some of his speeches into his own monologues and he himself ended a scene by saying, 'Well, I fair buggered that up,' not realising he was still on air. But he outdid himself when he invited Richard Burton to join him in watching the early scenes of a stage* play in which he was performing. He was still sitting enthralled by the action, and not yet wearing either his make-up or his costume, when he excitedly tapped Burton on the shoulder. 'This is where I come in,' he said.

Instead, let's remember a few more absentminded writers, starting with the famously dreamy La Fontaine, who called at the house of a friend he hadn't recently seen, was told the poor man had died six months earlier and said, 'True, true, I went to his funeral.' He also encountered a pleasant young chap at a gathering in the house of a Dr Du Pin, enjoyed his conversation, and asked who he was. 'What, do you not know your own son?' expostulated Du Pin. 'I seem to remember I have seen him somewhere,' replied La Fontaine. Another time, he appeared at one of his own dinner parties barefooted and wearing a nightgown and nightcap, strode through his dining room and disappeared into his study and reappeared half an hour later rubbing his hands with glee, and without another word went upstairs to bed. He had finished his story, 'Les Deux Pigeons'.

Even more eccentrically, Ralph Waldo Emerson is said to have gone to a funeral declaring that the man being buried was 'a sweet and beautiful soul but I have entirely forgotten his name'. It was, in fact, the poet Longfellow. But then Emerson was ageing and, as he himself sadly recognised, losing a memory that had once been reliable enough. As I've said before, we're not concerned with the problems of old age but with ingrained, habitual, persistent absentmindedness. And seldom has there been a better example of that than G.K. Chesterton, the early 20th-century essayist, critic and fiction writer who is still remembered for his Father Brown thrillers.

*He had an incisive, wide-ranging mind but suffered from memory lapses that were noticeable from the very start. 'He has an inconceivable knack of forgetting,' wrote his form master in a report from St Paul's, where he was sometimes to be found wandering round the playground under the misapprehension that it was Saturday and there were no classes, 'and consequently he is always in trouble'. As a young man, he wrote a long letter to his mother telling her that he had just got engaged to be married but without noticing that she was sitting in the same room. All this amused his friends but must have maddened his long-suffering wife, Frances. Often a 'bloodthirsty yell, like a werewolf' would come from their bedroom.*

*'Ah, that's Gilbert,' she would say. 'He wants his tie tied.'*

*And one evening she heard Chesterton, who was a large and heavy man, clambering out of the bath. There followed an almighty splash, which itself was followed by a cry — 'Damn, I've been here before!' — and possibly by a watery disaster, since her husband was apt to flood the bathroom floor, endangering the floor below.*

*He was very nearly late for their wedding, since en route to the church he had stopped for a glass of milk and forgotten where he was going. And when he and Frances lived in Battersea he became a familiar figure, walking around and laughing to himself while messily or even eccentrically dressed, on one occasion in a dinner jacket and cycling shoes.*

*When they moved to Buckinghamshire it was no better. Chesterton became a familiar figure in the refreshment room at London's Marylebone Station, alternately*

*supping cups of tea and glasses of wine from the bottle
he'd brought with him and never knowing the times of the
trains from London to Beaconsfield, where they lived. 'My
dear,' he told Frances, 'I couldn't earn our daily bread if I
had to study timetables.' He's also said once to have
asked for coffee at the ticket office and a ticket from a
waiter dishing out coffee.*

*Travel always caused him problems, even though he
did plenty of it, since he was much in demand as a
lecturer. That meant that he often left his belongings in
hotels, once forlornly saying to poor Frances, who had
asked him why he didn't replace his lost nightwear, 'I
didn't know pyjamas were things you could buy.' And it
was she who received the celebrated telegram, 'Am In
Market Harborough – Where Should I Be?' She replied,
'Home', thinking it safer if he returned to their house and,
even if it meant missing an engagement, restarted his
lecture tour from there. Unsurprisingly, he either missed
many engagements or arrived embarrassingly late, once
apologising to an organisation called the Knights of the
Blessed Sacrament with: 'As knights you will understand
my not being here at the beginning, for the whole point of
knighthood is that the knight should arrive late but not
too late. Had St George not been late there would have
been no story. Had he arrived too late there would have
been no princess.'*

*In London itself he wasn't more focused. He would
sometimes wander around for hours, enjoying the
sensation of being lost. He also found it difficult to
remember where he worked. After his own magazine, the
G.K. Journal, moved offices he was desperately late for
an important board meeting, explaining that he had*

hailed a taxi, couldn't remember the new address, went
to a tea shop, ordered a cup of tea, emptied his pockets in
the vain hope of finding something that would tell him
where to go, and then had an inspiration. He hailed
another taxi and told the driver to take him to a
newspaper stall. The first and second didn't stock his
journal, but the third did. He bought a copy – and at last
discovered the address.

It was Chesterton who ordered two eggs in a café,
didn't notice when they slipped on to his lap, and ordered
two more from a giggling waitress. It was Chesterton who
tried to open his front door with a corkscrew he'd
borrowed, fending off the obvious explanation with 'I
should probably have been more vigilant if I had been
drunk'. One of many likable things about him was that he
was self-knowing and, for all his gifts, pretty humble. As
he wrote to a friend: 'On rising this morning I carefully
washed my boots in hot water and blackened my face,
poured coffee on my sardines and put my hat on the fire
to boil. These activities will give you some sense of my
state of mind.'

One of many books Chesterton wrote was a study of
the medieval world's greatest theologian, St Thomas
Aquinas. It's a fine work, but also relevant to us in that
G.K. clearly identified with a thinker who was, like him,
large, awkward, bookish and abstracted, was derided as
a boy as 'the dumb ox' and, like him, became committed
to reconciling religion with reason, spirituality with
common sense. You can sense the English writer's delight
as he describes how Aquinas goes to the French king's
feast in his black friar's clothes and, ignoring the finery
and the grandeur, loses himself in his own deep, deep

thoughts. *Suddenly both king and guests are reduced to shocked silence when Aquinas brings down his huge fist with a mighty thump on the table, making the goblets rattle and leap, and roars in a loud voice yet still like a man in a dream, 'And that will settle the Manichees.'*

It was, wrote Chesterton, '*as if the fat friar from Italy had thrown a plate at King Louis or knocked his crown sideways*', yet that great monarch wasn't merely unoffended but fascinated and impressed. He told his secretaries to take their tablets to this strange, absentminded friar and make a record of the argument that had just occurred to him, to ensure he didn't forget it.

And that isn't just a nice story but an answer to those who sneer at the vague and the dreamy. Yes, we embarrass people and ourselves. Yes, we make mad social errors. Yes, we forget where we've left dogs, mug joggers, lose our keys, misplace our spectacles and try our bosses' patience by spattering them with their own vintage champagne. But, but, but.

But some of us are geniuses and, yes, one or two of us are saints. Don't forget it. Or at least try not to forget it.